FATE BY DESIGN

by

M J Walsh

Grosvenor House
Publishing Limited

Cover art by Roisin Martindale

This book is published by
Grosvenor House Publishing Ltd
Link House
140 The Broadway, Tolworth, Surrey, KT6 7HT.
www.grosvenorhousepublishing.co.uk

A CIP record for this book
is available from the British Library

ISBN 978-1-83975-254-4

To Tricia and our much loved family.

Contents

Part 1 – Survival 1

Part 1 – Chapter I 3

Part 1 – Chapter II 13

Part 1 – Chapter III 22

Part 1 – Chapter IV 32

Part 1 – Chapter V 39

Part 1 – Chapter VI 46

Part 1 – Chapter VII 52

Part 1 – Chapter VIII 59

Part 1 – Chapter IX 67

Part 2 – Transition 75

Part 2 – Chapter I 77

Part 2 – Chapter II 88

Part 2 – Chapter III 95

Part 2 – Chapter IV 103

Part 2 – Chapter V 112

Part 2 – Chapter VI 121

Part 2 – Chapter VII 126

Part 2 – Chapter VIII 136

Part 2 – Chapter IX 146

Part 2 – Chapter X 152

Part 2 – Chapter XI 161

Part 2 – Chapter XII 167
Part 2 – Chapter XIII 175

Part 3 – Resolution 187
Part 3 – Chapter I 189
Part 3 – Chapter II 198
Part 3 – Chapter III 209
Part 3 – Chapter IV 225
Part 3 – Chapter V 232
Part 3 – Chapter VI 237
Part 3 – Chapter VII 244
Part 3 – Chapter VIII 249

Author's notes 261

Bibliography 262

Acknowledgements 263

PART 1 - SURVIVAL

Part 1 – Chapter I

There was an awkward silence in the interview room. The woman had stopped mid-sentence and was searching in her handbag for a handkerchief, which she could not find. Casting aside the bag, she placed her arms on the table and laid her head down on her left forearm. The police sergeant pushed back in his chair and diverted his eyes to the grey filing cabinet standing against the whitewashed wall behind where the woman was slumped. He was unsure how to respond to what she had just done, with such calm deliberation. The constable, who was sitting next to the sergeant, took out a clean white handkerchief from his jacket pocket and reached over the table to hold it just above the side of the woman's head. She raised her right hand and accepted it without speaking. After a few moments, Sergeant Bates gathered himself and in a hesitant voice said,

"I am sorry about all these questions. The more information we have, the quicker we will find your husband. So, Mrs Gallagher, can you please tell us again how Eddie was behaving in the last few weeks?"

In her own time, she lifted her head from the table and sat up. Her honey coloured hair tumbled down in waves onto her shoulders. Her face was framed by her high cheek bones and was without colour; accentuating her blue eyes, which were red-rimmed from crying. The sergeant was struck by how fragile she looked and wondered if this made her look more attractive than she would do were he to meet her outside of this set of circumstances. After wiping her eyes with the handkerchief, she responded to the question in a steady, assured voice that the sergeant had not expected.

"For the last time! About three weeks ago, there was a change in Eddie that I did not attach a lot of importance to right away, but which I began to get more and more worried about over the weeks that followed. He would always be attentive and involved, but on that morning something was different. He hadn't said a word since he came downstairs. He was sat at the table in the kitchen, staring into the distance as if I was not there – as if he was not there!"

"What about the night before? Was Eddie withdrawn then, Mrs Gallagher?" Bates asked.

"He was working very late, or so he said, so I was asleep when he got home. That morning, I was in a hurry to get our son ready so that I could go out to meet friends at the café as I do most days. I didn't give Eddie's unusual mood any more thought – I assumed he would be fine when he returned from work."

Sergeant Bates rubbed his index finger back and forth across his lips and then asked,

"And when was that, Mrs Gallagher, can you remember the day of the week or the actual date?"

"It was the first week of this month and it was... it was Wednesday."

The sergeant scribbled down a few notes and then looked up, expecting her to continue. Mrs Gallagher was now staring out of the window at the puffy white clouds being blown at speed across the bright blue sky. Sergeant Bates wanted to reach out across the table to get her attention, but then thought better of it. He left her to look out of the window for a short period before he continued.

"And what happened after that, Mrs Gallagher?"

She turned from looking out of the window and appeared surprised at the question.

"I went shopping and met up with my friends. He didn't come back until late that evening, long after I had put our son, Neil, to bed. I remember that he was smelling of drink; of alcohol."

The sergeant interrupted her.

"Do you know what pub he went to and who he had a drink with?"

Cassie thought for a moment.

"I assume the Railway. He usually drinks in the Railway Tavern. I don't know if he went there that evening or whether he met up with anyone. There is a regular group in there when he goes on Saturdays."

"Do you know any of the group that Eddie drinks with, Mrs Gallagher?"

"There are a few. A man called Dobson, one called Elliott, and some others. I can't remember their full names."

"Ralph Dobson and Tom Elliott?" asked Bates with a frown appearing on his face.

"Yes! That's them."

"And does Eddie normally drink during the week?"

"No. He would normally only go to the pub on Saturdays. During the week he would come straight home from work and we would put Neil to bed together, with Eddie reading him a bedtime story, more often than I did. On the evenings he got home after Neil's bedtime – he often worked late – he would always go upstairs as soon as he got in to check on him."

"When did he come home that night?"

"That night he didn't come home until after Neil's bedtime – and now that I think about it – he didn't go upstairs to check on Neil."

"And what was he like when he came home that evening? What mood was he in?"

Mrs Gallagher thought for a few seconds. "Eddie's mood had never changed for as long as I have known him. He was normally cheerful and good company. But that evening he was... sort of cut off. He looked drained and a bit red-eyed; as if he may have been crying, when I think about it now. He did not eat any dinner. I told him he looked sad and asked him what was wrong."

"And what was his reaction?"

"He denied that there was anything wrong and said that he was just a bit tired from working so hard. When I asked him if he was feeling ill, he said he had an upset stomach, which he did have from time to time. He snapped at me when I suggested he should maybe see the doctor. But then he immediately apologised."

"And how were things after that?"

"Things continued much the same for the next couple of weeks, with Eddie hardly talking to me and barely looking at Neil. He was staying out very late, even more so in the week before he disappeared. I was getting more and more worried and spoke to my friends about it. They thought I should confront him and demand he tell me why he was behaving like this. I suppose I was hoping that it would pass and everything would return to normal. But it didn't!"

"So, did you confront Eddie?"

"I decided on Monday this week that I would have it out with him. But, on Monday night he didn't come home. I waited up half the night and was going mad with the worry of it all. The next morning, I was at my wits end so I went around to my friend Jenny's house. She persuaded me to go with her to the colliery and talk to him there."

"And you saw Eddie there?"

"No! When Jenny and I got there, I went into the colliery office and spoke with Mr Dewar, the manager. He told me Eddie had not come into work; nor had he the day before. I was shocked. I just sat there feeling a deep dread and hardly able to speak. Mr Dewar suggested I should get in touch with you, the police."

"So then you called us?"

"Not right away. Jenny and I still thought that he might just turn up, so I decided to go back home and wait to see if he did. He didn't, so this morning after dropping off my son with another friend, I came to Aylston police station to report him missing. The constable brought me here to the police station in Westpool."

Tears were now welling up in the woman's eyes and one or two were trickling down her cheeks. The sergeant looked at her as she bowed her head, wiping her eyes and cheeks with the handkerchief. He decided that he could not go on with the interview, cleared his throat and said in a reassuring voice,

"Mrs Gallagher, I think you should go home now. We will get on with finding Eddie – you can be sure of that. A few key details that I just want to check before you go:

- Your name is Cassie Gallagher and your date of birth is 25th February, 1923. You married your husband, Eddie, in March 1946 and your son, Neil, was born in 1947. You have lived at your present address in Aylston since 1948.
- On the 3rd May 1951, Eddie's mood suddenly changed and he became withdrawn for no known reason. This continued for the next few weeks. You have not seen Eddie for the last two days, since Monday 22nd May, when he left home to go to work at the Bridge Colliery. He has not returned home and has left you no message as to where he may have gone.
- Eddie is almost 30 years old and his birthday is 23rd June, 1921. He is Australian, 5 feet 10 inches tall, his hair is blond, and he is in good health, although he has a slight limp due to a war injury to his left leg.
- Eddie's parents are dead, but he has a twin brother called Harry who lives in Australia.
- Eddie drinks at the Railway Tavern only on Saturdays, but out of the ordinary he has been drinking during the week for the last three weeks. His usual drinking companions are Ralph Dobson and Tom Elliott.

Is that correct? Is there anything important I have left out, Mrs Gallagher?"

She shook her head and smiled at Sergeant Bates for a brief moment as she rose from her chair and said thank you.

"Constable Simpson will take you home in a police car. Can you give him a photo of Eddie to help with our search? And also, would you give Constable Simpson his brother's address in Australia?"

Cassie Gallagher nodded her head.

"We will do everything we can to find your husband – just leave it to us. We will speak to you at home no later than tomorrow afternoon to let you know how we are getting on."

It was evening on a windy day in May as she came down the steps of Westpool police station, after reporting her husband missing. Constable Simpson was waiting with the back door of the car open. It had been raining not long before and Cassie noticed that the roads and pavements were glistening wet in the bright May sunshine. She climbed into the back seat, took a long, deep breath and closed her eyes for a moment. There was a smell of fresh cut grass in the air. That fragrance always triggered an uplifting feeling in her; of winter being over and summer soon to arrive. But today, springtime did not raise her spirits.

Constable Simpson started the motor and turned to her, asking, "Thirty-two Lewis Drive, Mrs Gallagher?"

"Yes, that's right, thank you."

The drive would take Cassie the ten miles from the police station in Westpool to her home on the north-west edge of the mining town of Aylston, the largest of several mining towns in the county. They drove through the outskirts of Westpool and soon they were surrounded by fields showing signs of spring growth. Fresh green foliage was beginning to hide the branches of the trees, and leafy bushes were swaying to and fro in the gusty breeze. She could see rolling hills in the distance, set in a darker hue of blue than that of the bright, cloudless sky.

A heavy tiredness came over her and she was drifting in and out of sleep as the car rolled from side to side through the winding lanes on the road back home. Faded memories of teenage years came to mind, when she and her friends would wander in the meadows and hills beyond their home town of Aylston on bright, warming days such as this. Cassie had lived in the town for as long as she could remember. It had a population of just over seven thousand people and within a mile radius of the town there were five coal mines. The town had no other industry and the great majority of the men, young and old, had spent their lives down the mines.

The distinctive sights, sounds, and smells of coal mining prevented the town's inhabitants from ever forgetting how important mining was to their town in the past, present, and future. As the car approached the edge of Aylston, mine workings reared up into view and dominated the landscape. She was awoken by the intensity of the noise coming from the pit head operations, which could be heard even from within the moving car. On these southern and western edges of the town, there was no green countryside to be seen. Volcanic shaped slagheaps obliterated nature from view. Next to the towering cone of slate-blue slag, there was a giant, thick spoked, metal wheel supported on a black steel frame rising to about sixty feet above the ground. As the giant winding wheel span round, there was a nerve-shredding screech and strain of steel cables being wound and unwound, as they disappeared through the pit shaft enclosure, and from there descended vertically into the depths of the earth.

Adjoining the winding-gear enclosure were several blocks of dirty red brick, with a single row of metal framed windows that looked like they had never been cleaned. In front of these austere blocks, rusting and battered coal wagons were in constant slow motion, pulled and pushed by lumbering black steam engines. Wagons arriving empty were shunted from one set of track rails to another and others were departing full of coal. The coal crashed down from a mechanical hopper loading wagon after wagon, until each was filled to the top with glistening, black coal. The slow commotion of chugging steam engines generated a high-pitched screech of steel on steel as their wheels glided across a complex mesh of rails and points. They puffed out clouds of white steam and trails of dark grey smoke from their furnaces, into the now pristine May day sky. Carried on the air was a sickly-sweet smell of engine oil amidst the swirls of coal dust from the coal loading, which had a mildly nauseating effect on anyone other than miners, whose daily exposure to it had long made them immune.

They soon passed the mining operations on the fringes of town, and the car was now headed towards the centre of Aylston where the daily bustle of street activity in the centre of town even drowned out the pounding and screeching of the mine workings. Only in the quiet of dusk and dawn or if awake during the night, did one hear the metallic noise from the never silent mining operations on the edge of town. Cassie wound down the car window a bit further and it struck her that the air within the town was much more smoke filled than it was at the mine head workings. The streets on windless days in particular, were pervaded by the smell of coal smoke from chimneys of homes and those premises that emitted dirty grey smoke from dawn to dusk.

The car pulled up at a three bedroom council house on one of the town's newer estates, with a view extending for miles across open countryside. The landscape comprised a patchwork of fields – some arable, others for grazing – all demarcated by either hedgerows or low, drystone walls. In the distance, the Leidan hills rose up on the horizon from the valley floor.

The front garden stood out from the neighbouring gardens in how well tended it was. There were flower and shrub beds bordering a lawn with snaking edges, well stocked with a mix of mature shrubs and flowers, some of which were in early spring bloom and others only at budding stage.

She felt a mix of relief and longing to get indoors to see her son, Neil. The constable followed her through the front door and then into the living room where Jenny and Ellen, who were sitting supping tea, stood up when they entered.

"Cassie, how did it go?" Jenny asked.

"I am so glad to be home. Is Neil in bed?" asked Cassie

"Yes, I put him to bed just half an hour ago, as he was so tired. He spent the afternoon round at my house playing with the twins. He is just fine, though he was asking for you and his dad before he went off to sleep," replied Ellen. Cassie gave her a fleeting smile and sighed. She then realised that Constable Simpson was still standing just inside the doorway waiting.

"This is Constable Simpson. I just want to call in on Neil and then I need to give the constable a couple of things. I won't be a minute." Constable Simpson nodded to the women and shifted his weight from leg to leg, as he awaited her return.

"I don't suppose there is any news, Constable?" asked Jenny.

"No, madam, no. It is early days but we will be doing all we can to find Eddie. You can be assured of that."

Cassie entered the living room looking pale and staring with intensity at the photograph in her hand. She handed it to the constable together with a note of Eddie's brother's address in Australia.

"Is this a recent photo, Mrs Gallagher?"

"Well, it was taken over four years ago at our son's christening, but Eddie still looks the same as then."

The constable turned to leave after giving reassurance that the police would be doing all they could and that they would be back in touch tomorrow afternoon.

"How did it go at the police station? Let me get you a cup of tea," Jenny blurted out as soon as the front door was closed behind the constable. Sinking down onto the sofa and with tears welling up in her eyes, she started to tell Jenny and Ellen about all that she had been asked and her responses. What had been most difficult was being asked so many questions again and again, in the main about how Eddie had been behaving in the last few weeks.

"They said that they were confident that they would find Eddie, which I found comforting at the time; but now I am getting that feeling again that something terrible has happened."

"Don't think that! Jenny and I both believe that everything is going to end up fine. There will be an explanation – we are sure of it. You just have to hold on and keep your hopes up," Ellen said.

"Yes, Ellen is right. Don't forget that you have so many good friends in this town. Already today we had Jean Smart and Anne Higgins from down the street, call in and ask after you. Jean brought some cakes and biscuits round – she is so thoughtful," added Jenny.

Cassie nodded in agreement.

"Also, old Jim Reilly – he called to say that if there is anything you need, including money, then you must tell him and he will do what he can. They all said to remind you that there are so many folk in the town concerned and asking after you. Father Doherty called by too. He asked how you were but he wanted to know more about what was happening and what the police had found out. As if we should know! He said he would call round again soon," added Jenny.

"I am trying to be strong. It's just so hard not to feel overcome when something as dreadful as this happens. I don't know what I would do without you two and the other kind folk in this town. Old Jim Reilly! He lives on a pension and only just about manages, but he is offering me money. He was ever so kind to my mother," Cassie remarked.

"I am exhausted. I need to go to bed and I expect you two both need to get home too. Thank you for looking after Neil. It would be good if we could meet up tomorrow, although I have no idea what state I will be in."

Jenny and Ellen got up to leave promising they would call in as soon as their children went off to school in the morning.

"Try to get some sleep, and if you don't, I think you should go to the doctor's tomorrow," Jenny said as she stepped out the front door and followed Ellen down the garden path.

Cassie nodded and closed the front door behind them.

Part 1 – Chapter II

After washing up a few cups and saucers, Cassie turned off the lights downstairs and climbed the flight of stairs to Neil's bedroom. Sitting on the edge of his bed listening to the child's soft, rhythmic breathing, her focus was that no matter what happened, she would never be separated from her child. How they would manage without Eddie brought on angst again, but then an acceptance that this was hardly the time to be worrying about such things. For the first time since Eddie's disappearance she felt calm as she leant over the child, stroking his blonde curly hair while being careful not to wake him. Feeling reassured, she got up from the child's bed and walked across the landing to her bedroom.

Slumping down onto the stool, she leant forward and placed her elbows on the dressing table in order to support her chin in her cupped hands. The image in the mirror reflected just how worn out she felt. Her tumbling, wavy hair was bedraggled, with the ends matted together. It had been a day of so many tears. On the point of starting to comb and brush her hair, as was her custom every night before getting into bed, she became fixated with the thought that this trauma might change her looks forever. After a few moments sitting motionless, the decision was made not to go to bed looking like that, so she opened the top drawer of the dresser to retrieve her combs and hairbrush.

Taking hold of a comb, her eyes caught sight of a white envelope lying at the bottom of the drawer. She picked it up as if it were something fragile and placed it on the surface of the dressing table. The envelope had no writing on it. Some time was spent sitting and staring at it; she was afraid to touch it, let alone open it. It would have to be a letter from Eddie, but feeling so tired and weak, she couldn't face reading what would plunge her into despair. Yet the realisation that it had to be opened was too strong, so easing her finger under the flap, the envelope flicked open to reveal a wad of bank notes. She counted out £95 in five and one pound notes – but there was no letter.

Relief was followed in an instant by unease. The money amounted to almost three months' wages. The only conclusion was that Eddie must have left the money in the envelope and placed it where only she would have found it – but why had he, and where had the money come from? Why was there no letter, she kept asking herself. A feeling of agitated confusion came over her as she undressed and climbed into bed. Unable to fall asleep despite feeling so exhausted, her mind drifted back to when Eddie Gallagher first introduced himself into her life.

It was at a dance hall in Westpool, the county town, in 1945, just a month after the end of the war. The evening air was still warm, with sunset not arriving until after ten o'clock. Everyone was continuing to feel the relief and elation that had followed the ending of the war. The town was busy and noisy with people out to enjoy their Saturday night, which was the one day of the week when young people went out either to the cinema or more likely to a dance hall. Cassie recalled going dancing in Westpool on that Saturday night with Jenny, Ellen, and a couple of other girls from Aylston. Jenny was a friend from school and Ellen had lived next door to her and her mother, ever since she could remember.

They had travelled to Westpool by bus with what seemed every other young person from the town. The journey took half an hour and they would do that trip most Saturday nights, catching the last bus back home. They were joking and speculating about whom they might meet that night at the dance, and whom they didn't want to meet. She remembered that it was Jenny who had stated in that forthright certainty of hers, that this was the night when one of them would meet the love of their life.

Soon after they had paid their entrance fee and found a table in the dance hall, Eddie approached their group and homed in on her, asking if she would like to dance. He had a limp on the left side that was only just detectable. Eddie was of medium build, with strong forearms that filled out the sleeves of the white shirt he was wearing and he had thick blond hair that was neatly combed with a straight side parting, and it was gleaming with hair cream. His deep set blue eyes were what had struck Cassie most on that first meeting and that image evoked a faint smile as she lay in the darkness. He had kept on looking at her; his face locked into a rapt expression. She had blushed – and she remembered the irritation with herself for doing so.

It was the accent that stood out when he invited her to dance. She did not know where it was from in those first moments. There was an air of solidity and confidence about him, which was an attraction for her. Having accepted his invitation, they danced together without a break for the rest of the evening. What came to mind now was how inquisitive he had seemed, asking a stream of questions about her family, her job, her likes and dislikes, and about her friends. Cassie was happy to respond to his questions. In contrast, he was more reticent in response to what she asked him and had to be prompted to give even a little detail to his responses to every one of her questions. On that first night, she managed to find that he was from near Perth in Western Australia and that he had a twin brother called Harry. They had been adopted when very young, after his birth parents had died in a car crash when he was too young to remember. He said little of his adoptive parents, which left the impression that he did not much like them. Eddie had left home to join the navy aged sixteen. He had trained as a mechanical engineer and had served in the Australian navy as part of the Allied forces in the

Mediterranean. In late 1944, he had suffered injuries to his legs when his ship hit a mine, just off the coast of Sicily. After being treated in a hospital in Gibraltar for a few days, he was then transported to Exton, the naval dockyard a few miles from Westpool, for further treatment to his leg injuries at the local hospital. He had arrived for treatment in the hospital where she worked as a nurse.

After a few months recovering, he had resumed work at the naval base pending return to his ship. Eddie had told her that, although they had never met and spoken while he was in the hospital, he had seen her from a distance and had been struck by how beautiful she was. He recounted how he had asked other nurses where they and their colleagues would go at the weekend, in the hope that he would be able to meet up with her sometime in the future. Having looked out for her at every opportunity, he had never come across her until he caught sight of her that night in the dance hall. Cassie was flattered that there would be someone so committed to searching her out. As that first night progressed, it became clear just how attracted to her Eddie was. He was very careful not to offend her with any remark, nor to attempt any intimate contact that could have been construed as inappropriate. Smiling to herself, she wished that he had been more daring in how he held and touched her when they danced. How alluring Eddie had looked and smelled on that first meeting. He was wearing aftershave and that sweet, fragrant odour was something from then on that was always associated with him.

The first evening of their courtship was followed by months of meeting up in Westpool, every Saturday night. They knew that they had fallen in love after their second meeting. In those early months of courting, a lot of time was spent during the week thinking about him and longing for Saturday night to come along. Eddie was always so excited to see her when they met up. On those Saturday nights, they began to spend more and more time outside the dance hall in quiet alleyways, kissing and touching with an increasing intimacy that would have been an embarrassment if done in more public places. Soon they stopped going dancing and went to the cinema instead. It was much easier and more comfortable to be intimate there. They were now a couple and Cassie was more than happy to talk of Eddie as her boyfriend to her mother and friends. A month after that first dance hall meeting Eddie was introduced to her mother who had liked him right from that first meeting.

Everything then began to fall into place. Eddie never returned to his Australian navy ship as the war ended before he had fully recovered. Having applied for and been granted discharge from the Australian navy in late 1945, he decided to stay and work in the country, as he was so entranced. Being a qualified mechanical engineer, he had found work at the naval base but after falling in love, Eddie got a job in a local mine just outside Aylston as a mechanical engineer. They became engaged five months after that first meeting with a wedding date set for late spring in 1946. As she lay in bed reminiscing, the memory of their wedding reminded Cassie of her mother's unexplained change of heart about Eddie and then her death which had occurred without warning, that same day. She did not want to think about that now and set it aside.

It was Eddie's reticence to talk about himself that was uppermost in her mind. Ever since those first few months of their relationship, she recalled just how little he had divulged about his family and friends, or indeed his life in Australia. He had said that his adoptive parents had died a few years back and gave the impression that he had never gotten on with them, his adoptive father in particular; that was why he had little contact with them after leaving home. However, he did have some contact with his twin brother, of whom he said he was fond but not that close to. With those thoughts drifting in her mind, she finally fell into a deep sleep after a very long day that would never be forgotten.

All of a sudden she was awoken by noises of Neil talking and playing. It was already light though still only just after six o'clock in the morning. Throwing off the blankets and swinging her legs out of bed, she hurried to put her dressing gown on and rushed through to Neil's room to find him playing with his pet horse, called Sammy.

"Neil, Neil, darling, what are you doing up at this time of the morning?"

"I am playing with Sammy. He must have woken me up, Mummy. Is Daddy asleep? Can we go see him in your bedroom?" Neil asked.

Cassie's heart sank. She had to respond but dreaded the thought of causing distress to her son, doubting that she could hold herself together were Neil to become upset. Taking a deep breath to gather herself, she picked him up and sat him on her knee.

"Daddy has had to go away for a while, darling. But he told me to tell you that he loves you and he will be back soon. Shall we have breakfast? Are you hungry, darling?"

"Yes, Mummy – can I have some toast and egg? I think Sammy is hungry too. Where has Daddy gone?"

"He has had to go away to do some work in another place. He will be away for a bit. Yes, Neil, let's have some breakfast!"

Neil ate breakfast as he did any other morning. He played with his food some of the time, chatted to Sammy when not to his mother, and tested to see how much mess he could make before his mother intervened. After breakfast, there was clearing up to be done before first dressing Neil, then dressing herself. Neil seemed happy with her explanation for his dad's absence and was content to play and chat with his toys.

By the time Jenny and Ellen arrived it was mid-morning and Cassie was feeling in control of her emotions, for the first time since her realisation that Eddie had gone. She had Neil to look after and he was her priority over everything else.

"How are you, my love? Did you get any sleep?" Jenny asked as she and Ellen sat themselves down at the kitchen table. Neil was now amusing himself with his train set in the far corner.

"Yes, I got some sleep though it took me a while to get off. Last night I found an envelope tucked away in the bottom of my dressing table drawer."

"What do you mean, a letter?" Ellen asked.

"As I was about to go to bed I noticed this white envelope at the bottom of the right-hand drawer of my dressing table where I always keep my combs and brush. There was no letter inside – but there was ninety-five pounds. It must have been put there by Eddie and it must have been put there just before he left. He knows that every night I comb and brush my hair before getting into bed but since he disappeared on Monday night, I have only brushed my hair using a brush that I keep downstairs. That's why I only noticed it last night. I still don't know what to make of it."

Ellen and Jenny looked at each other as if willing the other to respond. Ellen took the decision to go first.

"That is strange. Especially there being no letter or note with the money. I don't know what to make of it either. As you say, it must have been Eddie who left it there, but why would he not have at least left a note? God! This is all so hard to understand."

"Well, two things are in my mind. Firstly, the money is not from our Post Office savings account as there is still the same amount in there as there was last week. I am relieved I have got some more money to be getting on with for the next few months at least. But deep down, I am beginning to feel… well, a bit irritated! I know that may sound harsh given that we don't know what has happened. But why would he do that? Why would he not leave me a note and where did he get that money from?"

"I have no idea – but it would have to be a man. It's like they always have to have their secrets – even kept from those they are closest to. My Alex can be like that, but he wouldn't have the guts to keep something like this from me. Sorry – I shouldn't say things like that. We still don't know what has happened to him," Jenny replied.

"No we don't," interjected Ellen. "We don't know anything for sure at this stage. It is good though that you have money to get by for a bit. You have had more than enough to put up with this far without money worries on top. Are you going to tell the police about it?"

"I don't think you should," Jenny stated firmly before Cassie could respond. "You are going to need that money and what if he stole it? The police will take it from you if it has been stolen."

Cassie looked perplexed. "I suppose you could be right about that. Eddie didn't have money set aside – or at least not that I know of. But maybe he did. I don't seem to know as much about him as I thought I did." A faint smile crossed her face as she added, "Are you suggesting, Jenny, that I should start to keep secrets like you say only men do?"

"Well it's probably true that men and women both have their secrets but women at least share their secrets with those closest to them. Men keep theirs in their own head until they get drunk and then let them out. Though as often as not, you can't understand half of what they are on about when they do. I have often wondered about those men who don't get drunk; they must go to their graves with so many secrets. What's the point of that!" Jenny responded, making them all smile.

"I am going to tell the police. I expect them to tell me everything they know and it wouldn't be right for me to do otherwise. The police are due to call this afternoon. Can either of you look after Neil for the hour or so that should take?"

"I can at any time this afternoon or evening. He can play with my two – they like having Neil around," Ellen said.

"Thanks, Ellen. I'll bring him round and collect him after the police go."

"We each had the police call on us this morning," Ellen said in an apologetic tone.

"The constable was asking me about Eddie. And also about how you and Eddie were getting on – especially in the last few weeks," added Ellen.

"I don't mind you telling them what you know," said Cassie.

"He asked me about Eddie's friends. I did say that he goes to the Railway Tavern on Saturdays and meets some mates there but I said that didn't know who they were. Although, I do know but I didn't want to say anything to the police about people I don't know well," Jenny added.

"They do seem to be very interested in his drinking mates for some reason," Cassie intervened to say. Ellen continued to explain what she had been asked by the police.

"He then wanted to know about how you and Eddie got on. I told him everything had been good until Eddie's sudden change a few weeks ago. And also, as Jenny told them, I said I did not know of any reason why things had changed."

"I am sorry you are being bothered by all this," Cassie sighed. "What are folk in the town going to be saying about this? I feel a bit ashamed."

"You have nothing to feel ashamed about," Jenny responded. Looking at Ellen she took up the conversation.

"All the people that we have spoken to are concerned for you and many of them are asking how they can help. Of course there will be a few who like to speculate and gossip maliciously – but it was ever thus in a small town like Aylston."

"People are so kind," Cassie said.

"Oh! That Father Doherty called again. He seemed very concerned about Eddie's disappearance and was keen to find out how you were taking it. He said he would return in the next week or so – once things had settled down," Jenny added.

Part 1 – Chapter III

Sergeant Bates pulled his seat up to the table where two constables were sitting, waiting for him to start the meeting. Although forty-one years old, he was often assumed to be no older than thirty-five. He stood out for his physical presence, being over six feet tall, square shouldered, and muscular. His dark hair was thick and unkempt. It was swept back in waves from his forehead, which contrasted with the neat and closely trimmed moustache. The complexion was florid and his facial expression was stern most of the time. Whenever Sergeant Bates caught sight of himself in the mirror, he was often taken aback at just how miserable he looked; even on those occasions when in a good mood.

Taking a cigarette from the packet, he tapped one end of it on the table, lit up, took a long slow inhalation, and breathed out a trail of blue tinged smoke.

"Right, men! Let's go through where we are and what we need to do next about the missing Eddie Gallagher. As I told you, any involvement with Dobson and Elliott causes me concern, given their violent, criminal records. Constable Simpson, you have been putting details together on Gallagher's past; tell me what you have got."

Constable Simpson opened his notebook and began to read out his notes. He recounted all the information that had been garnered in the interview with Cassie Gallagher when she had reported her husband missing, finishing with confirmation that a telegram had been sent to the police in Western Australia.

"Is that it, Simpson?" Sergeant Bates asked in a disgruntled tone.

"Well... he is a practising Roman Catholic. Also, despite his war injury, which has left him with a slight but noticeable limp, he has always been in good health, according to Doctor Stevens. The doctor said he hadn't seen him at the surgery for over a year."

"And did you ask the doctor about whether Gallagher had any history of depression and what the doctor knew of his marital relationship?" Sergeant Bates asked almost before Constable Simpson had completed his sentence.

"No, Sergeant. I should have asked that," Simpson said in a tone of voice devoid of the irritation he felt.

"Well, when a man leaves a woman as pretty as Cassie Gallagher, we need to find out about their relationship, whether anything was troublesome between them and in particular, whether there are any indications that either of them is having a relationship with someone else. Anything along those lines could throw something up that is of use to us. Get back to Dr Stephens and ask him."

"Yes, Sergeant."

"Also, speak to the priest and ask him about the Gallaghers. Constable Lee, what have you found out from Eddie Gallagher's employer, colleagues and friends?"

Constable Lee pulled in his chair closer to the table and sat up straight. He started to read aloud in a monotone voice, at the pace of a child who was in the early stages of learning to read. Recounting his interview with the manager of the Bridge Colliery, Mr Dewar, he set out that Eddie Gallagher had been promoted to senior mechanical engineer because of his hard work. Mr Dewar was complimentary of his work, pointing out that all his colleagues had a lot of respect for him. The manager had confirmed that there had been a change in Gallagher's behaviour in the last few weeks, during which he appeared to be depressed and not fully engaged in his work in the way he had always been until then.

"That change of mood; if only we knew what caused it," Bates intervened.

"Another thing the manager mentioned is that in the week before his disappearance, Gallagher had asked him for an advance on his wages."

The constable went on to explain that Gallagher had promised that he would pay it back in instalments over the next few months. The manager had been taken aback by such a request as no other employee had ever asked him for a wages advance. He initially said no, but as Gallagher was such a valued worker – his best engineer – he had reconsidered and talked further with him to see what could be done to help. The explanation given by Gallagher was that he needed to pay off a loan to some people who were putting pressure on him and demanding repayment. There was no mention of who these people were. He had asked for £100 and promised to pay it back in regular instalments. The manager had agreed to give him £55.

"I wonder if it was Dobson and Elliott that he owed money to. They are nasty bits of work," said Bates as Constable Lee turned over the page of his notebook.

"I also spoke to two of his colleagues who confirmed that he had been very withdrawn over the past couple of weeks. They told me that although they did not know him outside of work, they knew he liked to go to the pub at the weekend, and also liked to gamble on horse racing. However, they did not think Gallagher had a heavy gambling habit."

"This is much too vague on dates. We need to know precisely when he became depressed at work, when he asked for the money and the date it was given to him. We also need to know about his gambling and drinking in more detail; certainly more than you have just read out. Go to the bookmakers and the pub in town and ask."

"Yes, Sergeant – will do."

The last part of his report covered his interview with Gallagher's drinking companion, Ralph Dobson, adding that he had not managed to interview Tom Elliott as yet. They would all drink together at the Railway Tavern at the weekends.

Dobson did not express any emotion about Gallagher disappearing and when asked whether he had any idea why Gallagher had disappeared, he had been cold and unconcerned, saying that he had no idea why. Dobson had said they had last met on the Saturday night at the Railway Tavern and that he had left before Gallagher and Elliott, at about 9.30, and had not seen Gallagher since. Dobson said Gallagher was the same as normal on that Saturday night and denied noticing any difference in his mood over the last few weeks.

"He would say that, wouldn't he," Bates remarked.

"He did appear to me a bit uncomfortable and perhaps holding back on something, but that may have been just because I am a policeman. As for Tom Elliott, he was out last night when I called at his home, so I left a message with his wife for him to come to the police station after work. He is due to finish work at six this evening," said Lee as he concluded reading his notes.

Constable Simpson intervened; pointing out that two years ago Dobson and Elliott had been charged and found guilty of breaking and entering shop premises and also of grievous bodily harm of a local man, Joe Easton. They had served a six-month stint in prison for that assault, as Easton had been badly injured and had ended up in hospital with a broken arm and two broken ribs. Easton had owed them money, which he hadn't paid back as promised.

Sergeant Bates stroked his chin and said nothing for a few moments as he gathered his thoughts.

"Yes, at this point in time I think we should focus on Gallagher's relationship with his dubious friends, and also on his marital relationship."

He told the constables that he had discussed the case with Divisional.

"The plan is that we continue with our enquiries but that we bring in Dobson and Elliott for interview. I will also be interviewing Mrs Gallagher again but only after you two have completed your enquiries and reported back."

Constable Simpson walked up the drive of the Catholic Presbytery. The lawns behind the line of mature trees growing on each side of the driveway were trim and the borders were neatly cut. At the end stood a large, double fronted, three-storey building constructed of grey granite. As he stood on the doorstep Constable Simpson looked around at the gardens and then at the impressive house. He could not think of any other residence in the town that was as grand as this. He rang the bell. After a lengthy delay, the door swung open and a priest stood on the threshold.

"Good afternoon, Father Doherty. I am Constable Simpson, as you will remember. I would like to ask you a few questions in connection with the disappearance of Eddie Gallagher. It won't take long, I am sure."

Father Doherty opened the door wide and stepped aside, indicating that Simpson should enter. "We can talk in the parlour, which is the first door on the left there. Just sit where you would like."

Father Doherty was forty-seven years old and spoke with an Irish accent. He was a small, thin man with hands that appeared larger than they should be for his build. There was a faint smile on his face that remained unaltered no matter what he was saying or doing. He had been the parish priest in Aylston for almost eight years and was seen by his parishioners as a reserved, often awkward, man who only appeared a degree more comfortable when delivering his Sunday sermon.

"Of course I remember you, Phil Simpson. It's a long time since you have been to Mass and Confession. You are always welcome back; anyone can be forgiven for their sins; for being a lapsed Catholic. How can I help you then, Constable?"

Constable Simpson took out his notebook and pencil and looked over at the priest.

"Thank you for the offer of forgiveness, Father, but that's not what I am here about. I assume you are aware that Eddie Gallagher has disappeared, and we are trying to find out where he is. In cases like this, Father, we try to get as much information as we can so that we can form some ideas on the whys, hows, and wheres, so to speak. I understand that Mr and Mrs Gallagher are parishioners of yours. Do you know them well?"

"I do. Well maybe not as well as some in the parish, but I do know them, yes," replied the priest.

The constable looked at the priest expecting him to continue which he didn't.

"I need to get an idea of how well they were getting on, Father. Were you aware of any problems in their marriage?"

"No, no problems that I know of, Phil, sorry, Constable Simpson."

"As you have known them for many years, can you tell me what you know of their relationship – their marriage – and whether you have spoken with either one of them in the last few weeks in particular?"

"I should make you aware, if you have forgotten all these years you have been away from the Church, that I can talk to you generally about any of my parishioners, but I cannot divulge anything that one of my parishioners has told me in confidence."

"But I thought that only applied in terms of the Confession, Father. I am not asking you to tell me of any sins they may have confessed to, just whether you are aware of any problems they may have been having that would be relevant to this investigation. A man is missing after all and his wife is sick with worry," Constable Simpson replied, unable to conceal his irritation.

Father Doherty leant forward and started rubbing his thighs with his open palms. "Well yes indeed, there is nothing I could possibly divulge that was told to me in a confessional, but outside of that I can tell you what I know that was not told to me in confidence. There is nothing untoward about their marriage that I know of. Eddie was a bit down over the last weeks, but their marriage was fine."

"How did you know that Eddie was 'a bit down', Father? Did Eddie tell you or was it Mrs Gallagher?"

"Eddie told me. It might be more accurate to say he was angry rather than down," the priest responded, still with his fixed, smiling expression.

"And what exactly did Eddie tell you? Did he say why he was angry?"

"Listen, I cannot give you any clear reasons because Eddie did not give me any," Father Doherty said as he continued to rub his thighs, but with more vigour. "He was feeling very unhappy, but he was not clear with me as to why."

"So you can't tell me anything more than that? He told you he was angry about something but did not say what? Isn't it unusual that someone would tell you that they were angry without either them or you going into the reasons why?" Constable Simpson said in a tone of sarcastic disbelief.

"No. Sure it is not unusual, Constable, and I am surprised you think so," replied Father Doherty, in a sharp tone.

"When did you last see Eddie Gallagher, Father?"

"I think it was a couple of Sundays ago – Sunday 21st May. Yes, that's when he came to the presbytery and was so angry."

"Angry about something he failed to explain. So you cannot tell me of anything that may be related to his disappearance? The day after he sees you he disappears but I don't suppose he mentioned anything about leaving either. Do you have any idea where Mr Gallagher might be now, Father?"

"No, I don't, Constable. And I really don't think there is anything more I can tell you. I have some people I need to visit, as well as poor Mrs Gallagher herself," he said while getting up and indicating that the meeting was at an end.

"If there is anything that comes to mind, we would be grateful if you would contact us promptly, Father. There is a lot at stake. Goodbye and thank you for your time."

Constable Simpson arrived back at the station still feeling irritated. He prepared his notes and went to the sergeant's office to report on all the matters he had been asked to follow up. He knocked on the door and only entered on hearing the sergeant telling him to do so.

"Sergeant, I have seen all the people that you told me to speak to further. Do you want a briefing now or later?"

"Now will be fine, Simpson. Take a seat at the table."

Simpson opened his notebook and reported that he had seen Dr Stephens and asked him what he knew about the Gallaghers' relationship. The doctor was unaware of any difficulties between them and confirmed that the only time in the last year when he had seen any of the family was in December when Mrs Gallagher had called at the surgery in respect to their child's heavy cold. The last time the doctor had seen Mr Gallagher was well over a year ago and it was for a recurrent stomach problem – though nothing serious in his view. Dr Stephens had confirmed that he had never seen either of them for depression. As far as he was concerned, they were happily married and devoted to their child.

"That clears that up then," Sergeant Bates said.

"After a couple of attempts, I managed to see Father Doherty the parish priest of St Edward's. In my opinion, Sergeant, he was unhelpful and evasive."

"You are probably saying that about him because you are a former Catholic. I have often found that former Catholics are easily irritated by priests. Anyhow, what did the priest have to say for himself?"

"Not a great deal – and that's what annoys me as I think he must know much more about them than he was willing to tell me."

Simpson recounted that the Father Doherty had started off by saying he knew the Gallaghers, but not very well, and then had admitted that he was aware that Mr Gallagher was 'unhappy, even angry', but denied having any knowledge of the reason why. Eddie Gallagher had gone to the presbytery on that Sunday, the day before he disappeared from Aylston, to let him know how angry he was feeling, but for some inexplicable reason failed to tell him why, according to the priest. Having stated in a smug, self-satisfied manner that confidentiality was sacrosanct, Simpson recounted how the priest had brought the interview to an end by stating that he had nothing more to add on Eddie Gallagher's disappearance, nor did he know of his whereabouts.

Sergeant Bates leaned back in his chair and lit a cigarette. He also thought that Father Doherty was not telling the whole story, but he could not settle on what information he might be withholding, or why. Were there troubles in the Gallaghers' marriage or was there some other trouble that only Eddie Gallagher was in? He tended towards the latter but did not discount the former. He decided that there was a need to question Mrs Gallagher further about their relationship; and also to get a better grasp of who Eddie Gallagher really was; his history, his habits, and his interests. He stubbed out the half-smoked cigarette and turned to Constable Simpson.

"Thank you, Simpson. Get in touch with Division again and press them for a response to the telegram requesting they contact Mr Gallagher's brother in Australia. We could do with knowing whether there has been any recent correspondence between the brothers that may throw some light on the matter. Getting a response may take some time so we need to push this."

A short time after Simpson had left the room, Constable Lee knocked on the door.

"Sergeant, have you got a minute? I have interviewed those people again as you requested and there may be something of interest that has cropped up."

"Okay, Lee. Have a seat. What have you got?" Sergeant Bates asked as he lit up another cigarette.

"Well the important thing first. I spoke to Mr Gallagher's colleagues at the Bridge Colliery again. Ted Moyes, who is also a mechanical engineer, told me that Eddie Gallagher had borrowed his car overnight on two days in the week before he disappeared – Tuesday 16th and Thursday 18th."

Lee went on to explain that this was the first time Gallagher had asked to borrow Moyes' car. Gallagher had said he needed it to meet up with some ex-colleagues, whose ship was berthed at Exton Dockyard for a few evenings last week. Constable Lee reported that he had checked with the dockyard and there was no record of any ship arriving or leaving last week – let alone an Australian navy ship.

"Does Mr Moyes know how many miles Gallagher's use of his car put on the clock?" asked Sergeant Bates.

"No, he doesn't. I did ask but he says he seldom checks the milometer. He also said that Mr Gallagher had filled up the petrol tank as thanks for letting him use it."

"So, we know he used the car to go somewhere on two evenings last week and we know he didn't use it for the purpose he told his colleague. What else do you have to report?"

"I couldn't speak to the manager of Doyle's Bookmakers on the High Street as he is off sick. The person I spoke to at the bookies said that Gallagher was not what could be called a regular gambler – he placed a modest bet no more than two or three times a month, but much more in the last few weeks. He said he would check with the manager and get back to us if there was anything else to add."

Sergeant Bates got up to leave.

"Thanks for that, Lee. Interesting, interesting... We will go through what we have got after I have interviewed Mrs Gallagher again; and Dobson and Elliott of course. We will see how things look then and decide what to do next."

Part 1 – Chapter IV

Someone was knocking at the front door. Cassie opened it to see Sergeant Bates standing with his police hat under his left arm and reaching out to shake her hand. She extended a limp hand, feeling awkward with the formality.

"Can I come in, Mrs Gallagher? Just got a few things to ask you and to update you on what we are doing – though at this point in time we have nothing new to report on Eddie. This may take up to an hour so I don't know if you want to get someone to look after your child? I could drive you and the child to a friend's place and drive you back to collect him."

"That's fine. Can you drive us around to my friend Ellen's place? She has agreed to look after Neil. It's not far."

"Of course, I can. No problem."

The trip took no more than a few minutes and when they returned, she offered Sergeant Bates a cup of tea, which he accepted. He explained that he needed to better understand the sort of person Eddie Gallagher was to have more chance of solving his sudden disappearance. The sergeant started off by asking her to tell him of the time when she and Eddie had first got together. She recounted in detail how they had met and how they had fallen in love.

"I do understand, Mrs Gallagher, that you were both very happy together right from the start. Were you living with your parents when you met Eddie? How did Eddie get on with them?"

"I was living at home when I met Eddie. Just my mum and me. My father was killed in a mining accident, or that's what they call it. It happened not long after I was born so I have no memory of my father. I don't like the term 'accident' when it is applied to deaths and injuries in the pits – there is always something that should have been done to prevent the vast majority of those so-called accidents."

"And how did your mother take to Eddie? Your mother is dead now isn't she?"

Cassie turned to look out the window and sighed. After a little time she turned back to address Sergeant Bates' question.

"That was a very sad time – my mother had died suddenly only a month before we were to be married. There is something I will never understand about that. She really liked Eddie right from the first time I brought him home. Mum was so pleased and happy for me when we announced we were getting married. But something happened."

"What do you mean, Mrs Gallagher?"

"When I had got back from work one evening, Mum, without any explanation, told me she disapproved of the wedding and begged me to call it off. I was taken aback and asked again and again why she was saying such things. All she would say was that she no longer thought that Eddie was a suitable person for me to marry and that she could never agree to it."

"That is very strange."

"As you can imagine I was completely thrown by her sudden change of opinion about Eddie. We had a bitter argument that night. I stormed out, shouting at her that I was going to marry Eddie whether she liked it or not. Later, after a lonely and tearful walk around the town, I returned home to find Mum dead on the bathroom floor. She had had a massive heart attack. I have always felt responsible for that, albeit that I still can't understand why my mother turned against Eddie in the way she did," Cassie said as she turned away to look out of the window again.

Sergeant Bates felt uncomfortable and reached for his cigarettes.

"I am sorry, Mrs Gallagher. That must have been dreadful for you. And you still have no idea why your mother turned against Eddie?"

"No. And I don't suppose I ever will. Maybe she was beginning to get confused – that could be an explanation. She was also beginning to forget things. I told Eddie and we discussed it at length. He was intrigued about it for a good while after. In the absence of any other explanation, we both settled on the cause being the first stages of dementia."

Sergeant Bates sat back in his chair and asked if it was okay to smoke. She nodded and he lit the cigarette he had been holding for some time.

"And you married as planned?"

"Yes, we did. But it was certainly not the wedding day I had hoped for. I was still in a state of shock and mourning my mother's death, and how it had occurred. That eventually eased, not least due to Eddie's kindness and patience. We were so happy together. And since Neil arrived, I haven't given the circumstances of my mother's death any further thought – until now that is. It has suddenly come back to me just how strange all that was."

"And now that it has come back to you, have you any new idea as to why your mother changed her mind about Eddie?"

"No, none," replied Cassie without hesitation.

"And what do you know about Eddie before you met him, Mrs Gallagher? What do you know about his background, his family, his childhood, and how he ended up here? I know you have already told us something of his past but can you just set out all that you know or can remember?"

There was irritation at Sergeant Bates' question.

"Well I will tell you what I know but I find it hard to see how that is going to help."

She gave an outline of all that she knew about Eddie's childhood. From what she understood, Eddie's and his brother's upbringing was not a happy one, though she stressed that he had never actually said it was happy or unhappy – he just hadn't said very much about it. He had hardly mentioned his parents when talking about his life after leaving home and it was clear that he had very little contact with them – although he had always maintained some contact with his twin brother, Harry. His adoptive parents died while he was serving in the Australian navy. Their deaths were close together, due to some virus that had swept through the area where they lived. Eddie had said he was unable to go to the funerals as he was serving in the navy at the time. Cassie stopped to drink from a glass of water. Sergeant Bates had his eyes fixed on her and did not appear to notice that she had stopped talking. After a few seconds he became aware that she was looking at him with unease.

"Sorry, Mrs Gallagher. I was just thinking about what you have told me," he lied as he felt his face blush. "And what do you know of Eddie's life in the navy up to the point when you met here a few years ago?"

"Again, come to think about it, I know the outline but not a great deal of detail. Men are like that, don't you think, Sergeant? They give you the bare facts or a brief description of events, but they never tell you much about their own feelings nor about the feelings of others who were involved in those events?"

"Some men do. Some men don't. I know what you mean but I wouldn't make a rule about how men can be," said Sergeant Bates as his face broke into a smile.

Cassie proceeded to explain what she knew of Eddie's navy career. He had started his war in the Indian Ocean as a ship's engineer, but in 1943 his ship had been transferred from there to the Mediterranean, to help with the Allied invasion of Sicily. His ship was assigned to minesweeping duties and in 1944 it hit a mine off the coast of Italy. He had suffered bad leg injuries, which required specialist hospital treatment, and that was why he had ended up at Exton naval base, and then spending several months recovering in Westpool hospital nearby. After Eddie recovered, he stayed in the country.

"And Eddie never wanted to return to Australia?"

"Just before we got married it did come up, but it was me who was interested, not Eddie. I don't know; maybe the effect of my mum's sudden death made me think about leaving here, and emigrating to a new life in a faraway country. It did have some appeal. Eddie was neutral about the idea. He said if that was what I wanted then we would go and live in Australia. I suppose I realised that I had good friends here and that if Eddie was happy then there seemed no good reason for giving everything up and moving to the other side of the world."

"I don't mean to upset you, Mrs Gallagher, but do you think that perhaps Eddie did harbour thoughts or dreams of going back to Australia that perhaps would explain why he has disappeared?"

She leant back in her chair and turned her head to look away. Her eyes were glazed with tears. After a few moments' silence, she replied without averting her gaze.

"I find it impossible to believe that he actually wanted to go back to Australia. So, no, I don't think that has anything to do with his disappearance. But perhaps I did not know him all that well. I was never brought up with men in the house as my father died when I was a baby and I had no brothers. Maybe I just don't know men all that well. Eddie was the first man whom I ever got close to, but he wasn't a friend like my women friends. I can speak to them about everything in detail, about how we are feeling and what we worry about. I never had that with Eddie."

Sergeant Bates scribbled a few notes in his notepad and then lifted his head to look at Cassie.

"I understand what you are saying, Mrs Gallagher. One final thing – how did Eddie get on with colleagues and friends? Was he close to anybody or was there anybody he mentioned whom he did not like?"

"Eddie seemed to get on with everyone at work. As you know he had friends he met up with at the weekend but he never stayed in the pub until closing time. I don't think he had really close friends like I have, but maybe I have gotten that wrong too. I certainly don't remember him ever talking either that fondly or badly of anybody. But, there is something that I should tell you."

"What is that?"

She set out in detail the discovery of the money in her dressing table drawer, explaining that it could only have been left there by Eddie, for her to discover a short time after he disappeared.

Sergeant Bates was now sitting upright in his chair.

"That is interesting! Do you have any idea where the money came from?"

There was a slow shake of the head.

"I don't. I know that none of the money was taken from our Post Office savings account as I have checked that and it shows that no money has been taken out of that account since Christmas, when I took some out."

Sergeant Bates was silent as he scribbled some notes in his notebook.

"Mrs Gallagher, we have found out that Eddie arranged for an advance payment of wages of fifty-five pounds from his boss at the Bridge Colliery. His boss agreed to it on the basis that Eddie would be paying it back at five pounds per week. Eddie told his boss that he had some debts to people who were pressing him. Do you know anything of this or of any other debts he had?"

"No, no, I don't know about any of this. He had no debts that he made me aware of. Something else I just don't understand!"

"I do appreciate that this has come as a shock, Mrs Gallagher. We need to do a bit more work focusing on where the other forty pounds may have come from. However, getting this money together for you suggests to me that he was planning to leave. We'll stop there so that we can go and collect Neil and bring him home. Shall we go?"

She nodded in a resigned manner and got up to leave still looking perplexed.

Part 1 – Chapter V

Ellen walked at pace down South Street towards the centre of town as she was running late for meeting up with Jenny and Cassie. Thoughts of Eddie Gallagher filled her mind and she could not rid herself of the feeling that something bad had happened to him – even that he might be dead. There was no reason to be thinking such a thing, she kept on telling herself to no avail. Her thoughts moved on to her friend. How distraught she had been in the last few days and how much more grief might come for her, and her son Neil. She felt a touch of guilt at how fortunate she was in comparison; how her husband Bill, who was a fireman in the mines, was ever reliable and good natured, and how their six-year-old twin girls were now settled and coming up to the end of their second year at school. Ellen was trying to come up with ideas on how she could support her through this but was unable to settle on anything specific. What was important, she decided, was to be attentive as things unfolded. She affirmed to herself that she would help out where she could; undertaking any practical tasks that Cassie needed doing.

Turning into Main Street, she was quickly distracted from her thoughts by the bustle and noise that only the centre of town generated. As with every morning apart from Sunday, Main Street was busy with women carrying shopping bags, some pushing prams, and all going from shop to shop. The prevailing sound was of women either greeting those they knew without stopping, or others who were standing chatting. Only occasionally was this background hum of conversation disturbed by the noise of passing traffic. The few men to be seen on Main Street at this time of day were older men. They were mostly retired, wandering along the street without any clear purpose. They would be standing in small groups chatting, either outside the bookmakers or by the Miners' Institute, where many would spend their leisure time, reading newspapers or playing dominoes or cards.

Before reaching Bertoni's café where she was due to meet up with her friends, Ellen was stopped several times by people asking about the Gallaghers. A few wanted to express an opinion on Eddie Gallagher's disappearance. In the last few days she had been stopped so often, with most people expressing concern at Cassie's situation and expressing the hope that everything would turn out well. However, there were some who wanted to speculate about possible reasons and focus on the morality of what happened – mostly critical of Eddie but a few hinting that Cassie must have contributed to him 'choosing to leave her'. Ellen's tendency for politeness was tested by such comments, but she did not allow herself to respond. She would bring the conversation to an end by citing the need to get shopping done and walking off before the person could respond.

On entering the café, Ellen spotted Cassie and Jenny sitting at a table at the far end. Neil was playing with some toys in the adjacent corner.

"Hello! Sorry I am a bit late. How are you, dear? And you, Jenny? Hello, Neil!" she called out.

"Not a problem dear – and anyway we know your clock always runs at least ten minutes slower than everyone else's for some reason," Jenny said with a broad smile.

"Last week you said last it was fifteen minutes slower – Ellen must be getting better," Cassie intervened to say.

Have I missed anything?" asked Ellen.

"Oh don't concern yourself, Ellen. Jenny and I agreed that we would wait for you before I set out what has happened since we last met. Get yourself a drink and I will tell you both what has happened."

Ellen went to the counter and returned with her coffee.

"Well, as you know I had Sergeant Bates come around yesterday. He wanted to know more about Eddie's past or at least all that I know about it. I told him of Eddie's childhood, his adoptive parents, and his time in the Australian navy. As I was telling him what I knew, it did strike me how little I actually know about Eddie's past. I also told him about Mum's sudden change of mind about us getting married which he did find strange. I had forgotten all about that – but it is strange isn't it, even after all this time? But probably not as strange as Eddie's disappearance now."

"And did you tell him about the money?" asked Jenny.

"Yes, I did. He said that they had already found out from his boss at the colliery that he had borrowed fifty-five pounds in advance wages. He asked if I knew where the other forty pounds could have come from, but I have no idea. Sergeant Bates thinks that leaving this money in a place where only I would find it, shows that Eddie must have been planning to leave."

At that point, tears began to well up. She bowed her head, trying to conceal the tears from others in the café. In response, Ellen put her arm round Cassie's shoulder as Jenny placed her hand gently on her forearm.

"I need to face up to it. He has left me and he has abandoned his young son. I can't even imagine why. I feel like I did when Mum suddenly turned against Eddie. It's the not knowing, the not understanding why things have suddenly changed – that's what's so hard."

"It is; it is. And it's so unfair on you. You have done nothing wrong. And don't let any bad-mouthing make you think otherwise," Jenny stated with her characteristic firmness.

"Are folk bad-mouthing me? What are they saying?"

Ellen glanced at Jenny with her lips pursed and quickly took the responsibility of replying.

"The vast majority of people who have spoken to me – and there have been many – have expressed their concern for you.

That has been the same for Jenny. This is a small town – you know that there are always a few who will take any opportunity they are given to gossip and speculate unkindly. It's not worth bothering with. There are so many more who are concerned for you. Isn't that right, Jenny?"

"Yes, that is right. I don't know why I mentioned it. As Ellen says, it's few and far between and nothing worth even mentioning, let alone bothering about. Me and my big mouth!"

They all smiled. Cassie wiped her eyes with her handkerchief and continued.

"You are right about how good folk are in this town. I do need to start to face up to what has happened and start thinking about the future – but I feel so exhausted most of the time. I can only concentrate on Neil and make sure he is okay. He doesn't seem bothered and although he asked about his dad, he seems happy with the explanation that he has gone away for a while to work elsewhere. It is surprising how carefree and trusting very young children seem to be."

"And what exactly are the police doing now, Cassie? Did they say? I see in the newspaper they are asking for anyone who may have some information about Eddie to come forward, but you would think they could do more than that," Jenny remarked with a degree of irritation in her voice.

"I don't honestly know what they are doing but I trust them. I trust Sergeant Bates. He told me they would do all that they can and I have no reason to doubt him. But if someone chooses to leave – and plans it well – it can't be easy to find them. Who knows where Eddie is now. He could be on his way to Australia for all anyone knows."

Neil had wandered over from the corner and started to complain that he wanted to go. Cassie picked him up and put him on her knee. Neil broke into a smile when he saw Ellen and Jenny, but soon reverted to whining that he wanted to go.

"I need to get going and do some shopping on my way home. Call round tomorrow morning if you can and we can go for a stroll in town and end up here as usual."

Cassie lifted Neil off her knee and on to his feet.

"Say goodbye to Jenny and Ellen, Neil."

"Remember, Cassie, If you need anything doing, like washing, looking after Neil, or anything – either Jenny or myself are only too willing to help, Aren't we, Jenny?" Ellen said as she got up to go.

"Of course! Anything – just ask," Jenny added.

Later that day, Ralph Dobson walked out of his house, closed the garden gate and turned left to walk into the centre of town. He had been feeling agitated since he returned home from work in the early afternoon, when the day shift finished. The police had called at his home again that morning while he was at work and told his wife that they wanted him to go to the police station. He knew it was about Eddie Gallagher's disappearance and was trying to work out what the police would want to talk again to him about. He made his way through the new council housing estate, coming across only a few boys playing football in the traffic-free streets. His step quickened as he approached the town centre. A group of teenagers was hanging about a bus shelter making the only noise that he could hear as he crossed Main Street and pushed open the side entrance door of the Railway Tavern.

There was only a half dozen men in the pub when he arrived just after seven o'clock on a Thursday evening. He approached the bar, which was the stand-out feature of the Railway Tavern. It was constructed of dark-stained hardwood with carved oval panels, reaching from below the sill of the bar down to just above the floor. The polished wood gleamed, in sharp contrast to the dirty wooden floor, covered with an uneven smattering of sawdust. There were four wooden tables and benches that showed years of use. In the far corner was a grubby darts board with a chalk slate for scoring. The large windows fronting on to the street had frosted glass in order to preserve the anonymity of those drinking in the bar.

"A pint please, Joe. Has Tom Elliott been in?" asked Dobson.

"No, not yet, Ralph. He usually appears nearer half seven."

Dobson sat down at a table in the corner by the darts board. After a few minutes Tom Elliott came through the door, looked around, and on spotting Ralph, quickly turned towards the corner and took a seat at the table his friend was sat at.

"I have been asked to go to the police station tomorrow morning before I go to work," Elliott blurted out.

"Keep your voice down, man. What are you thinking of? What do you want to drink?"

"The same as you, but also a whisky," replied Elliott.

Ralph Dobson ordered the drinks at the bar and walked slowly back to the table, careful not to spill the brimming glass of beer.

"They have also asked me to go to the police station tomorrow, so it's not just you, Tom. We need to agree what we are going to say. It doesn't need to be identical but what we say does need to fit with – or at least not contradict – what the other is saying. They are going to ask about when we last saw Gallagher and they are probably going to ask about how he was when we last saw him. This is what I—"

Tom Elliott interrupted before he could finish what he was saying.

"I am worried about this, Ralph – really worried. They are going to try to fit us up with something; like they tried to do last year, when there were those break-ins that we had nothing to do with. Why did Gallagher want us to do it anyway? What did he get out of it? And he still owes us for helping him! And with him still missing, they are going to focus on us – I know they will!"

Ralph Dobson took a long slow sup of his beer and looked around the pub, with a casual movement of his head from side to side. Neither the small group chatting at the bar, nor the two men sitting in the far corner seemed to be paying any attention to them.

"Listen, Tom, keep your voice down – and keep calm for Christ's sake. There is nothing the police have got on us. We tell them that we normally have a drink with him here on a Saturday night and we also did last week on Tuesday and Thursday, but that was because he came into the Railway during the week which was unusual for him. We deny that we saw him or were with him at any other times, especially any time after 7.30 last Tuesday and Thursday nights. The last we saw of him was on Saturday night here – that's what we say, Tom. Remember that!"

"Okay, I will remember all that."

"If asked, we deny any involvement in any break-ins, though I think it is unlikely that they will raise that, given that he didn't appear to take anything of value. Get your wife to confirm this account of what happened so that she keeps to it, if she is asked by the police. I have already got my Irene up to steam on all this. When they ask about how Gallagher was, we don't wander down that path. We say he was much the same as usual – no different. Right, Tom, tell me what you are going to say then when questioned."

Tom went through his story much as Dobson had outlined.

"That's fine. Remember – the police will always go fishing, but they have nothing on us. Just keep it matter of fact, tell it how we have agreed, and deny anything they suggest. There's nothing to worry about if you do that. I need to drink up and get back home. See you Saturday here or possibly we may bump into each other in the cells at the police station. No worries, Tom, – I am only joking!" He smiled, finished off his drink, and left Tom Elliott looking as worried as he was when he arrived.

Part 1 – Chapter VI

Sergeant Bates sat at his desk bent over interview notes and the reports from his two constables. After a few minutes, he sat up in his chair and stared out of the window while he took out a cigarette from the open packet on the table and lit it, only averting his gaze briefly in order to put lighted match to cigarette end. He sat very still as the blue cigarette smoke snaked its way over his head. He was thinking about Eddie Gallagher and was wondering whether he was still alive or not. After a few moments, he stubbed out his half-smoked cigarette and got up to go out to the main office in order to call in the constables for a meeting.

When he and the two constables were seated at the table in his office, Sergeant Bates began.

"Let's list the possible explanations for Eddie Gallagher's unexpected disappearance. And I say 'unexpected' not only because no one had prior warning of it but because it is out of character for a man who was happy and dutiful both at home and at work – until a few weeks ago. But before we weigh up the possible explanations, is there anything that has come in this morning that I don't already know about?"

Constable Simpson cleared his throat and stated that there had a been a telegraph response from the police in Perth, Australia earlier that morning saying that they had spoken to Eddie's brother but that he had not heard from him for almost six months. Constable Lee then reported that he had gone back to speak to the barman who was working evenings at the Railway Tavern last week. The barman told him that Eddie Gallagher had been drinking there with Ralph Dobson and

Tom Elliott early evening on both Tuesday 15th and Thursday 17th. He was sure as they were virtually the only men in the pub at that stage of the evening. They had left about 7.30 on both those evenings when Gallagher had borrowed the car from a colleague at work. The barman said that on the Thursday evening he had heard them having a heated argument or at least Ralph Dobson was being heated in what he was saying to Eddie Gallagher. He could not make out what it was about as they kept their voices low, but his impression was that Dobson and Elliott were the ones who were angry and Gallagher seemed to be the cause of their anger. The barman had been too far off to hear the conversation. All three were again in the pub on the Saturday evening although he can't remember for how long. It had been a busy session, as Saturdays normally were, and there were so many people in the pub. However, he had confirmed that all three again did not seem too happy together.

Sergeant Bates was nodding his head. After considering what he had just been told for a few moments, he shuffled the papers on the desk and began to read through the three possible explanations for Eddie Gallagher's disappearance.

- Gallagher's behaviour changed significantly because he became very depressed, three weeks prior to his disappearance. It may have been that he had suffered from depression in the past and this was a recurrence. Nevertheless, it does seem unlikely that anyone suffering from depression would have the energy and planning to up and leave as he did. As to possible suicide as a result of his depression, no body has been found, although it is possible to commit suicide without the body being discovered for a period of time.
- Gallagher may have got caught up in something that he had decided to escape from. He mentioned to his boss when asking for a wages advance that he had gotten into debt. He was with Dobson and Elliott on those two

nights in the week before he disappeared when he had borrowed a car. His wife confirmed that Gallagher stayed out very late in that week. Dobson and Elliott have criminal records for theft and for violence. Hanging around with them raised the possibility of him 'being disappeared', as well as that of him choosing to disappear.
- Something or somebody from Gallagher's past re-surfaced suddenly and that was the reason why he fled. Perhaps he was involved with another woman – possibly someone from the past with whom he had recently made contact again. The sudden change in his behaviour and mood in the last few weeks could support this. The fact that he got together a large sum of money and left it where only his wife would come across it, suggested that he planned to leave due to something that had occurred all of a sudden.

"So, let's go through each one of these possibilities. And I want you both to give your views regardless of what you think or imagine my opinions to be. And Simpson, can you take notes as you are well capable of doing more than one thing at the same time. So, taking the first scenario – depression and possible suicide. What do each of you think about this as a possible explanation? Lee – you first."

Constable Lee fiddled with the buttons on the cuffs of his jacket.

"Well ... I don't know what to think. I never considered that as a possibility. Oh yes; we do know that his doctor said that he did not suffer from depression. He had no history of depression, so I can't see how this could be the explanation."

"There was no suicide note left, Sergeant," Constable Simpson interjected. "Isn't there usually a note left by the person committing suicide? Maybe not always, but usually that's the case isn't it?"

Sergeant Bates thought for a few moments then spoke.

"Good point, Lee, the medical evidence does not suggest that he suffered from depression. But remember; the doctor has only known Gallagher for a few years and it may be that he has suffered from depression in the more distant past. Can you check with the Australian navy and Westpool hospital if there is any record of him suffering from depression in the past?"

Bates went on to agree with Simpson, that usually, but not always, there would be a suicide note left. However he didn't think that suicide fitted for other reasons. Gallagher was not so overwhelmed with suicidal thoughts that rendered him incapable of thinking of others. After all he had gotten £95 together and left this where only his wife would discover it. That did not fit with a suicidal mind as it suggested too much planning and too little motivation to leave a suicide note. He admitted that this was not conclusive and suggested leaving this until Constable Lee has done those checks on Gallagher's medical history before he arrived in Aylston. He then asked for the constables' views on the scenario that Gallagher had got caught up in something that may have resulted in him fleeing. Constable Simpson leant back in his chair and looked up at the ceiling for a few moments before responding.

"Well, the heated discussions in the pub last week certainly suggest that something had happened to cause bad feeling among them. Dobson and Elliott, especially Dobson, are capable of turning nasty and they both have records for theft, threatening behaviour, and serious assault."

His view was that the £40 that remained unaccounted for must have been either stolen it or it was gambling winnings. He suggested a check of all the thefts and break-ins within the district, not only since Gallagher had suddenly got depressed, but in the weeks before then. While there had been no break-in or theft in Aylston in the last couple of months that remained unsolved, there was a need to check if there had been thefts further afield, given that Gallagher had use of a car and may have had use of some other car at times that they did not know of.

"Yes, I agree. We should do those checks. But what about the possibility that Gallagher did not flee but was the victim of a serious assault that may have resulted in his death? I wouldn't rule it out that Dobson and Elliott are capable of such a thing, given how badly that guy Easton was assaulted by them, not that many years ago. No body has been found obviously but could a body lie hidden around these parts?" asked Sergeant Bates.

There was silence around the table before Constable Lee spoke. He recounted that fifteen years ago a local man, Barney Low, had disappeared. The rumours were that he had gotten on the wrong side of some local men to whom he owed money, and they had forced him down one of the many abandoned mine shafts in the district, and killed him there where it is unlikely for a body to ever be discovered. No body was ever found but that could have been because it was well-nigh impossible to do a thorough search of all the abandoned mine shafts within a few miles radius of the town. Despite that, Lee added, there were a lot of people who believed that he had been thrown down a shaft and some of the town's older people had told him that Barney Low wasn't the first to be killed in this way.

Sergeant Bates sighed and lit up a cigarette.

"There is a difference between following up a line of enquiry and setting off on a wild goose chase because of some local hearsay. So, before we consider embarking on a body search in God knows how many disused mine shafts or searching anywhere else for that matter, let's see what our further checks throw up."

Constable Lee nodded and looked embarrassed as Bates continued onto the third scenario.

"What about the possibility that something happened or re-surfaced that was totally unexpected? Something that compelled Gallagher to up and go. It would have to be huge given that he appeared to be happy with his life and his wife. And who wouldn't be – she is a beautiful, attractive woman."

Both constables looked at each other, then at Sergeant Bates again, who was gazing down at his papers on the table surface. They felt safe enough to share a smile without him noticing. Sergeant Bates returned his focus to the meeting. He stated his belief that the key to the mystery lay with Gallagher's sudden behaviour change. There was no evidence that he had been involved with any other woman in the time he had been living in Aylston, pointing out that had Gallagher gotten involved with someone in the town, everyone would have known no later than the next morning. He then reported that Mrs Gallagher had told him that her late mother suddenly turned against Eddie Gallagher, just weeks before they were due to be married. Her mother had given no reason for it and died of a heart attack on the same evening that she had begged her daughter not to marry him. She never gave any explanation of why she had suddenly gone from liking Gallagher a lot to then turning against him and their imminent marriage. Bates speculated that it may have been down to dementia, which Mrs Gallagher had said was the only explanation she had come up with.

"Notwithstanding all of that, we don't have anything concrete to go on that suggests Eddie Gallagher departed due to someone or something attached to either the past or present, so I don't see how we can pursue that line any further. We have enough to do on the other two lines of enquiry. Let's get these outstanding matters checked out and we will review where we are after we have interviewed Dobson and Elliott."

Part 1 – Chapter VII

She had put Neil to bed a half hour ago and was listening to the evening news on the radio. Feeling weary as she washed up the supper dishes in the kitchen, there was a knock on the front door. She opened the door to find Father Doherty standing with his hat in his left hand and a faint smile on his face. Cassie's heart sank at the realisation that she would have to invite him in, thereby preventing her from going to bed early as intended.

"Hello, Mrs Gallagher, I thought I would call to see how you are. This must be such a terrible time for you."

"Come in, Father. That's very kind of you," replied Cassie as she held the door open for him to enter. She directed him through to the living room.

"Have a seat, Father. Do you want a cup of tea?" she asked, hoping he might say no.

"Yes please. Milk and two sugars."

On returning with the tea, the priest sat down on the sofa next to her.

"You must be feeling lonely and desolate, Cassie. It's at times like these that you need comfort and support and that's what I am here for. Someone you can trust! Tell me, how have you been?"

Bowing her head, she felt tears welling up in her eyes, triggered by the priest's words of concern for her.

"It has been the hardest period time of my life in all honesty. Even harder than my mother's sudden death five years ago. I just don't understand why Eddie has left. Do you have any idea, Father? You have known him for a good few years now. Did he say anything to you?"

Father Doherty put his cup down on the serving tray and turned to face Cassie, which brought on expectations that he was going to tell her something that would give her an understanding of why Eddie had left.

"I did notice that he was not his usual self so I spoke to him after Sunday Mass a couple of weeks ago. He told me that he felt unhappy for the last few weeks, but he wasn't clear why. I tried to get him to talk to me but he didn't make a lot of sense. I expect he is one those people who thinks that it's best to resolve things themselves, and not to share them. He didn't confide or trust in me." The priest stopped talking as he put the cup of tea to his lips.

"You see, Cassie, the advantage is that everything is confidential with a priest; you can open up in total confidence, which you cannot do with a relative or a friend – or even with your spouse. Do you see that? You can always confide in me knowing that no one else will ever know anything that was said between us."

There was disappointment that the priest could not offer anything more informative, but she was touched by how considerate Father Doherty was being. She was beginning to feel pleased that he had called after all.

"It's very kind of you to call, Father. I am just at a loss to make sense of it all. My life with Eddie has been so good. I was happy; Eddie was happy – or at least he appeared to be all these years since we first met. That's what really throws me. Could it have been that I just didn't notice that he was unhappy? Something happened but I have no idea what. If you can help me with that, Father, I'd be eternally grateful."

The priest was staring at her intently and suddenly realised she had stopped talking.

"Well I am not sure… but maybe, just maybe I can."

He then recounted that he had often found marriages went wrong because one partner is unhappy, which the other partner had been unaware of. On several occasions he had found that it was because one of them was unhappy about the couple's sexual relationship. The priest suggested that this may not have been the reason in their case, but that would only become clear one way or the other if she was willing to talk openly about it.

"Would it be okay to ask you some personal questions? As I said, you can trust me, Cassie, I am a priest, and everything we talk about will be in confidence between you and me."

There was brief silence as she considered what he had asked. She desperately wanted to understand why Eddie had left and could see no good reason for not talking to the priest, given the guarantee of confidentiality.

"I am fine with that, Father. Go ahead and ask me, if you think that may help."

The priest leant slightly forward and looked into her eyes for the first time.

"I suppose the first thing we need to talk about is how you and Eddie have been together. I mean, I know you say that everything has been good but we need to explore just how close, how intimate you have been together. As you know, a marriage is a happy one when the husband and wife get on in every way. I have found so many times that marriage problems are often caused by a husband or a wife just being unaware that they are not communicating well and particularly in the matter of sex." He stopped to put his cup down.

"I have often had to work hard to get a married man or woman to tell me how things have been in the bedroom but when I have managed to get them to speak openly, I have been able to help them understand what the problem is and how to resolve it. I know that you don't understand why Eddie has left, and you did say that you wanted to find an explanation, so I think that it's worth exploring, in order to see whether this was the cause of his disappearance or not. Just remember, you shouldn't feel embarrassed telling a priest about these things."

However there were signs of embarrassment with the priest noticing that she was fidgeting with strands of her hair.

"Honestly, Cassie, you will feel so much better talking to me about these intimate matters, than you would with anyone else. Remember, it's all confidential, just between us – never to be shared with anyone else. So just tell me everything in as much detail as you can. The detail is very important in all of this. Let me make it easier for you by asking some questions about your sexual relationship. How often did Eddie and you have sex?"

She cleared her throat and looked down at the floor before replying.

"Most of the time he would want to at least three or four times a week. But in the last few weeks before he left, he showed no interest."

"If he showed no interest then it does suggest that your sexual relationship was a problem. And what about you before Eddie lost interest: did you want sex – did you enjoy it?"

"I did. I have always enjoyed it."

"And what about Eddie before he lost interest; did he enjoy it? How did he show you that he enjoyed it? Can you tell me, in a bit more detail about how you would make love, right from the initial stages?"

"Oh Father, I can't do that – it's too private," she replied as she looked away.

"Cassie, I understand. Believe me, I don't want to cause you any embarrassment, especially at this time when you are feeling so alone and without anyone knowledgeable in these matters to confide in."

He went on to express the view that with her help he would be able to work out whether this was the underlying issue that had caused Eddie's disappearance. In his role as a priest, men and especially women, had told him all sort of detailed things about their sex lives and felt so much better for it, because as a result of them opening up, the priest had been able to help them resolve the difficulties they had been having in their marriage. He was confident that he was best placed to help her to better understand what had happened – but he stated that he would understand if this was all too difficult for her to talk about with him.

Cassie felt Father Doherty put his hand on her shoulder. She was thinking of her intense frustration with having no understanding of why Eddie had left. She so wanted to have some explanation of the reasons for him leaving.

"I know you are trying to be kind, and I appreciate it. I will open up about this with you on the basis that you are a priest, who wants to help, Father. Eddie and I both enjoyed making love. I always assumed that he liked it as he would always initiate it. And I know—"

"How did he initiate it? Just tell me how it would happen, how it would be initiated, Cassie," the priest interrupted.

"Well he would kiss me very passionately, then he would… he would touch my breasts with one hand and then lift my dress up with the other, and… he would stroke the inside of my thighs."

"That's good. You are doing well. This is all in confidence between us, remember. And what would happen after that?"

"Eddie liked to take his time. He would start to unbutton my dress or my top, and would slip his hand inside my bra, while his other hand would—"

Cassie froze. She felt a hand on her left breast and a hand on the inside of her thighs. She immediately jumped up from the sofa.

"What are you doing?" she cried out at the priest.

The smile had departed from the priest's face.

"I am just trying to help. I was doing what I thought would comfort you. You gave me the impression that is what you wanted me to do – to comfort you. Why don't you just relax and enjoy what you told me you always enjoy. Remember what I said, this is in confidence between you and me. You have nothing to feel bad about. I am a priest just trying to help you."

"I think you should leave! You can't come into my home and do this," she added, struggling to keep her voice from faltering.

Father Doherty got up from the sofa with the smile now returned to his face.

"As you wish. I was only trying to help you and as you know yourself, you were inviting me to do so. But as I said before, this is all confidential and if you want me to help again, you should know that I am happy to do so – as your priest. You can come to the presbytery next time if that makes it easier. I do think I can help you, Cassie. Just keep that in mind. Good night, my dear."

He made his way to the front door, opened it, and departed without looking back. Cassie locked the door behind him. She turned around, leant backwards against the door, and started to tremble. After a while, she made her way to the living room, still in shock, and slumped down on a chair at the dining table. Her eyes were fixed on the sofa and her head was shaking from side to side with ever more speed. The thought of what had just occurred filled her with disgust and shame. An image formed in her mind of the priest's faint smile turning into laughter while scoffing at her attempts to plead innocence! She kept on asking herself if she had invited him to touch her as he had claimed. Feelings of shame and naivety enveloped her as she recalled telling the priest such intimate details of her sex life. Maybe he was right, maybe she had invited him to touch her in the way Eddie did. No matter how many times she went over it in her mind, she could not decide if she was blameless for what happened. Cassie felt more forlorn than at any time she could remember.

She got up suddenly from her chair and rushed upstairs to the bathroom. Taking off all her clothes, she washed and dried her thighs and breasts several times. After putting on her dressing gown, she took the dress downstairs and started to wash it in the kitchen sink, draining and then filling up the sink several times to rewash the dress. After the third washing she slowly ground to a halt with her hands and forearms in the water, her eyes fixed on the dress. She began to cry and started to slowly wring the water from the dress as best she could. Opening the back door, she stepped out and dumped the still dripping dress into the rubbish bin.

Returning to the unlit living room, she lay back on the sofa and stared out of the living room window. It was dark outside but there was a glow in the sky from a full moon, with a few stars shimmering in the darker reaches of the night sky. The outline of the Leidan hills in the distance could be made out. Breathing in a slower rhythm now, she felt a calm come over her. She ran and re-ran in her mind what had happened and found herself shaking her head. Why would I have ever invited a priest to behave as he did, she asked herself. Her mind was clearing now – it was the priest who had pressed her to talk about intimacy between her and Eddie. He had said several times that this was to help her make sense of Eddie's disappearance. This had all been set up by the priest under the guise of helping her. She could now see a clear difference between what she had done and what she had not done. It was never her intention to encourage that priest to do what he did. 'It was not my doing; it was not my fault'; she found herself repeating. Cassie felt defiant as she climbed the stairs. Having made a final check on Neil to find him sound asleep, she departed to bed with a determination that she would never allow herself to be set up in a situation like that again.

Part 1 – Chapter VIII

"Right, let's go over where we are with this, and decide what we do next – if anything," Sergeant Bates said to Simpson and Lee who were sitting on the other side of the table.

"We interviewed Dobson first and although we then asked Elliott much the same questions, there were of course different follow-up questions arising from their responses. We asked them about specific meetings with him in the last three weeks, and we put to each of them that they had had a falling out with Gallagher over money and that they were linked to his disappearance. Let's first go through what Dobson said. Constable Simpson, you took the notes for each interview."

Constable Simpson flicked back several pages in his notebook. He read out that Dobson had said that Gallagher had been an acquaintance for years, but not a particularly close one. They had met at work and although they did not see each other that often – as Gallagher was a mechanical engineer and Dobson a coalface worker – they had gotten to know each other better because they drank in the same pub, the Railway Tavern. They would meet regularly on Saturday afternoons and evenings, placing some bets at the bookies and having a few pints. In reference to the last few weeks, Dobson had said that he was not aware of any change of mood in Gallagher. He continued that Eddie Gallagher was behaving much the same as always – cheerful and jokey – even when it was pointed out in the interview by the sergeant that he must have been the only person not to have spotted that Eddie's mood had changed from a generally cheerful disposition, to one where he was distant and perhaps depressed. Dobson denied that Gallagher had been like that with him and Tom Elliott.

On events during the last week before Eddie Gallagher disappeared, Dobson had admitted that he and Elliott had a few drinks with Gallagher early evening on the Tuesday and the Thursday, but was adamant that they had departed from the Railway Tavern at 7.30 and that he, Dobson, had gone home. He said he didn't know why Gallagher had been in the pub on those evenings in the last few weeks when he normally drank only at the weekend. Dobson had then challenged the police to check with his wife who would confirm that he was at home from just after 7.30 in the evening on both those days. He denied going in any car with Gallagher on any occasion both in the week before Gallagher disappeared or at any other time.

In response to the suggestion that Gallagher owed him money and that he had fallen out with him over this, and had taken his revenge on him – Dobson denied it all. He had said that he and Elliott did not have an argument with Gallagher in the pub and that anyone saying otherwise either misunderstood it for a disagreement about football or they were lying. He challenged the police to provide proof that any falling out had occurred and said that it was just untrue to suggest that Gallagher owed him money. He was insistent that the last he saw of Gallagher before he disappeared was on the Saturday evening as usual in the Railway Tavern and that things were as always – relaxed and friendly. Simpson quoted Dobson as saying: 'You lot are making things up as you go along. If you have any proof of wrong doing, then show me it. No, I knew it – you don't have any proof of this and yet again you are trying to pin things on me and Tom Elliott for our sins of the past.' Dobson had left the interview with a satisfied smile on his face. His wife had confirmed his story about being at home from no later than 7.45 on the Tuesday and Thursday evenings of the week before Gallagher disappeared.

Sergeant Bates blew out a trail of smoke and then took a slow, deep inhalation of his cigarette. He tapped his fingers on the table and then stubbed out the half smoked cigarette.

"I don't believe Dobson but let's move on to Elliott's interview rather than get into that."

Constable Simpson started flicking through the pages of his notebook but not looking at any page in detail, while continuing to talk at the same time. He said that Elliot had told it much the same as Dobson; denying anything untoward either about Gallagher's mood in the weeks before he disappeared, or in relation to any money owed by Gallagher, or as to a falling out amongst them. But, a couple of things were different. When Sergeant Bates had contradicted him about being in Eddie Gallagher's car, claiming that Dobson had said that Gallagher had given them both a lift home in the car he had borrowed both on the Tuesday and the Thursday evenings, Elliott stated in response that he had forgotten about that and yes, Gallagher had given them a lift home. Also, Elliot's wife had been very nervous when Simpson checked what time her husband had arrived home on the Tuesday and Thursday evenings and she had ended up saying she could not remember as she had gone to bed early those evenings because she had a headache, but funnily enough, she had not had a headache on any other evening of that week.

Sergeant Bates got up out of his seat and started pacing around the table.

"Constable Lee, have you checked again with Division on any break-ins or thefts that week before Gallagher disappeared – in particular on the Tuesday or Thursday nights of that week? And did you speak to the manager of the bookies about the betting habits and winnings over the last month for Gallagher, Dobson, and Elliott?"

The constable said that with regard to break-ins or thefts, there were none on those particular days. There had been a couple on Friday night of that week in Westpool but a man had been charged with those. There were no unresolved break-ins in the weeks before. He then reported that he had had a word with a Mr Doyle, the manager of the bookies. The manager had told him that Gallagher had been placing bets virtually every day in the last couple of weeks before he disappeared; whereas before then he would only make a few bets on Saturday each week. The manager reckoned that Gallagher has won over £40 in those last few weeks but he wasn't sure of the exact amount. He also said that Dobson and Elliott always made some bets on Saturdays and that's what they continued to do over the last month. He thought they jointly might have had winnings of about £5 maximum.

"In that case, we cannot connect Gallagher getting use of his friend's car on those two days with any break-in or theft. So why he borrowed the car and where he drove to remains a mystery. Maybe he went to see some woman he had fallen in love with."

Bates concluded that there was nowhere else to go with the suggestion that Gallagher was involved with Dobson and Elliott in some robbery, or that Gallagher owed money to Dobson and Elliott. That being the case it also left no motive for Dobson and Elliott assaulting Gallagher – or indeed anything worse. Despite the barman saying that they had argued and had a falling out, Bates didn't think there was any basis for continuing with the foul play line of enquiry, and therefore there were no grounds to conduct any search for a body in disused mine shafts or the like.

"So what do we know about Eddie Gallagher's past that would explain his disappearance? Simpson, weren't you doing some checks on his mental health history?"

Simpson replied that he had checked with Gallagher's doctor again and with Westpool hospital, where he was treated for several months following his war injury. There was no record of Gallagher having any mental health problems in the past. The hospital also confirmed that they had never been informed by the Australian navy that he had any mental health problems, which they expected they would have been if Gallagher had had problems in the past.

Sergeant Bates stopped pacing around the table and took his seat again.

"Well that is more or less definitive and in effect ends the line of enquiry that Eddie Gallagher's mood change and his disappearance were related to mental illness. It also rules out any basis for suspecting that he may have committed suicide due to mental health reasons. That leaves us with the cause of his disappearance being that somebody or something from Eddie's past resurfaced suddenly – and he fled because of that."

"It's beginning to feel like searching for a needle in a haystack! Sergeant, how can we take that line of enquiry further?" Constable Simpson asked.

Bates recounted again what had come up in his interview with Cassie Gallagher with respect to her mother suddenly and without any explanation turning against her proposed marriage to Eddie Gallagher. He speculated that there could be some connection; perhaps her mother had discovered something about him that no one else knew. However intriguing though that was, it amounted to nothing more than something strange which happened five years ago. It did not help them solve why Eddie Gallagher's mood had suddenly changed a few weeks ago.

The sergeant pointed out that it was of course no crime to leave a marriage and disappear and that despite all their efforts there was no further line of enquiry to pursue on why Eddie Gallagher had suddenly changed from being a happily married man, with a very attractive wife and young son, to a man who in a short space of time became deeply unhappy to the point of abandoning his family and life in Aylston. Given that Gallagher was together enough to leave a fairly large sum of money for his wife and son, it led him to conclude there was nothing more that the police could do other than to put this down to a man leaving his marriage and not wanting to be pursued and found.

"Have either of you got anything to say to challenge that conclusion?"

Constable Lee shook his head, but Constable Simpson responded.

"I still suspect that the priest knows more than he is letting on, as to Eddie Gallagher's reasons for up and going as he did; but I agree that there is nothing more for us to do other than to close the case."

Sergeant Bates nodded and replied, "Yes, I will speak to Division to get formal approval to do that. I will also inform Mrs Gallagher of our conclusion. Poor woman. She doesn't deserve this."

It was almost eight o'clock on a July evening when Sergeant Bates pulled up outside Cassie Gallagher's home. The sun was still high above the horizon. After switching off the engine, he sat looking out over the verdant fields of Summer, stretching to the distant Leidan hills. He was thinking how fortunate Cassie Gallagher was in having a house that overlooked such a striking landscape. His mind then turned to what he had to tell Mrs Gallagher, which he was not looking forward to. He comforted himself with the thought that at least he was not about to convey news that Eddie was dead. Besides, seeing Cassie Gallagher again was a pleasure and with that thought he got out of the car, walked up to the path, and knocked on the front door.

After waiting a few seconds, he knocked again. The door opened and Cassie Gallagher was standing in the doorway looking stern at first but then with a warm smile she invited him in.

"Take a seat in the living room, Sergeant. Is there anything I can get you to drink?"

"No thank you, Mrs Gallagher. Sorry to call so late but I thought it would be best to call after you had put your son to bed. Is he in bed?"

"Yes. I put him to bed at seven in the evening and he normally sleeps through until at least six o'clock in the morning. I assume you must have children to have thought to plan your visit around children's bedtimes?"

"No, I don't. Mrs Gallagher, I have come to update you on the results of our investigation."

Bates explained that despite the police's efforts, they had not been able to find Eddie or to come up with any explanation of why he had left. They had looked at a number of possible reasons behind Eddie's change of mood a few weeks back and his subsequent disappearance and had ruled out anything untoward having happened to Eddie – at least physically. Bates was sorry to say it, but the police had now exhausted all lines of enquiry and had concluded that Eddie Gallagher had chosen to leave for reasons that only he knew. The evidence suggested that he made the decision to leave by making sure he left his wife with some money to tide her over, at least for a few months. The money appeared to have largely come from the £55 wages in advance and also from at least £40 winnings from betting, which Eddie had done a lot of in the last couple of weeks before he left.

"Am I in trouble over his wages paid in advance? Will I have to pay that back?"

"Well, it's certainly not a criminal matter that we will be following up. It's a civil law matter, which means that it's for the employer to take action on that matter in the civil courts; if that is what they decide to do. The employer will have huge difficulty recovering this from you as it was a matter related to an agreement solely between your husband and them. I can't tell an employer what to do but I could have a word to see if they would give you some reassurance quickly so that you have nothing to worry about. Would you like me to do that?"

"I would really appreciate that. I know that I will need to go back to work now but I need money to tide Neil and myself over for a bit. The money left by my husband will help with that. So yes, please see what you can do with Mr Dewar. I don't want this hanging over me with all I have had to cope with."

"I understand and while I can give no guarantees, I will speak to the manager and do what I can to persuade him of the difficulties he will have in recovering money from you, given the agreement was made with Eddie. I will let you know what he says."

"That is so kind of you. Thank you very much, Sergeant Bates."

Sergeant Bates smiled and got up to leave.

"I am sorry about what has happened to you; you do not deserve this, Mrs Gallagher. If you think there is anything else we can help with, please get in touch. I will of course contact you after I have spoken to the manager at the Bridge Colliery. I could call in from time to time over the next few months if you think that would be helpful."

"Thank you again for being so considerate, Sergeant. I will be happy to hear what the colliery manager says. As to the future, I know I have to move on. I don't want any regular visits as I need to leave all this behind and get on with finding a job and looking after my son. Does that make sense? I don't want to sound ungrateful for your kind offer."

"That does make sense. But feel free to contact me in the future if you think I can help with anything. Good night, Mrs Gallagher, and I wish you all the best in getting back on your feet. I feel sure that you will do, and with success."

Cassie reached out to shake hands, which Sergeant Bates reciprocated. He departed feeling pleased that he had something he could do to help her. It was clear in his mind that, if necessary, he would put whatever pressure was required on the colliery manager to get him to drop any idea of pursuing Mrs Gallagher for the wages paid in advance. Then he would be able to return to see her in order to provide the assurance that she had nothing to worry about, at least on that score.

Part 1 – Chapter IX

After putting Neil to bed, she was busy in the kitchen preparing a meal, having invited Jenny and Ellen round to her house for supper that evening. The evening play on the radio was on in the background for the first time since before Eddie had left. Prior to that, the radio would always be on in the evening but one of the effects of the recent trauma was that she had found it difficult to muster the interest and concentration. That was changing now as several other things were. In the last week, she had spent a great deal of time working out what she would have to do now that she was left on her own to bring up her son. It was over two months since Eddie had left without explanation and it was now clear in her mind that he had chosen to leave. Cassie had always tended to confront the reality of any situation she was faced with, and not to pretend it was not what it was. Sometimes it took her a bit of time, but there was no avoiding the compulsion she felt to face up to difficulties, regardless of how frightening they may be. Although there were still moments of fragility, there were more times now when she felt irritation, if not anger, that Eddie had left without any warning or explanation. She felt no appreciation to him for the money he had left but was aware that it did give her some leeway in getting a job and securing a regular income that would sustain her and Neil. Contact had been made with both Eddie's trade union and also a trade union official from her former work as a nurse in Westpool hospital. A plan for the future was forming and she wanted to talk this through with her friends and then hopefully to make a start on what she was beginning to refer to as her next life.

Jenny arrived first. As always, Ellen arrived about ten minutes later.

"Come through to the kitchen, girls. Less chance in there of Jenny waking Neil up."

"I don't talk that loudly, do I? The only person I raise my voice to is my Alex. But he never hears what I say anyway, no matter how loud I get," Jenny said.

They sat down at the table and began to eat.

"The police have closed the case. They think he just up and went for some unknown reason. They didn't quite put it that way but that's the way it is, in reality. They don't know and I don't know the reasons why. He chose to leave – he planned it – as leaving that money in the drawer of my dressing table shows. According to the police he got the money together by borrowing wages in advance from his colliery boss and through his winnings on the horses over the last few weeks. All very well planned, you could say," Cassie said.

"Will you have to pay that money back, Cassie? The wages money, I mean," asked Ellen.

"Surely not. I think you should refuse to pay that back. It's Eddie debt – not yours!" Jenny stated.

"Sergeant Bates had a word with Mr Dewar, the manager of the Bridge Colliery, and he called in earlier this week, Sergeant Bates that is, to tell me I don't have to worry about being pursued for the money."

"That was nice of him," Ellen added.

"Yes, that was good of him to put himself out for me."

Cassie then explained that she had been the recipient of another act of kindness by a man – old Jim Reilly who lived nearby. Someone, she didn't know whom at first, was leaving a small bag of groceries; vegetables, bread, milk, and tinned meat, which appeared on her doorstep every couple of days. After a week, she had so much food that she couldn't get through it. Cassie had caught Jim Reilly doing it early in the morning the following week. He had told her that he could easily continue to do this as he only had himself to look out for and that he didn't eat much so was able to give her at least half his rationed food. She explained to her friends that Jim also worked an allotment and produced more vegetables than he could eat. They had agreed that he would provide a grocery bag just once a week, including all the vegetables from his allotment that he could not eat. Jim had also been very encouraging of Cassie, pointing out that she had strength of character and quick intelligence; and that she was even more beautiful than her mother.

"The kindness of some people! And often those with little or nothing to share," Ellen said.

"What's more, Jim has always been a keen reader of all sorts of books, mainly novels but also including a collection of socialist and anarchist books that he gets from a specialist bookshop in Westpool. He used to talk to Mum about books all the time and would regularly give her books that he recommended. He has offered to do the same for me and I have accepted. He suggested that I start with a woman author and he has given me a book called *Silas Marner* to start with."

"He is viewed as being very knowledgeable and people reckon he has read more books than everyone else in the town put together," said Jenny.

"So, you are going back to work?" asked Ellen.

"Yes, that's what I intend. I need to. I had Mr Graham, from the miners' union at the colliery, call at the house last week. He was very nice. He brought me ten pounds that he said had been collected from colleagues at the pit. He said they would be doing other collections over the next months. But he also wanted to help me with advice on what social security benefits I would be entitled to, now that I was on my own. No Widows Benefit unfortunately. Can't get that unless there is proof that Eddie is dead. And of course you only get Family Allowance on the second and subsequent children."

"That doesn't seem right. Why no help with the first child?" Ellen asked.

"That's the rules, but don't get me wrong I am so grateful I have only one child to see through all this. So, although I now get some benefits, including help with the rent, it wouldn't be enough. Or at least not enough for me, which means I really need to get back to work. But at the same time, I had always intended to go back to work once Neil started school, so it's no different to what was always going to happen anyway."

"That will be easier said than done for a woman with a child," Jenny remarked.

"As you know, Neil is due to start school after the summer holidays and as soon as I can after that, I am determined to go back to work. That's the first thing I wanted to talk about with you both. I will need help with looking after Neil until I get home from work, which should be no later than six o'clock in the evening."

"Listen, I can help with that, no problem. Neil will be going to St Joseph's as my Charlie does, so he can come home with him and you can pick him up from my house. Alex will be fine with that," Jenny said.

"That's so kind of you, Jenny. But the thing is, Neil won't be going to St Joseph's. He will be going to the West School," replied Cassie with firmness in her voice.

There was a momentary silence, before Jenny spoke.

"But you and Neil are Catholics."

"Well... that's something else that has changed. I was never a strong Catholic anyway. A bit like my mother maybe. She stopped going to church in her later life. You can remember that, I am sure."

"I know these last few weeks have been a nightmare for you, Cassie. But do you think this is a time for making such a decision? Have you spoken with Father Doherty? He said he was going to call round. I think you ought to have a word with him about how you are feeling," Jenny suggested.

"Never! I will never do that," Cassie spat out with anger in her voice.

There was a silence among them. Ellen and Jenny looked at each other with bewildered expressions on their faces. Then Ellen leant over to take hold of her hand. Jenny followed by reaching over to put her arm round her shoulder. Cassie could not hold the tears back and she broke down. She cried like she had not cried at any time before then. Eventually she sat up and wiping her eyes with a nearby dish towel, said, "There is something I need to tell you."

She recounted to them what had happened when the priest had visited, telling them everything in as much detail as she could remember. Her friends' expressions turned from concern to horror as they listened. They were sitting in a state of shock until Jenny broke the silence.

"How awful! I am shocked. For a Catholic priest to... I can't believe it. Sorry, Cassie, I do believe you, it's just... well... it's unbelievable that he would do such a thing. He can't be allowed to get away with this," Jenny said, moving from a state of shock into anger.

"Jenny, I thought you would believe me but I know you are a much stronger Catholic than I and knew you would find this so difficult to hear. No doubt he and indeed many others in the parish – were this to be made public, which I definitely don't want – would put it down to a woman disturbed at her husband's sudden and unexpected departure. No, there is nothing I can do about it. But I don't want anything more to do with him and I don't want Neil anywhere near him."

Ellen nodded in agreement and got up to pace around the table.

"This is just so awful. You having to make sense of the worst thing that has happened to you in your life and he... a man of religion, takes advantage of you in such a manipulative way, when you are so vulnerable. It's making me angry, thinking about it and I am not one to get angry. But this! Listening to what you have just said, Cassie, I think you are right. There is not a lot you can do. He will deny it and were it to become public, there is a real danger of you not being believed and being seen as some hysterical woman in distress at your husband's disappearance. Hard as it is, I don't think there is anything you can do without probably making it worse for yourself."

"Yes, Ellen is probably right. But it does not lie well with me that he gets away with what he has done. I can hardly blame you for wanting Neil to go to a non-Catholic school. I am still happy for him to come to mine after school if that works. There are several kids in my road who go to the West School and of course they all walk home together after school," Jenny said.

"I am also more than happy to help out with him after school until you get back home from work. We can work it out between ourselves. Jenny and I could share what needs to be done. What are you thinking of in terms of a job, Cassie?" asked Ellen.

Cassie pointed out that to look after a child on her own, she certainly could not do shift work as she had done all those years ago when nursing in the hospital. She had contacted Bob Andrews, who was still the union convener at the hospital. He had been helpful by telling her that the county council was about to set up a district nursing service as a result of the National Health Service changes. The council would be establishing district nursing units in several towns and would be advertising for staff in the next couple of months with each unit being established around late September. The hours of work would be 8.30 to 5.30, Monday to Friday. Being a county councillor, Bob Andrews thought that Cassie should apply for one of the posts as she was a qualified and experienced nurse, at a time when there was such a big shortage of qualified nurses for the expanding health service. He had promised to provide a good reference for her, given how highly thought of she had been by everyone at Westpool hospital when she worked there during the war. Her preference was to get a job based at Westpool town hall. Ellen and Jenny both expressed the view that the job sounded ideal for her and agreed that the council would be foolish not to appoint her.

"And another thing. The job also includes financial help to buy a car as the job will require a bit of travelling around. I have decided that I am going to use some of that ninety-five pounds to learn to drive and get my driving licence. I am going to start that next week. So, although I won't need any help with Neil after school until late September, I will need some help with him while I take a couple of driving lessons a week. I would like to start next week. Would either of you be able to look after Neil while I am learning?"

"Of course I would," Jenny and Ellen said in unison.

"I honestly don't think I could have gotten through the last two months without you two. Thank you – I will never forget this." There was a silence as they all smiled at each other with their eyes glazed with emotion.

"We need a toast. Another bit of luck I have had is that Eddie Gallagher left a full bottle of whisky. He may have done so thinking I would need some comforting in my sadness. Well I have had too much of sadness. Let's drink to my future!"

Cassie poured out three large glasses of whisky. Raising their glasses, she made the toast.

"To the next life!"

And they all laughed out loud for the first time in what seemed like an age to each one of them.

PART 2 - TRANSITION

Part 2 – Chapter I

The letter arrived a few weeks before Christmas, the year after Eddie had left. Cassie had collected Neil from Ellen's house after driving home from work. As was her routine, on opening the front door she had put aside any mail that had arrived that day until she had kindled a coal fire in the living room, made supper for her and Neil, and put him to bed. As they sat at the kitchen table, she and Neil were talking about what they had each done that day. Every evening they had this same form of conversation; his mother telling him about what she had been doing in her work and in turn, Neil was expected to tell her about his day at school, and the games he had been playing with Ellen's daughters after school. On her prompting, he would then recount the story that Ellen had read to the children, as she always did, just before he was collected by his mother.

There was a ritual for bringing each day to an end. After finishing their meal, there was always clearing up to be completed, as Neil played until it was his bedtime. Without exception that would involve his mother reading a story, pronouncing every word with clarity, while drawing her finger along the line as she spoke it. Although Neil was just five years old, most of the time he was able to read the book aloud along with her. At the end of the story, Neil was half asleep and by the time his mother had kissed him, put out the light and closed his bedroom door, he was fast asleep. After finishing the preparation for the next day, there were a few hours of relaxation, before going to bed herself. She would start her relaxation time with reading any mail that had come, while listening to the radio news followed by a radio play or some programme on current affairs. There would then be at least an hour in bed reading a book that had been suggested and often provided by old Jim Reilly.

Having completed her household tasks, Cassie opened the single letter that had been delivered that day, which had her name and address typed on the brown envelope. Her assumption was that it would be a bill. On opening it, she found it wasn't. Inside a single sheet of white writing paper were four ten-pound notes. The accompanying note contained four short sentences in typed text:

From now on, £40 will be paid into the Post Office account on the first day of every month. It will be paid until Neil becomes eighteen years old. The monthly payment will only alter in proportion to any increase or decrease in my income. This promise will never be broken.

Picking up the envelope to decipher the postmark, she could just make out 'London' over the postage stamp. After sitting, pondering for a few minutes, she got up, turned off the living room light and sat at the table by the window looking up to the star-lit sky. After her eyes became accustomed to the dark, the wintry countryside became visible, extending to the faint outline of the Leidan hills in the distance. Eddie was in her mind for the first time in a long time. There was an intrigue now rather than the anger she had felt for most of the year after his walking out and leaving them. Her thinking was that he must have been someone she had never known; not deep down. She could not understand how he could have such a strong sense of duty yet disappear out of her and Neil's lives without any warning or explanation. What began to irritate her whenever it came to mind, was that there was still no understanding of the reason why. And not understanding something would always be the hardest thing for Cassie to live with.

For some time now she had settled on the idea that there may have been something wrong with Eddie – something troubling in Eddie's mind that he had kept concealed from her. Whatever it was, she now accepted she would never know. Time had given her a degree of distance from those traumatic events. Looking up at the stars, she began to wonder about London. What was Eddie Gallagher doing there? What sort of life was he living? But she could not come up with any ideas or images and soon tired of the effort to do so. However, she was surprised to realise that she had a firm belief in what was stated on the sheet of paper: that she would be receiving this money for many years to come until Neil turned eighteen. The only reason why he may fail to send the money would be if he became an invalid and as a result could not work. The other possibility would be if he died before Neil reached the age of eighteen. But she had long decided that possibilities were of no consequence to her. Since Eddie had disappeared out of her life, she had resolved never to worry about what might happen, but only to concern herself with what was happening, as she knew that she had very little time to spend worrying about anything at all.

She turned the lights back on and closed the curtains to the night and began to think about how this money would make her life so much more comfortable. Having been working for well over a year now, she was managing, albeit with nothing left at the end of the week to put by as savings for harder times or for future needs. The £95 Eddie had left in her dressing table drawer together with most of the £100 in the Post Office savings account had been spent, mainly on her car. The car not only made her job easier, travelling from household to household each work day, but it made commuting to and from work and the collection of Neil from either Jenny's or Ellen's home, so much easier. Her first thought on what this new money could be used for, was payment to both Ellen and Jenny for the childcare of Neil – without which she could not go out to work. For a while now there had been a feeling of taking advantage of their friendship and giving nothing in return. Apart from after school care there was the reliance on them to care for Neil during the day in school holidays. Not being able to spend much time with Neil during school holidays had on occasions made her envious, and even sometimes a little resentful of Ellen and Jenny, given they were in the position to spend all day with their children during the holidays. Nonetheless, she not only needed to work, but she wanted to go out to work. For her, working was a vital part of her life and her future.

There was a realisation that she would now have more than enough money to live in relative comfort and also be able to make some payment for the contribution of her friends. There would be considerable difficulty in getting them to accept any money from her, but she felt confident that if they would not take any money directly, agreement could be had for paying money each month into a savings fund for their children. Their agreement to being paid would also make it easier to ask them to look after Neil for an extra couple of hours on Saturday mornings, to allow her to do one of the many courses at the Workers Educational Association in Westpool that had caught her interest. She decided that some of the money would also fund a washing machine and a fridge, which would make running the household on her own so much easier. Even with this expenditure, there would still be some money left over for a little savings, which could cover one-off expenditure on things like holidays, car repairs, and Christmas presents – in a way that had not been possible until now.

With an increased sense of security about the future, it was time for bed. The holiday break over the Christmas and New Year period would be a time to relax and to enjoy time at home with Neil. She was looking forward to telling her friends about the money and being able to offer something back to them that would make their lives easier. Besides that, there were other things that awaited over the holiday period. Jim Reilly would be coming around on Saturday evening, as he now did on a regular basis. His company was the highlight of her weekends. As Cassie was undressing for bed, Sergeant Bates took the focus of her thoughts. He had sent her a short letter saying he would like to call in over the festive period to see how she was doing and to update her, though he had made it clear that there had been no new developments. In the letter, he had asked that she contact him by leaving a message at the police station if she preferred that he didn't call on her. She had gone to Aylston police station to leave a note in an envelope suggesting he should call any time after 7.30 in the evening on the Sunday before or after Christmas. Cassie was looking forward to that visit to a degree that surprised her.

The next day she was up early and was energised by the day ahead that she had planned out. She cleaned out the ashes from the grate before lighting a fire, which not only provided heat but was the source of hot water in the house. The prospect of spending so much time at home with Neil and with her friends over the festive period, was already exciting her. With the windfall of money arriving, she had decided early that morning that she would take Neil by car into Westpool to do some shopping; spending some of the money she had received on clothes for both her and Neil. The purchase by instalments of a washing machine and fridge was also something she wanted to complete today. She had arranged to have Jenny and Ellen, with their children, around to her house for lunch. And of course Jim Reilly was coming round tomorrow, so there was a great deal to be done.

They set off for Westpool after breakfast with Neil still complaining that he wanted to go to either Ellen's house to play with the twins, or to Jenny's, where her boy, Charlie, would be happy to play football with him in the street outside. Neil's complaining began to relent once he was in the car when he became distracted at travelling with his mother; not in any car, but in his car, as he referred to it. Cassie was enjoying having someone to talk to while driving and she pointed out the mines on the edge of town and a few other landmarks on the journey from Aylston to Westpool. When they arrived there, she knew exactly which shops to go to and in what sequence as she could not afford to spend much time shopping, with so much happening that day. The first shop she called into was a draper's shop where she got new clothes and shoes for Neil. After completing the purchase agreement for the fridge and washing machine, the next port of call was her favourite bakers in Westpool, in order to buy some pies and cakes for her visitors arriving later. Cassie then called into her favourite women's clothes shop, where after trying on two dresses, she settled on the dark blue, linen dress that she felt best accentuated her figure and her honey blonde hair. In the shop, Neil sat quietly with his book as agreed, in return for the promise that if he did so, he would be allowed to sit in the driver's seat and play with the steering wheel before they started the drive back home.

Neil had fallen asleep in the car on the return journey and Cassie found herself thinking about Aylston and how strong the attachment was to her home town. She had no recall of living anywhere else, although the first year of her life had been spent in a coal mining village, called Mapleside, which was in a different mining area, a long distance away from Aylston. Her mother, who had been brought up in Aylston, had married and moved to that village just after the First World War. Cassie was not yet one year old when her father was killed while working in the mine at Mapleside, having been struck by a coal hutch near the coalface where he was working. At the subsequent accident enquiry, the judgement had been to absolve the employer of blame but to find her father guilty of negligence. Not only had her mother lost her husband but she was denied the compensation the mine owner would have had to pay had he been judged to be negligent. That meant destitution and loss of their home, so she had to return with her young child to Aylston, as her only available option was to move in with Cassie's grandmother. Her mother never lost a deep seated resentment as a consequence of what she had been condemned to. Being so young when they had moved back to live with her grandmother in Aylston, she had no memory of those times. However, in her teenage years a clearer understanding had been gained of just how much of a struggle the years since had been for her mother. The outcome was that Cassie had been brought up in the town where her mother had found refuge and that was why she was so bonded to Aylston. As she was driving through the outskirts of the town, she was shaking her head at the memory of what she would always perceive as a brutal injustice her mother had endured.

Her mind then settled on the town itself and in particular what had changed from how it had been when she was growing up there. The centre of Aylston was a hub of activity on weekdays and Saturday mornings – with the streets busy with women doing their almost daily food shopping in the mornings and early afternoons. The car turned into North Street and passed through The Crossing, which was the heart of the town, where the two principal streets dissected each other. These two streets were where the few buildings in the town of any presence were located. The Co-op building dominated The Crossing. Constructed of red sandstone with ornate mouldings in complex floral forms above every window, it was the only three storeys edifice in town and stood out for having a turret at each end, with copper roofing that had turned a watercolour green over time. At street level all along the terrace from one turret to the other, were the shops, which comprised the largest food and general provisions store in town, a bakery, a butchery, and a draper's.

Across from the Coop was the post office, which was an austere building of dull grey granite, built in Georgian style. There were so many people coming in and out as Cassie drove past at a low speed, which made her realise just how busy the post office was throughout the day. The town's leisure facilities were also to be found in these two busy streets. There were several pubs of course but there was also the cinema, which stood out for being the only avant-garde building in the town. It had a whitewashed central tower soaring above the roof line, with symmetrical glass panelling on each side. It was busy every weekend and holiday of the year. The other stand-out construction was the Miners' Institute in High Street. It was rectangular and had a striking façade framed in darkened sandstone with three tall windows each comprising over twenty rectangular glass panes, set on either side of a stone arched entrance. On the upper floor just below the sandstone roof line, there was a row of oval shaped windows, which were also framed in stone. The frontage was of white pebble-dash, which accentuated the darkened stonework.

Cassie began to realise just how restricted was the range of shops and facilities in the town; there were no more than that required to fulfil the basic needs of the resident population. As a consequence, local people had to do a great deal of travelling to other larger towns on a regular basis, often for shopping but also to access those services that the town did not provide. While there were sufficient primary schools in Aylston, on completing primary school education, children then had to travel out of town for secondary education. This weekday travelling by children had increased with the passing of the Education Act only a few years ago, which required all children to stay on at school until aged fifteen. Although there was an adequate number of general practitioner surgeries within the town, local people also had to travel to larger towns in the region for hospital and other medical treatment, which with the creation of the National Health Service, local people were now accessing to a much higher degree. The one provision for which there was no shortage in the town was religion. There were churches of all denominations so nobody ever had to leave the town for life's rituals of christening, marriage and burial.

This frequent and essential travel to neighbouring towns was primarily undertaken by means of cheap and regular bus services. The railway station, which was now coming into sight at the far end of North Street, was another mode of transport available for the town's residents. However, it was seldom that local people would travel by train, although the transportation of coal from the local mines ensured the line was busy day and night. The exception would be summer holidays when families would holiday or day trip to the pretty coastal towns that were within reach by train, or when they travelled further afield such as the very occasional trip during the year to the city.

Of all the local towns larger than Aylston, the most visited by local people was the county town of Westpool. Apart from giving access to a wider range of shopping and required services, this was where young people in particular would go most weekends for its dance halls with live music, its cinemas, and its wide range of clothes shops; all of which Aylston lacked. As a consequence of having to travel to neighbouring larger towns, local people developed a sense of belonging not only to the town or village that they lived in, but to the wider district and its main town. Cassie was struck by the thought that as Aylston was far from self-sufficient in respect of shops and services, should the single local source of employment come to an end and people then had to travel out of town to other places to work, there would be no anchor to keep the young and able bodied living there.

Having driven through the centre of town, she was now driving on the road north through the small affluent part of town where the merchant and professional classes lived. There was no mistaking that this was where the few well-off residents of the town were located. The houses were stone built, detached, and all had their own driveways, with gardens big enough to contain extensive lawns as well as substantial trees and shrubs. Residents in this part of town could afford to buy their own, much more spacious housing and they were also much more likely to own a car. The road here was wider to accommodate a tree-lined footpath on both sides and several of the churches and the doctors' surgeries were also situated in this area. In the rest of the town, the vast majority of the dwellings had been built to a minimum standard at the end of the last century and maintained no better. They had been constructed by the mining companies to house miners and their families, as an essential investment to attract and maintain a workforce. For the last three years, there had been a start to the demolition of this damp and dilapidated housing and an ever-increasing number of new dwellings were being built by the local council. A generation had passed in which there was little if any building going on in the town, but the last few years had seen a striking change in the town's housing stock. There was still a great deal of poor standard housing to be cleared, comprising mainly one bed, terraced houses with outside toilets, but it was what politicians were promising would be done in the years to come. Since 1947, new council housing estates had been emerging mainly on the edges of the town, most constructed in pristine red brick; all of which suggested the arrival of a modern and expansive era. The new housing was largely semi-detached housing of two or three bedrooms with front, back, and sometimes side gardens – all with inside toilets and bathrooms. Each housing estate had a road network and a small park or green recreation area for ball games. As a consequence, the town had an air of optimism that local people could not recall in living memory. Cassie concluded that the new housing was without doubt the biggest change to the town; not only in terms of the expansion and the look of the town, but also for the impact of this new housing on the quality of life of local people.

They were now driving up to their home, which was a semi-detached house on the edge of a council housing estate, facing northwards and overlooking an expanse of countryside that extended to the distant Leidan hills. They arrived just as Neil was waking up.

"Can I go around to either Aunt Ellen's or Aunt Jenny's, Mum?" Neil asked with a yawn.

"They are all coming around here in about an hour, Neil. I need to get the lunch prepared."

Part 2 – Chapter II

The coal fire was stacked up and glowing by the time Jenny arrived with her son, Charlie.

"How are you doing, Cassie? My, it's good to get in from the cold. I am sorry I am twenty minutes late. Ellen always makes me feel that I arrive too early so I thought I would get here after her for a change. Where is she?"

"I'm afraid you have still managed to arrive before her. She probably waited until she saw you passing her door before she got ready to leave. Look, I can see her coming down the road with the twins. Jenny, come in and warm yourself by the fire."

Ellen arrived with her girls less than a minute later.

"Good to see you, Ellen. Hello, girls! Come in! Jenny is already here, having tried so hard to arrive after you – but to no avail," said Cassie trying to suppress her laughter.

"Ellen, my New Year's resolution will be to arrive later than you at least once in this coming year," Jenny replied.

"You don't want to take on any of my bad habits of being late. Surely you must have enough of your own!" Ellen responded.

"Talking about bad habits, my Alex's are getting worse. You know how he makes deliveries for the Co-op to outlying villages on a horse and cart? Well on Fridays he always gets home a bit later than on any other day of the week. He says he celebrates the end of the week on Friday afternoons, with a bottle he has on the cart. I reckon he would never make it back to the depot on Fridays but for the horse returning him there, asleep on the cart. Just as well horses don't get drunk on the job!" Jenny recounted.

They all laughed.

There were not enough chairs to seat them all round the kitchen table so the children were allowed to eat their lunch in Neil's room.

"Such lovely cakes, Cassie. You can't have gotten these in Aylston," Jenny commented.

"That's right. I got them from my favourite bakers in Westpool this morning. They are so good aren't they?"

"You surely didn't go all the way to Westpool just for these, Cassie?" Ellen said.

"Well no, I went in for some other shopping. Listen, I have something to tell you. Last night when I got home from work, there was a letter on the floor. It was from Eddie!"

Ellen and Jenny stopped eating instantly and were staring at her.

"Or it must have been from Eddie – although there was no signature. There was £40 enclosed – in a single, folded, sheet of paper with a short typed message saying – oh let me get it, I don't want to get this wrong."

She went to the drawer of the sideboard, took out the typed note and passed it to Jenny who read it and then handed it to Ellen.

"Well… what do you make of that!" Jenny said.

"Yes, I was as taken aback as you. It's not something I expected. I have thought about it and I am inclined to believe what is said in the note. I could make out 'London' on the postmark so he's well away from these parts now."

"London is a long way away. I wonder why he went there," Ellen said.

"The fact that it is so sparse – typed and not signed – makes it cold and impersonal. That confirms my view that Eddie Gallagher was someone I never really understood. I think something happened to that person but I have no knowledge of just what that something is. I don't think I will ever know why he left us. It's all a great mystery."

"And a great pity! But this money coming in now on a monthly basis – that will make a big difference, won't it?" Ellen asked.

"I am going to be much more than comfortable as a result. I suppose you will be thinking that I cannot rely on it, given Eddie Gallagher's track record, but the thing is, before he did his disappearing act Eddie was always reliable on money matters. He handed over the bulk of his wages without fail, which is a damn sight more than can be said for the majority of husbands in Aylston."

"Do you think he might ever return? He is clearly not abandoning you with this promise to send money?" asked Jenny

"Well, I think he is being clear that he is not abandoning Neil, at least in a money sense. It's for Neil's benefit. But yes, I have thought about the possibility that he could return – on a number of occasions since he left. My feelings now are that I would not want that."

"Really?" Ellen asked

"I can't think of any explanation that he could give that would make me forgive him. I don't want to sound hard and vindictive, although maybe I can get that way at times. It's just that I am beginning to realise that time moves everything on in a way that makes it impossible to return to the past."

"I can understand a bit of what you are saying. I suppose I come to it thinking, 'never say never'; that maybe things can be recovered," Ellen replied.

"My recovery is down to other things such as good friends. That brings me to a matter I need to talk about with you both," Cassie said, changing the subject.

"I will be getting forty pounds a month in addition to what I earn. That more than doubles my income and means I can live a very comfortable life. I want to pay something back to you both for the childcare you do, without which I could not work and live as I can now."

"No, no. We can't accept money from you for doing no more than you would do for us, were we in your situation," Jenny intervened.

"Hear me out, please. I knew you would say no and state that you will not be paid for friendship, but I am asking you to consider this. This is about friendship and honour for me too. How am I to feel if I am living in a much more comfortable way than you are when that is only possible through the hours you put in looking after Neil? Okay, if you don't want money, I can make my contribution by paying into a savings account for your children."

Both Ellen and Jenny sat in silence, looking pained. Ellen replied first. "Cassie, I have listened to what you have just said. I just find it very difficult to accept money."

"And that's my point. Were you in my shoes you would feel uncomfortable, if you ended up well off because of what I was giving to you. It's about friendship – not about money," Cassie said, sounding a little agitated.

"The money may not continue as you think it will," Jenny said.

"So, how about we wait for a period? If it does continue, then here's what I want to do. I am suggesting that I pay eight pounds to both of you every month, either in cash or a payment into a savings account. Contributing that amount to each of you still leaves me doing very well in terms of a standard of living – it's not as if I am sacrificing a lot."

"Okay. I will think about it. I can see now what you are saying about friendship and the position this puts you in, but I still feel very uncomfortable with what you are suggesting," Ellen said.

"Thanks, Ellen. I really appreciate that. And you, Jenny?"

"I go along with what Ellen has said. I will think about it. If Ellen decides no, she cannot accept anything, then I will also say no."

"I am happy with that. On another matter, it's time to be honest with Neil about his father not coming back. He has not asked for a while but the next time he does, I will tell him the truth that's he not going to come back. I will tell him that his father still loves him and shows this by sending money every month. It's best to be honest and it's best to do that when a child is very young where it does not seem to matter as much as it would do if I kept the truth from him until he was older."

"It is true that his father cares. Sending money shows that," Ellen added.

"Secrets and lies, even those done in order to be kind, hurt a lot more and for a lot longer than any initial pain of being told the truth. That's how I see it and I could not do it any other way with my son."

"When you put it like that, who could disagree?" Jenny replied.

After Jenny, Ellen and their children had departed, Cassie told Neil that they would be buying a Christmas tree tomorrow and asked him if he wanted to help decorate it. She reminded him that Father Christmas would be calling on Christmas Eve night with his presents and that they would be going to Ellen's for Christmas dinner. Neil was excited and wanted to help to decorate the tree.

"Will Daddy be coming home for Christmas?"

Cassie was taken aback. She knew she had just told her friends that she was going to be open with Neil about his father, but she had assumed that the next time he raised it would have been a long time in the future. At first there was a reluctance to inform Neil about his father's permanent departure, but she decided she had no option but to tell the truth.

"Neil, Daddy won't be coming home for Christmas. He has sent money to buy you some presents though."

"Why is he not coming back, Mummy?" Cassie heard him ask as she realised the full dread she had always thought this moment would bring.

"Your dad has decided to live in London. I don't understand the reason why myself, darling, or I would tell you."

"But why does he not come home? Everybody else's dad is at home for Christmas," asked Neil as he began to cry.

She took him onto her knee and hugged him and kissed the top of his head.

"I don't know, darling. What I do know is that he still loves you and every month he sends money to me so that I can buy your clothes and pay for us to continue living here. A dad would not do that if he didn't love you," Cassie said trying hard to keep any trembling from her voice.

Neil did not respond.

"Will Daddy come back next year, Mummy?"

"I don't think so, darling. It is sad but your mum will always love you. I will always be here with you. Always!"

Neil was sat on her knee sobbing for a while before she asked, "What would you like for your Christmas present with the money your dad sent?"

"I'd like a pair of football boots... and a football... and a bigger train set... and a..."

"Well let's go out tomorrow to get those. We have just about enough money to get all those things," Cassie intervened in order to prevent Neil adding to the list.

"Christmas will be so exciting this year, darling. Apart from all your presents, we are going to Ellen's house on Christmas Day and to Jenny's house the following day. So, you will have lots of friends to play with. And lots of your favourite things to eat. All that will make you happy, don't you think?"

Neil did not respond until his mum tickled him, which made him laugh, though it did not make him get down from her knee. After a few minutes he slid down and started to play and chat with his toys. After tea, his mum told him he would have to be up early tomorrow so that they could go and buy his presents. Neil's reaction was to complain about how long it would be before tomorrow would come. His mother suggested it would come a lot quicker if he went to bed, as a minute after falling asleep he would wake up to find tomorrow had arrived. Neil was convinced and took his pet horse, Sammy, to bed with him. While being read a Christmas story, he fell asleep holding on tightly to Sammy.

That night, the decision was made to postpone Sergeant Bates' visit until sometime in the new year. The next day she left a message to that effect at the police station. Neil had to be the focus of her attention given how upset he had been when told his father would not be returning. Christmas was spent without further incident. Neil was thrilled with his presents and spent many hours playing with his extended train set. His mother had also given him a framed photo of him sitting atop his father's shoulders, which she put on his bedside table. He had seemed pleased with that. Over the festive period, despite clinging to his mother more than normal, he showed no other sign of being upset. By the time the new year arrived, the sadness about his father appeared to be fading. His mother was relieved that the issue of his father's absence was now out in the open as it gave Neil the permission to ask further questions whenever he wanted to in the future.

Part 2 – Chapter III

Jim Reilly had become a stalwart friend to Cassie. He had lived all of his seventy-one years in the town and Cassie had known him since she was a child as he had been a good friend of her mother, who used to say that she had more respect for Jim than for any other man she ever knew. From the age of fourteen he had worked in the mines, although in the last fifteen years of his working life, he had been employed by the miners' union, as an organiser. Sacked and blacklisted for his trade union activism in the 1920s when the coal mines were privately owned, he had been able to earn a meagre living through his employment with the union, which took him up to retirement age. Although a long-time member of the local Communist party, Jim had never been very active in the party. Over many years, he had spent much more of his time serving on the committee for the Workers Education Association (WEA), to which he was committed, like nothing else.

Reading books was a major part of his daily existence. Apart from being an avid reader of fiction, a lot of his time was spent in the reference library in Westpool. Educating oneself was a life-long commitment and the benefits of reading he extolled to anyone who would listen, at every opportunity. To that end, he helped out at a bookshop in a nearby town that specialised in anarchist and left wing literature. In addition, through his efforts a reading room had been established in the Miners' Institute in Aylston and now contained an ever expanding stock of fiction and non-fiction books. Rare amongst the men of the town, Jim was a teetotaller. He often complained that men wasted so much of their energy on drinking, which without fail led to pointless arguing and fighting about things they had little if any knowledge of in the first place. The rest of Jim's diminishing energy was spent on his allotment growing vegetables, which he had worked on for over forty years. He had very recently given it up for a new responsibility; that of keeping Cassie's garden in trim. He loved gardening and being in the open air. His wife was long dead and for many years now he had lived alone. There was a married daughter who lived in Westpool with her husband and their three children, whom Jim was fond of, with no week going by without him seeing them. His only son, Laurie, was dead. He had been killed fighting on the Republican side in the Spanish civil war; something that stirred immense pride in Jim, but which he was forever sad about at the same time.

Cassie admired Jim Reilly for his stories, his wide knowledge of literature, and his well-argued views on political and economic matters. She had never met anyone like him and never tired of listening to him talk. Always encouraging and prompting Jim to give his views or to tell stories about times and events in the town long gone by, they would end up discussing books, radio programmes, or sometimes politics. Jim seemed like a personal teacher who never failed to be kind and encouraging. Although she had known him for most of her life, it was only shortly after Eddie had left, that a full appreciation was gained of the person he was. For some time now, Jim had been coming around to her home every weekend, spending a couple of hours there on Saturday evening or occasionally a Sunday morning. She trusted him like no other man and had come to fully understand why her mother had liked him and had confided in him so much.

His knowledge of literature was having an impact on Cassie. She was now reading every evening of the week due to his encouragement. Suggestions would be made by him as to what she might find interesting and he would give her a brief outline of what a book was about. Every weekend they would talk about the book she was reading or else discuss authors such as Dickens, the Bronte sisters, Hemingway, Foster, Kafka, and Joyce. Jim would often bring his dog when he called round. Neil loved the dog and that was the only time he was interested in staying in the room when Jim called. Cassie was always keen to go walking with him and his dog in that rolling countryside that was so accessible to her. On those walks they would have long and intense discussions about books and politics.

On a bank holiday Monday, they had agreed to meet up for an afternoon, while Neil was at Ellen's home playing with her children. Being a day of unbroken sunshine, it was decided to take a longer walk than usual. Cassie was keen to talk about a radio programme that Jim had flagged up as worth listening to, when he had come around to her house the previous weekend. They had agreed to listen to the programme and talk about it when they next met. It was about social and economic change in the UK since the end of the Second World War in 1945; with a discussion panel of four men expressing a range of opinions on the impact of the many changes on the lives of ordinary people.

"I listened to that programme on the radio about social change since the war and I learned a great deal that I didn't know. I knew about the National Health Service, the new housing, and something of the nationalisation of the mines, but there has been so much more than that. What did you think of the programme, Jim?"

"Well, I thought it was good in many ways, but I have one criticism. To understand the present, you have to know about the past. One of the things that could have been talked of more was why and how the scale of the recent changes are so very different to what happened after the end of the Great War in 1918."

"So, what is very different this time round? And why do you think that is?"

"Similar, big promises were made by government following the end of the Great War. It promised to improve the living conditions of working people, the unemployed, and the sick. Look at what actually happened! Nothing of any substance! The government in 1919 even accepted a report, which recommended that the mines should be nationalised. But they quickly reneged on that; just as they reneged on so many other things! Yes we had the beginnings of council housing being built for working people in the early 1920s – but that soon was reduced to a trickle of what was promised."

"I was growing up in those inter-war years so don't have any real appreciation. What was it like then?"

"The 1920s were as bad as any time I recall; certainly in the period that I remember before the Great War. Things were so bad that only eight years after the end of the war in 1918 we had the first General Strike in this country. That lasted for only ten days nationally, although the miners battled on for well-nigh eight months. Despite some heroic battles and the appalling hunger and hardship, we lost and had to return to work defeated."

"That must have been hard to take."

"Yes it was. Following a humiliating return to work on the mine owners' terms, some of us were then blacklisted because of our union activities. I was one of them, but I had the good fortune to be taken on as an organiser with the Miners' Union. The bitterness of the defeat in 1926 continued for several years and just when we thought things could only improve, the Crash of 1929 hit us. Life became even worse for our people. Unemployment, under employment, and poverty were rife, and most families had no security; not knowing how they would cope with the next week, never mind the next month or year."

"Is there a good book to read that recounts those times during the miners' strike?"

"I can't think of anything specific that was written about what happened in the mining villages around here. Of course,

I could tell you lots about what I witnessed and was party to; and there is a lot to tell. But as I have said before, Cassie, a good novel is often better at conveying reality than any so-called historical accounts, including mine. Certainly better than newspaper articles! So, I would recommend you read Emile Zola's novel, *Germinal*."

"Is that a novel about the strike in some other mining community in the UK?"

"No. It's a story of a strike in a mining town in northern France before the turn of the last century, but it's as true an account of what happened here almost thirty years ago in this century, as anything else you are likely to come across. I have a copy at home – you can borrow it."

"I'd like that. It seems strange to think that reading a novel about what happened at the end of the last century in northern France is a reliable way of understanding what happened right here, not so long ago."

"Getting back to why things are different after this latest war; in a nutshell I would say it's because people were never going to accept a return to how the world had been pre-war, in the way they had been cheated into after the Great War ended in 1918. Think of the scale of what had happened in 1945 with so many dead and so much suffering after two World Wars only separated by a long period of economic depression and widespread poverty. A radically different, more just world was being demanded," explained Jim.

"That suggests that only through massive wars and suffering can come progress. I'd like you to be wrong about that."

As they continued on their walk, they talked about what had featured in the radio programme, in particular, the changes in housing, social security, education, health, and in government taxation. They had heard how the government had committed to building 300,000 new council homes a year in 1947. Years after that commitment, that target was often being met and even exceeded on occasion. It was on social security changes where most disagreement had featured within the discussion panel on the radio. The disagreement had been on the extent that poverty was being alleviated. The state was now paying Family Allowance for each child after the first and there was unemployment pay for six months and sick pay in place. Another major change had been for those long-term unemployed not entitled to National Insurance with the new National Assistance scheme to fall back on – instead of the poor law.

"I don't think the new benefit system is in any way generous or even adequate – certainly for some of the people I see in my work. There are still a lot of people living in dire poverty," Cassie said.

"I don't doubt that, Cassie. Perhaps it would be more accurate to say the government has ended destitution for most families. It has provided the security of a safety net from destitution, although it has hardly started to tackle poverty."

Their discussion then moved on to the changes in education and the funding for all the social and economic change since the end of the war. The school-leaving age had been raised to fifteen, with free education for all and there were now opportunities for working class children to get a better education and even to go to university. The panel on the radio had been unanimous in the view that these changes would enable working class children to access further education and enter the professions. The programme had ended up by reviewing and assessing the changes in taxation and government spending. The more progressive tax system now in place meant the wealthy were paying much more tax. The top income tax rates had risen from thirty per cent in 1930 to ninety-eight per cent in 1950. In addition, inheritance tax rates for the wealthy had risen in much the same way. The panel had largely agreed that with such a progressive tax system, a huge increase in government spending, and almost full employment with earnings rising by about four per cent per year, it was little surprise that working people and pensioners were feeling much more secure and better off.

"That change in government spending and in taxation is the big difference from what has ever happened before. Has this only happened here, in this country?" asked Cassie.

"No. You will be amazed to discover that America is no different and in fact introduced a far more progressive tax system before this country did. President Roosevelt introduced these higher rates of taxes on the wealthy in the 1930s, well before the war started. He did it in response to the country wide poverty that the 1929 crash caused there. And now, despite such higher taxes on the wealthy, the USA is the most powerful economy in the world."

"Well at least what happened in America in the 1930s suggests that there doesn't need to be war for a government to be forced into progressive social change – although widespread suffering caused by dire poverty would appear necessary."

"A big unknown not touched on in the radio programme is whether all this progress will last."

"So are you predicting that these big advances for working people won't last, Jim?"

"I am saying that at some point the welfare state could be rolled back and there could be a return to levels of inequality and insecurity, akin to what they were prior to the Great War. Not likely in the foreseeable future, granted, but it can't be ruled out in the longer term. The wealthy have hardly been stripped of their hold on power."

"One thing the radio programme did not mention is that so many women have lost their jobs since the end of the war. The nursery provision that allowed women to go out to work during the war has ended and women are largely unable to earn a living and remain dependent on the fickle generosity of their husbands. That's where the focus should be now, though I am not sure it would be the priority of those in power who are almost solely male."

Jim smiled and nodded in agreement.

"I can't disagree with that. Men are indeed running almost everything, including the trade unions and often very badly. I agree with you that the one backward step the end of the war has brought is that there are much fewer women in the workplace now. Isn't it ironic that it takes a war for women to have opportunities to earn their own living?"

"Or sometimes it takes a man to walk out on their family! Being serious, it's the inequality that women face at every turn; that's something that has gone backwards. It's no surprise that the all-male panel on the radio programme failed to mention that."

Part 2 – Chapter IV

After tidying up the house and stacking up the coal fire, Cassie had a long, relaxing bath. She felt a touch of expectancy when putting on her new navy blue dress. The idea of dressing up for Sergeant Bates appealed, as she knew he found her attractive. Her face broke into a smile at the thought of 'how scandalous' it was that she, a still married woman, was looking forward to seeing another man. Following her bath, some time was spent on doing her nails, followed by applying her favourite lipstick. Pouring herself a whisky, she sat by the fireside waiting for his arrival and began thinking of what had been said about divorce on the radio some time ago. It had explained that until 1937, it had only been possible to get a divorce on the grounds of adultery. The change to divorce law had introduced additional grounds for divorce, namely: cruelty, desertion and incurable insanity. As a consequence, she was now aware that divorce was an option that was available to her. The thought had come to mind on a few occasions, but after Eddie had started paying the money every month, she had decided there was no hurry to do anything that might disturb that source of stability. This evening, sitting in front of the fire awaiting Sergeant Bates, she speculated on whether she might change her mind sometime in the future.

There was a knock on the front door. She took her glass into the kitchen, checked her appearance in the hall mirror while making a few adjustments to her hair, and then opened the front door.

"Good evening, Mrs Gallagher. How are you?" Sergeant Bates asked. He was dressed in a dark checked suit that accentuated his white shirt and red tie.

"Come in and sit yourself down in the living room. I am well. You look very well."

"I brought you a bottle of malt. I hope that's okay, Mrs Gallagher, can I call you Cassie?" asked Bates, as he swept back his jet black hair with his right hand.

"Of course, but only if I can call you by your first name. What is it? It seems odd that I do not know it."

"Ronald – but I prefer Ron. Tell me how you have been. Before you do that though, I should say that there is nothing more that we have found out since I last saw you, other than that Rob Dewar, the manager of the Bridge Colliery, phoned me a few weeks back to say he had received fifty-five pounds in the post accompanied by a short, typed note thanking him for the wages in advance. I asked him to bring in the envelope and could make out it had been posted in London."

"Eddie Gallagher pays his debts then."

"I could get the police in London to make some enquiries or at least alert them to the fact that he has disappeared. We could ask them to keep an eye out and let us know should they ever come across him. What are your thoughts? I am happy to do what you think is best, as there is no crime to speak of in this case."

"Just give me a few moments to think about what you have just told me. Would you like a drink? Whisky or something non-alcoholic? Have you eaten?" Cassie asked getting up from her seat to go into the kitchen.

"Thanks. I have eaten but I wouldn't say no to a whisky, with a little water please."

"Good. I'll join you."

She returned from the kitchen with a tray containing two whiskies, a jug of water, and two slices of cake.

"Good health, Cassie."

"And good health to you! I wouldn't want you to do anything at all concerning Eddie. As you say, he has not committed any crime by leaving me. For my part, I cannot see the point of searching for and possibly finding someone who has chosen to leave his son and his wife. That might sound harsh and heartless but I don't mean to be – it's just how I feel."

"No, that doesn't sound harsh to me."

"Feelings change! I was deeply hurt at first, and then I began to feel angry. But having a child probably quickens the recovery. I should tell you that a few weeks ago I got a letter and money from Eddie. The envelope also had a London postmark. He has committed to paying me forty pounds a month. The money makes things a lot easier. But it has been my good friends who have pulled me through all this."

"As far as I am concerned then, we won't be contacting the London authorities, given that is what you want. I already knew that you had picked up your life and were getting on with things. I understand that you are working and driving a car. This is a small town, as you know. Here's to you and your future."

They clinked glasses and smiled at each other. As the evening wore on, they continued drinking and talking, with her doing the bulk of the talking, if not the drinking. After explaining what her job entailed, the conversation then moved on to her enthusiasm for the books she had read. She told him about Jim Reilly's role in her reading and the stories he told that she found so interesting; stating how amazed she was at how much he knew about books and history. Ron was an attentive listener and seemed content to be listening rather than talking himself. Cassie continued for some time before she became aware that she was the one doing all the talking.

"And what about you? I have been going on about my life all evening. There must have been a woman in your life?"

"I was married but my wife died about five years ago. She had a heart attack and died at the age of thirty-five. We did not have children. Like you I have moved on from the trauma, though it did take me a while. I do a bit of reading, though not as much as you do. Also, I like to go on long walks in the country."

"Oh I am sorry. That's awful about your wife dying – and so young. How long had you been married?"

"About ten years. It was a long time ago now. As you say, time does move things on. I live on my own and I am used to that now. Listen, I ought to get going as I have drunk enough. It's been very enjoyable. I like your company, and I like you, Cassie. Could we meet again soon?" he asked, hoping that she would agree.

"I would like that a lot. The only thing is when and where. I would only want to meet up at a time like this, after Neil has gone to bed. I suppose that would mean you coming here again, which is probably not what you want to do. Can't you stay a bit longer while we talk about this?"

"Yes I can, but I'll have a cup of tea, please."

Cassie meandered into the kitchen feeling a bit drunk, but very pleased with how the evening had gone. She made the tea and brought it back into the living room.

"Thanks for staying a little longer. I like the idea of meeting up regularly, but I need to talk more with you before deciding whether it's the right thing to do. I am not in the position to start going out with a man with the expectation that it could grow into something bigger. It's too soon and I don't see how it's possible with my commitments. So, if that is what you have in mind, I should say no."

There was a silence for a few moments before Ron responded.

"I came here tonight looking forward to seeing you. I won't deny that I find you hugely attractive. I am well aware that you have a son who needs a lot of care and attention, and my presence may not help you in that. I don't know what we should do – I just know I would like to see you again and on some sort of regular basis."

Ron sat back on the sofa and looked at her, awaiting her response. Cassie began to smile.

"Isn't life full of surprises! I won't lie. I was also looking forward to your visit tonight but with no thoughts beyond that. You have been very good to me, Ron."

"Have I? I was just doing my job."

"You were very kind and you did more than your job. For example, you had a word with Mr Dewar about the wages money. I know you made it plain to him that he had no claim on me for returning the money – he told me so when I met him by chance one day in town. I appreciate what you did there. So, what are we to do?"

She got up, sat down next to Ron on the sofa. He pulled her close to him and they began to kiss.

"This is certainly better than talking about difficulties," she commented as they lay back on the sofa.

She felt his hand just above her knee and did not resist it. As he slowly raised his hand up the inside of her thighs, Cassie sat up and took his hand away.

"It's not that I don't like that, but let's decide what we are going to do. I am not concerned personally about gossip, but I am concerned about how Neil could be confused and hurt by it. I would like to meet on a regular basis – but let's take this slowly. We hardly know each other. Maybe you could come round every fortnight to begin with?"

"I find you so attractive, so perhaps it is best to slow this all down. The best evening for me to call round is Thursday. I will be discreet and park around the corner. Would that be okay with you?"

"Yes, that would suit me fine. Maybe we shouldn't drink as much next time." They both smiled and kissed again.

Cassie pulled herself away and stood up.

"Come on, Sergeant Bates – I'm calling time. I look forward to being interviewed again by you in a fortnight's time, but it has to involve lots of kissing." She took his hand and led him to the front door and he departed with a broad smile across his face.

Almost six months had passed since that first meeting at her home. Their relationship amounted to Ron calling at Cassie's home every week now, on a Thursday evening after work. She would start to look forward to his visit several days before it was due. His visits never seemed to last long, although he would stay for at least three hours. Most of the talking was done by her but he was now contributing more. He showed an interest in what book she was reading and they would often talk about a radio programme, as they both listened to the radio every evening. There was still a reluctance from him to talk in detail about his past, and especially his wife. That caused feelings of caution in her which were associated with the aftermath of what had happened with Eddie. She told herself that it was no bad thing to be cautious, given how strongly attracted to him she had become.

Some time had been spent on talking about the difficulties of having a relationship – of how she could not leave Neil in the evenings at least for the foreseeable future. They also talked about the impact on each of them of the gossip that at some stage was bound to start and to spread in such a small town. Without coming to any resolutions, the meetings continued because they liked so much being in each other's company. It was clear in her mind that if things continued to go well in the next year or so, then she would want him to come around earlier in the evening so that Neil could meet and spend some time getting used to him being around.

At their last meeting, it was Cassie who had raised sex. Ron was surprised and then pleased that he had been relieved of having to raise what had been on his mind for so long, but which he lacked the confidence to raise. It had not been the simple agreement that he had hoped for. The matter had been raised after they had ended up kissing on the sofa. She had sat up to prevent the intimacy going further and said that it was clear they were both attracted to each other, but they needed to agree on some rules if they were to start a sexual relationship. First, she had set out that there was no possibility of having sex unless he was willing to use a condom. There was a firm insistence that no risks would be taken in getting pregnant. Second, that until and unless Neil had gotten to know Ron and felt comfortable with him, then they had to be very discreet which meant that he could not stay overnight. And third, there had to be a promise made to tell no one about their relationship other than very close friends, and that any friends told, should be made aware that they must tell no one else. Ron agreed to the conditions without hesitation. Her response was that he should bring condoms when he called round again in two weeks' time. They had parted that night both looking forward to the next time they would see each other.

Cassie had spent a great deal of time preparing for his next visit. Having managed to get Neil off to bed half an hour before his usual bedtime, she had used the extra time to have a long, relaxing bath, and to do her hair. She was now sitting looking at herself in the dressing table mirror and felt content with what she saw. There was a knocking on the front door and she rushed to open it.

"Come in! Come in! It's so good to see you."

As soon as she had closed the front door and without him saying anything in reply, they kissed. Cassie could smell that he had been drinking, which made her feel a little disappointed.

"I brought a half bottle of whisky."

"Thank you. You've already had one or two, haven't you?"

"Just the one! It's a big night this, for me," Ron said, looking sheepish.

"Well I suppose it's a big night for both of us. I think we should just see how things go. We don't need to do anything if we don't want to. Let's eat and chat, and not drink too much – as we do too often."

"You look beautiful. But would it be okay if, perhaps, we end up not having sex this evening? I'm not saying definitely not – just maybe not?"

"Of course, that would be okay. Is there anything worrying you?"

He looked pained and sat down on the sofa and stared at the floor.

"I feel a bit strange about this... it being the first time... since my wife died."

He remained looking at the floor and did not add anything more.

"Of course; you would be feeling a bit strange. I should have thought," Cassie said as she took his hand. "Listen, I am just happy that you are here. Let's spend the evening as we normally do; chatting, laughing, and making each other feel good. I always think it's best to talk about feelings with someone you trust, especially feelings that cause sadness or difficulty."

Ron took time to respond.

"I'm not very good at that. I don't know what to do with feelings. I suppose I am in the business of finding solutions to crimes, and I don't spend a lot of time on feelings – or at least not on my own feelings. I am surprised that this has happened – feeling this way, that is. It is a long time ago since I have been in bed with a woman. Maybe we can come up with a solution."

"You know, you don't need to find solutions. My friends and I... we just talk about how we feel without thinking about whether there is a solution or not. We may then start to talk about the best way of dealing with things – with our worries or our hopes – but sometimes we don't come up with a clear way forward, at least not right away. And that's fine."

"I suppose I feel I am betraying my wife, in a way. Betrayal is probably a bit strong. It will be the first time I have had sex since she... well, departed. Maybe I am also worried about not being able to do it."

"If you feel that way, it's not a problem for me. That's not to say that feelings won't change. They do. Time changes everything – not quite everything but it certainly changes how we feel. Let's leave time to take care of this. Would you like a drink of this fine whisky you have brought?"

"Yes, please. I only had one in the pub. You are such an open and honest woman, and a beautiful looking one to boot."

She brought the bottle and two glasses from the kitchen, as well as some sandwiches. The evening proceeded as was the norm with Cassie doing most of the talking about her work and the issues she had to deal with. Moving on from that, she began to talk in her usual animated way about the book she was reading, which was *Dubliners* by James Joyce.

"It's different from most of the books I have read. It's a set of short stories for a start. But when Jim Reilly suggests something, you know it will be worth reading. It doesn't really have an intense focus on social conditions like a lot of the books I have read, Dickens especially. I am not sure what it is about, but what I like is that it focusses on how ordinary people deal with their lives."

"And how does it do that?"

"It sympathetically exposes their weaknesses, their sadness, and their passions. The writing is so beautiful. I don't know precisely how his style of writing generates so much intensity, but it does. The final pages of the story called 'The Dead' contain some of the most moving writing I have ever come across."

Cassie's voice tailed off as she seemed wrapped up in another time and place. He had sat captivated by how Cassie expressed herself and felt a surge of emotion. He put his arm around her and they kissed. He moved his hand up between her thighs, which she opened up to.

"You know something, I think I may be up for it after all. Can we go upstairs?" he whispered into her ear.

"Well, only if you are sure. I am glad you have managed to find one of your solutions. I was thinking for a while that I was going to have to come up with one. Yes, let's go to bed."

They climbed the stairs holding hands making as little noise as they could manage.

Part 2 – Chapter V

It was almost a year after Cassie had received the first of the monthly payments from Eddie that her friends agreed to accept money from her. Both of them had needed a great deal of cajoling to get them to the stage of agreement. They had insisted that they wanted to wait for a period to see if the payments from Eddie continued on a regular basis before agreeing to take any money from her. Ellen had opted for taking the money in order to open up a savings account for her children. She and her husband were comfortable relative to many families in the town, with his level of earnings and their Family Allowance payments. Her husband, Bill, had a well-paid job compared to miners, working as a fireman, which involved safety inspection and rescue duties underground. He was also offered plenty of overtime, which he tended to accept.

Jenny did not have the option of using the money to open a savings account. It had become apparent to Cassie over the last year that life was becoming more and more difficult for her. Alex, her husband, liked a drink and that had been joked about down through the years. On several occasions in the last year, Jenny had confided that he was spending a sizable chunk of his wages on his drinking.

"I think it's gotten a lot worse in the last two years, if I am honest, Cassie. It's a never-ending struggle," Jenny said as her voice began to waver.

"How awful. What else is he doing to you?"

"It's not like that. Alex is not violent like a lot of men are in this town. He never really gets angry. In fact, I can hit him when I am angry – and I do – but he never hits me back. He just sits there and apologises, then promises that he will try to stop drinking."

"Well at least you don't have to put up with drunken threats and violence, as so many women do."

"But his trying never amounts to anything. Nothing changes! Week in – week out. He now takes about a third of his wages before I get the remainder. He is out in the pub Friday night and all of Saturday, drinking with his mates. That makes it so difficult for me to manage. I have looked for work that I could do while our boy is in school but there are only full-time jobs available and few of them are for women. I don't know how things are going to get any better."

"Have you spoken to your doctor? Is there anything he has suggested?"

"I talked to Dr Stephens about it again this morning. He was very sympathetic as he always is. But his view is that unless Alex wants to seek help with his alcoholism, through AA or something like that, then there is nothing that can be done."

"That's the truth of the matter. There isn't any more a doctor can do."

"I told the doctor that I was struggling because of the amount Alex was spending on alcohol. To my surprise the doctor replied that he now needed a cleaner at the surgery for a couple of hours on weekdays and asked me if I wanted the work. He said that the cleaning was required in the evening between five and seven o'clock."

"And did you take up his offer?"

"I said I needed to think about it and would get back to him tomorrow. But I don't see how I can. Ellen and I share the looking after of Neil until you get home just after six so I can't see how I can say yes."

"Oh yes you can! I am sure that Ellen will be fine looking after Neil at her house, Monday to Friday."

"But I have come to rely on the money you give me now for looking after Neil 'til you get home. And also, it wouldn't be fair on Ellen to have to do it all."

"Listen, Jenny. There is no way you cannot take that cleaning job. I can and I will keep paying you the eight pounds for what you do for me. I now need more help with Neil for a few hours on one evening and on some Saturday mornings as I want to do some courses. You and I both know that Ellen will have no problem whatsoever looking after Neil every day after school until I get back just after six o'clock."

"If I took the cleaning job I would still be able to have Neil round at mine on mornings and afternoons during the school holidays."

"And now that I have a love interest in my life, I could do with a babysitter in the evening when Neil is asleep, so that we can go out sometimes. We can't go on only seeing each other at my house. It will drive me crazy if we don't have at least an occasional venture out together, although he possibly won't want to, as he is happy enough just staying indoors for the sex. So, how about that babysitting?"

"Well, it would let me take up Dr Stephen's offer of the cleaning job. And yes, Saturday mornings are no problem at all. The evening babysitting would be fine also as Alex will be at home. He is at home evenings of the working week, and sober, as he only drinks on Friday evenings and Saturdays from lunchtime onwards."

"Right! Let's go round to Ellen's to get her agreement and then you can go back to Dr Stephen and take the cleaning job."

"Thanks. You see things so clearly."

"And what would I possibly be able to do without you and Ellen doing the same for me?"

"And how is your romance going, Cassie? As you have probably guessed, mine has seen better days."

"As I said to Ellen last week, it's good, but I don't want to rush things."

"What do you mean rush things? If it's good, why hold back?"

"Well I am not holding back on everything. The sex is good. I enjoy his company. He continues to come around every Thursday now. But, why rush into something more permanent? He seems a good man but I thought that Eddie was a decent, reliable man. And then, out of the blue, the whole thing was lying in ruins. I don't want Neil hurt – probably more than I worry about myself. Let's see how things go over time."

"What you say makes sense, as usual. Men can be useful but it's never wise to become reliant on one, if you can avoid it. Maybe in the next life women won't have to rely on men for a living and will be able to live independently," Jenny said as she broke into a smile.

"I am in the next life already. Let's go round to Ellen's," Cassie replied, taking Jenny by the arm.

Ellen agreed without hesitation to care for Neil after school, Monday to Friday.

The next day, Jenny started the cleaning job at the doctor's surgery. That same day Cassie drove to the psychiatric hospital a few miles outside Westpool. She was going to see a woman whom she had been visiting at her home, until being admitted to hospital a few weeks back, suffering from a mental illness. The woman was the mother of three young children and since she had been admitted to hospital, her husband had been struggling to cope with looking after them on his own. The county's Children's Department was concerned and consideration was being given to removing the children from home. In her role as a district nurse, she had had been asked to attend a meeting at the department, the following week. Her opinion was that everything should be done to keep the children at home, which she thought was feasible if support services were provided by the department. However, the mental health of the woman in the longer term would be crucial if Cassie was to convince the department manager that the children should not be taken into care. Before seeing the woman, Cassie had an appointment with her psychiatrist, Dr Mike Bennett.

"Nurse Gallagher, pleased to meet you. Have a seat," Dr Bennett greeted Cassie on entering his room.

"Pleased to meet you. As you know, I am here about Mrs Irene Banks. The Children's Department is considering taking the children into care as her husband is struggling to cope. I need to understand just what the prognosis is for Mrs Banks, and specifically whether she will be able to return home soon without the mental health problems she has had. I may as well say at this point that I am keen to avoid the children being taken into care," Cassie stated.

"Well, I'll tell you what I can but as long as you understand that I can't give any firm assurances about the future. That's especially the case because of this new drug that became available recently, which we have just started to use in the treatment of schizophrenia. That's what Mrs Banks is suffering from."

"And this new drug, does it work?"

"Good question, and one that I can only give a qualified response to. How much do you know about mental illness and the treatment of it?"

"Well, I have a broad knowledge from my nursing training but in all honesty not a lot."

"I am not sure I know that much about it. There are as many questions as answers in psychiatry – but let me give you a broad outline both of schizophrenia and this new drug that is now being used – Largactil. Have you got enough time for me to explain – it should take no more than five to ten minutes?"

"Yes, certainly. That would be helpful."

The doctor set out how schizophrenia can cause marked changes in behaviour, through delusions, confusion, and hallucinations; pointing out that there are variations in impact from one person to another. He then went on to describe the traditional treatments for schizophrenia which always included lengthy – usually permanent – admissions to an asylum or a psychiatric hospital, as they had recently been renamed after being transferred from local authorities to the NHS. He described the treatments in use in the last fifty years, including insulin coma treatment, electroconvulsive therapy (ECT), sedative drugs, and lobotomy.

"Am I boring you?" asked the doctor.

"No, not at all. I am interested."

"Very recently the first drug for the treatment of schizophrenia, as opposed to mere sedation, has become available. This drug, Largactil, has been found to be effective in treating hallucinations and delusions as well as confusion and agitation. We have been using it for the last six months in this hospital. I have been prescribing this for Mrs Banks since she came in three weeks ago."

"And is it working? Is Mrs Banks improving and will she be able to return home soon as a result?"

"Is it working? Yes and no. It differs from one person to another in how long it can take to have an effect. For some it works well, for others it results in limited improvement in some behaviours, and for a few the impact is negligible."

"And for Mrs Banks?"

"It's too early to say. She has been less agitated but her confusion and delusions persist most of the time. We will have to see how things go over the next month or so."

"So, you can't be any clearer than that, Doctor? Sorry, I don't mean to be abrupt. It's just that the decision about taking the children into care is probably going to be taken in the next couple of weeks – not in the next few months," Cassie said, with a sigh.

"I appreciate your concern to prevent the children being taken into care. But on the time frame for her recovery or the prospects for her longer term mental health – I cannot be any clearer at this stage. One of the problems is that there are a lot of claims being made for this new drug but made without the benefits of extensive trials, which would have taken years to do. Consequently, it's a matter of building up experience and knowledge as we use it. I am sorry I cannot be more helpful."

"And what if the drug treatment does not work – will you try the more traditional treatments of ECT or lobotomy? Not that I like the sound of them."

"I agree that they are not ideal – the results are so varied. Indeed, somewhat haphazard. But if Mrs Banks' condition does not improve, I would want to discuss with Mr Banks the possibility of trying ECT. It will be his decision; I won't try to convince him one way or the other. I will only try it once. If it does not result in any improvement, I won't try it a second time. I would never consider a lobotomy."

He went on to put the view that a lobotomy was nothing more than a stab in the dark and it often had disastrous consequences. Too often it resulted in leaving the patient in a permanent vegetative state and that was the reason he would never consider it a legitimate medical treatment – though most of his colleagues would disagree with him on that, he added.

"It must be a bit lonely – working with colleagues you disagree with."

"More frustrating than lonely. So, if Mr Banks ever wanted me to consider a lobotomy, I would have to transfer her to the care of another psychiatrist who does lobotomies. But let's see how things go in the next month or so. Sorry I cannot be more helpful. Nice to have met you – I enjoyed our discussion. If you want to discuss anything else, you are welcome to come back to me."

"Thank you, Doctor. I may take you up on your invitation. Meanwhile I need to go see Mrs Banks on the ward. Thanks for your time."

As she walked through the door of the ward where Mrs Banks was, Cassie found herself immersed in thinking about Dr Bennett. How different he was from all the doctors and consultants she had come across in her career. He seemed so honest and forthright in his opinions and there was little concern that he did not conform to the accepted views within his profession. As she was walking down the long rows of beds on the ward still thinking about Dr Bennett, Cassie suddenly stopped. At the bottom of the ward, by the side of the last bed, next to the one that Mrs Banks was in, sat Ron Bates. He was holding the hand of a woman who was lying motionless on her bed, staring at the ceiling. Cassie was unsure what to do. Being some distance away, he had not seen her so she decided to turn back and walk at speed out of the ward and into the corridor. She felt a mixture of confusion and anxiety for the first time since Eddie had walked out without explanation. She knew that visiting time was due to end in about thirty minutes and Ron would have to leave then so she went to the canteen and sat down at a table on her own. Cassie felt irritated with herself that she had become so anxious all of a sudden. Questions surged in her mind: Why had she not just gone up and spoken to him? Why couldn't she have been open and honest as she would be in any other circumstances? Who was that woman – a relative? Why had he never mentioned her before?

After forty-five minutes in the canteen, she went back to the ward to see her client. Mrs Banks was uncommunicative. After a period of trying to converse and getting little response from her, Cassie's attention was diverted to the woman in the next bed, whose hand Ron had been holding. She was still lying on her bed motionless and was staring at the ceiling. Cassie thought her age would be somewhere in the late forties, although it was difficult to be confident about it as the woman looked so pale and thin, and her expression was fixed and lifeless; all of which would make her look older than what she was, in all probability. There was a thin line of saliva running down from the edge of her mouth onto the pillow. The woman looked like one of those patients who had had a lobotomy, as described by Dr Bennett. She was keen to know who the woman was and considered looking at the notes board attached to the base of her bed. After musing for a few moments on whether she should, she decided not to. She would ask Ron about the woman – he ought to be the one to tell her.

Part 2 – Chapter VI

Feeling agitated, Cassie poured herself a glass of whisky. Almost a week had passed since that day of the visit to the psychiatric hospital and seeing Ron sitting at the bedside of the woman whose hand he was holding. In that period so much time had been spent on wondering and speculating over those scenes. As she sat waiting for him to arrive at her home, there was a sense of relief that the matter would be resolved tonight. How it would be resolved, she had no idea. What was important to her was that soon she would no longer be in the dark. There would be no more wondering who the woman was and why he had never mentioned her.

Ron was excited as he drove towards Cassie's house. He always was when the day arrived for them to be spending the evening and part of the night together. Over these last few weeks, he had been thinking of how he wanted their relationship to be closer, with them spending more time together, and in particular for him to spend time with Neil. He knew that without that development then the relationship could not move on to the level he wanted. On stepping inside the house he noticed straight away that Cassie did not give him the warm welcome that she always did. His optimism drained from him as he followed her into the living room, feeling uncomfortable.

"Are you okay? You don't seem yourself tonight. Is there anything bothering you?" asked Ron.

"Well there is something on my mind. But let me get you a drink. A whisky?"

"Yes please – if that's okay?" he replied, while remaining standing.

Cassie brought the whisky and handed the glass and the bottle to him.

"Sit down, please. A couple of weeks ago I was visiting one of my patients in Furlong hospital. I saw you there visiting someone. A woman! I did not want to interrupt you as it looked very private. It appeared to me that it was someone you knew well – someone you seemed very attached to. I was intrigued. I remain intrigued. I don't understand why you have never mentioned her to me."

Ron froze. He stared at the floor and said nothing.

"Are you going to tell me? You have been hiding something. I know you have been."

"How much do you already know?"

"I want to hear the truth from you and not some part truths. I think you owe me that," replied Cassie growing more vehement.

He took a drink from his glass and put it on the table.

"I was going to tell you about her – about my wife – I mean my ex-wife. Do you already know that she was my wife?"

Cassie sat motionless. She had lost all colour in her cheeks.

"No," she heard herself murmur.

"I am sorry you have found out like this."

"Don't! Don't be sorry. Just tell me – just explain what has been going on."

"My wife – my ex-wife – we are divorced – has a long history of mental illness. It started before we had been married a year. It happened out of the blue – although looking back now, I should have seen the early signs. She began acting strangely, hearing voices, and becoming paranoid about going out. Some days, she would be having conversations with invisible people. They existed only in her head. I was completely thrown by her behaviour, by her deterioration, which was swift. It was like I was paralysed with dread every day as it all got progressively worse. She became unable to do even simple tasks like go shopping as she was terrified to leave the house."

"How did you manage?" asked Cassie

"I tried to cope as best I could. I got a cleaner and helper in on a daily basis. But it was no good. Things went from bad to worse. I tried so many times to get her to go to the doctor but she wouldn't. I did not know what to do. Well to be truthful, I knew what had to be done but I could not do it. Until one night when I returned from work to find her terrified, cowering in a corner of the room, begging the voices inside her head to leave her alone. It was so pitiful…" Ron ground to a halt and could not continue, looking to be on the verge of breaking down.

"I am sorry. Take your time. Do you want another drink? Listen, if this is all too much we can leave it for now," Cassie said, feeling guilt for pressing so hard for an explanation.

"No, I know I need to tell you this. Just give me a moment. And yes, can I have another whisky?"

Cassie poured a generous amount of whisky into his glass.

"I called the doctor out and together we took her to hospital. To Furlong hospital where she is now."

"And when was this?"

"Almost six years ago. She did not want to stay in hospital even overnight, but I agreed with the psychiatrist's insistence that she be kept in for treatment. I knew that was the right decision, but it felt so cruel. Since then, she has had lots of treatments – none of which have resulted in any improvement whatsoever. In fact the truth be told is that she has gotten worse since she entered hospital all those years ago. She has had ECT countless times. There was no improvement that I noticed. Eventually, the psychiatrist suggested a lobotomy."

"She had a lobotomy?" Cassie asked with alarm.

"As I remember it, the psychiatrist said there was a reasonable chance that this treatment would result in an improvement in her condition – or at least that is what I thought he said. Maybe he only said could – not would. Anyhow, I agreed. The lobotomy certainly stopped her fear and paranoia. She has never heard any voices in her head since she had it."

"So was it a success – or at least an improvement?"

"It has left her a shell of the person she was. She barely speaks now. I am not sure she knows who I am – though sometimes I think she does recognise me. The psychiatrist has told me that the chances of any improvement are not high. Though he will not say there is no chance of improvement. Funny that; how doctors are never definitive! Lately, they have put her on this new drug, called Largactil. But I don't think they can ever undo the damage of the lobotomy. I don't blame the psychiatrists. I suppose they have to try every treatment available."

"That's so awful. I am sorry I was so short with you," Cassie said as she put her arm round his shoulders.

"I was going to tell you eventually. I should have told you before. I just found it easier to not talk about it. And the more time went by without telling you, the harder it was to tell you. I go and see her every month."

"Even though it appears she does not recognise you; that must be comforting for your wife."

"She is no longer my wife. I decided shortly after starting to see you that I should get divorced. You may or may not know, but one can get a divorce on the grounds of insanity. I suppose I thought I should get divorced as I was now seeing you – especially as we had started to sleep together."

Cassie withdrew her arm from his shoulders. She felt uncomfortable and faint but could not pin down in her head precisely why.

"You don't think I should have gotten a divorce? It made no difference to my wife. She didn't…"

"What's your wife's name? You haven't told me that," interrupted Cassie.

"Peggy. It's Peggy."

"Tell me a bit more about her – about your life before she got so ill. I'd like to know more about her."

"Do I need to? What's the point of going there? It's been a nightmare for me. Can we agree that we leave that to another time?"

"Of course you don't – need to. It's just that I am interested. I don't want to make things any worse for you. But you need to understand that this has all come as a huge shock to me. I have to understand – it's not making sense to me yet. It's unclear why you kept this from me. You say you were going to tell me eventually – but would you have?"

A single tear began to run down his cheek. He took out his handkerchief and shielded his eyes.

"Sorry! I can see just how tragic this has been for you – and for Peggy. Let's leave it for tonight. We can continue this the next time we meet. Can I get you anything to eat or any more to drink?"

"No thanks. I don't feel hungry. I am so sorry that you have found out this way. I should have told you. I suppose the truth is I didn't want to do anything that might result in losing you."

"Why would telling me the truth about your life result in you losing me?"

"Well, you putting it like that… I don't know why I did not tell you. I can only apologise, Cassie. Can we go up to bed?"

"Okay, but I am just going to have a cup of tea; then we can go upstairs. Not quite the enjoyable evening we usually have. One other thing. You know how important it is for me to be able to talk to my friends. Would it be okay if I talked to only my close friends about this? They would be sworn to secrecy. We never talk to anyone else about what we have discussed among ourselves. You can be confident that nothing will be said to anyone outside our friendship group."

Ron looked troubled and thought for a few moments.

"I don't feel comfortable with that. This is all very private to me. I would prefer this remained between only you and me. Anyway, as you say we need to talk further first."

Cassie felt aggrieved. Not being able to talk to her friends about how she was feeling was not a situation that she had ever been in – in her entire life. They finished their drinks in silence then went upstairs.

Part 2 – Chapter VII

In the weeks following the revelation about Ron's wife, it was difficult to make sense of how she felt about their relationship. There was no doubting that it was a terrible tragedy for both him and his wife, but referring to his 'ex-wife' – that just did not feel right. She had feelings of sympathy for him but other thoughts were troubling. Episodes of guilt erupted from time to time, which she knew emanated from his admission that he had divorced his wife because she and Ron had formed a relationship and had started sleeping together. That thought could not be erased for long from her mind. The ensuing unease had impacted on that last night in bed with him when she had feigned a headache and nausea in order to avoid making love.

Something had changed between them. The trust and confidence that had been growing in strength ever since they had started meeting was now ebbing away fast. There were nagging doubts that left her wondering whether she even wanted to try for a future to their relationship. What was compounding her state of mind was being unable to talk to her friends about something so troubling. She resented his refusal to agree to her speaking to friends about the matter. Having kept all this hidden from her, he was now insisting on her complicity in keeping it concealed by preventing communication on the matter with those she most needed at this time. Ellen had already noticed there was something wrong when she took Neil round to play with her children. She had remarked that Cassie was quiet and uncommunicative unlike any time she could remember. Even in response to her friend's invitation to open up, Cassie had felt constrained to mention what was troubling her. That was the first time in her life that she had hidden feelings from her friends, and that was in turn generating anger towards Ron.

Having woken up feeling irritated that morning, a relief swept over her when she remembered that Jim Reilly would be calling soon. They had arranged to go for a long walk to the Leidan hills that Saturday, for which she had prepared a picnic of sandwiches and a flask of tea. It was a bright day with not a cloud in the sky when they set off together, accompanied by Jim's arthritic dog, making their way down the narrow path with fields on either side full of near ripe, golden barley that was swaying in the light breeze. As they rambled on towards their destination, the hills became less blue and more detailed and multicoloured – with the woods, streams and rocks becoming more distinct as they got nearer. Cassie was feeling better for the first time since finding out Ron's secret. As usual, the talk between Jim and her was about what each of them was reading presently. Unlike the normal pattern, today Jim was leading on that topic. He was enthusing about Hemingway's most recent novel: *The Old Man and The Sea*. The source of his animation was how much the character in the book, Santiago, had an understanding of life that so mirrored his own, and Jim put this down to them both being of similar, old age.

"Hemingway's novel reflects in that lyrical and economical way of his that when one is old, what is important is being committed to one's beliefs and way of life, retaining the passion and determination to keep going until the end, and never losing sight of the wondrous beauty in this world. The outcomes one achieves become less important than continuing to put in the effort. After all, outcomes are determined by many more factors than those most of us can control."

"That's certainly true."

"Another key aspect of the book in my opinion is that one should never lose respect for all those other species in this world. We are all in a battle to survive and to gain some security against adversity and death. An inevitable failure, though never a futile effort! That aside, I can't help but notice, Cassie, that you seem troubled about something today. Do you want to talk about it?"

"Well, just listening to you talk makes me feel better. You are right though – I don't feel at my best. The fact is that I am not at liberty to tell you any more than that as it concerns another person's private life."

"You can talk in a general sense about what's troubling you, without giving away personal details of others and thereby betraying any confidences. And anyhow, you know that anything you say to me will never go further."

"You are probably right. You may guess who it concerns, because of what I say, but so be it."

"You know, this brings to mind your mother and the last time I saw her before her sudden death. She said she had deep concerns that were very personal to others but was not at liberty to tell me. Maybe she would have eventually. I think you can talk about your own worries and troubles, without trampling over another person's right to have their personal affairs kept private."

"I didn't know you were aware that something was troubling Mum just before she died. She told me she was troubled about Eddie and me planning to marry."

"What has remained in my mind about your mum is that she had, up until then, always confided in me; but on that occasion for some reason she didn't. I don't know why."

"I have lost trust in someone that I had come to deeply trust. The thing is it's not because that person has done anything directly harmful to me. It's because they have kept something from me – something that I would have shared with anyone who was so close to me."

"I certainly think you have a right to talk with your family and friends about what's troubling you."

"After what happened with Eddie, I suppose trust has become crucial. And trust is not simply about having secrets;

it's also about deciding in your own head what family or close friends should be excluded from if you think that knowledge could have a negative impact on your relationship with them. That secrecy and control does not sit well with me. Does that make sense?"

"It does. I think it's legitimate to feel like that. That being the case, the focus needs to be on whether this can be resolved. And it can only be mended by talking to the other person involved and each one setting out their feelings and seeing if there is a common agreement about expectations and behaviour in the future. Have you talked this through with the other person yet?"

"No, we haven't – though we are due to fairly soon."

"Well, hopefully it can be resolved fairly soon."

"I am not so sure it can be. Can I can find the confidence to trust someone again after they have betrayed my trust in them? I don't think I am the unforgiving type when it comes to making honest mistakes, but when it comes to intentionally keeping something from me that could affect our relationship, that's another matter. I can't see that as an honest mistake."

"I see what you are saying. The thing about men is – I suspect it is a man in this case – is that they tend to think that everyone, men and women, have secrets and that concealing a secret is not a harmful act in itself. I am not saying I agree with that. I would say that attempting to control matters through keeping information to themselves; well, it's not uncommon for men."

"Why keep something concealed in the first place, unless you are ashamed or you want to keep sole control, even over the people you say you love? It's men who tend to think and act like that. The reality is that most women have to accept how men are given that they are often completely dependent financially on them. I am not in that position, nor am I ever going to be one to conceal things that are troubling me – even if I wanted to."

"I know that about you. You are so honest about your feelings and that's one of the things I admire about you. I would be so proud of you if you were my daughter," Jim said, breaking into a smile.

"That's such a lovely thing to say. But you already have a daughter to be proud of."

"I do – and I love her dearly. I am also proud of my son. It's the anniversary of his birthday next weekend."

"You shouldn't spend that day on your own. If your daughter is not calling round, why don't you come over for a meal next Saturday night? You have never told me the full story of Laurie. I'd love to hear you tell it in detail. What do you think?"

"I would be more than happy to spend the evening telling you about my son, who was an exceptional young man in my view. Linked to what we were talking about; it's ironic, but this last week, after a lot of deliberation, I have also decided to bring a relationship to an end, as I suspect you are about to. I have decided to leave the Communist party after being a member for over twenty-five years."

"What? Really?" gasped Cassie.

"Yes. The invasion of Hungary by Russian troops to suppress the people's rising there is something I cannot acquiesce in, never mind support, as the party does. I just can't be a member of a party that fails to support the right to protest against those in power, whether in a capitalist or socialist society."

"What does this mean for you, Jim? Is it a radical change in your thinking?"

"Certainly not! I will always support a strong state acting to oppose those who want to assert the right of an individual or a company to exploit others in the name of liberty. However, there is all the difference in the world between the state intervening on the side of the people who need protection from all powerful capitalism, and the state and its armed forces intervening to deny people the right to challenge dominant power. The same old problem I am afraid; people treating what is essentially a means to an end, as an end in itself."

Cassie was thinking about what Jim had just said and did not respond. They had reached the Leidan hills and after climbing a little way up they sat down and admired the views, both up towards the hilltops and down over what looked like a flat valley stretching out to Aylston on the distant horizon. There was a comfortable silence between them as they took in the views, with the dog appearing grateful for the rest as he lay on his side in the grass. After sharing the picnic of tea and sandwiches, they turned for home. On the return walk, Cassie spoke about the book she had just finished – her first Jane Austen novel, *Pride and Prejudice*. It had affected her like few other books had, even though it was set in a time and place with characters so different from her life here in Aylston. She was of the view that the strong impact on her was because the story had been written from a woman's perspective, which was still seldom the case in more or less all the books she had read. Cassie recounted a conversation in her head with the main character, Elizabeth Bennet, about mistaking bad character in a man's actions, when in fact the man was of good character. However, she was still not convinced of having mistaken the real intentions of Ron in him omitting to tell her the truth about his wife.

Soon after her walk with Jim, Ron received a short note at his workplace from Cassie marked private and confidential. In it she had stated the need for more time to think things through but that she was confident that her mind would be clear on the matter in a fortnight's time. The suggestion was that they meet then, at the same time as usual at her home. In the weeks after their last meeting, there followed an endless period of turning things over in his mind. He had swung from feeling confident that he could fix things so that they could move on from this, to doubting that he would able to do so. At times, he arrived at a view that she was being unduly harsh. After all, he hadn't been unfaithful to her. Instead, she had come to learn of the huge tragedy of his wife becoming mentally ill. Surely it was understandable that he could make an error of judgment in concealing this from her? At other times, he had found himself in a state of anxiety that Cassie was about to end their relationship. He had become dependent on their relationship to a degree that caused him a foreboding for the future. As had been the case ever since first meeting Cassie Gallagher, he was unable to get her out of his mind. However, it was a fear of losing her that permeated his thoughts now. The days before they were due to meet up, he was bordering on a state of panic about how to cope if it all came to an end. The thought of having nothing in his life other than dutiful visits to see his ex-wife in hospital filled him with despair.

On the evening of their meeting, he was feeling nervous, yet trying to be resolute. Cassie would forgive him, he told himself. After all, she was hardly in a position to throw up their relationship, being a lone parent. What other opportunities would she have? He had been kind and considerate and she had always said she liked the sex. He resolved to do whatever it may take to keep her. The plan was to work on her feelings by stressing the pain and loneliness caused by his wife's long illness; he would then make a marriage proposal to her. In order to bolster his courage, he stopped off at a pub on the way and had two whiskies.

Ron arrived at the door of her house with a huge bunch of flowers.

"So good to see you, Cassie. These are for you," Ron said handing over the flowers and attempting to kiss Cassie for longer than she wanted.

She asked him if he wanted a whisky and he replied that he did. Having put the flowers in a sink of cold water, she returned to the living room with two glasses of whisky and sat in the armchair across from the sofa where Ron was seated.

"I have spent so much time thinking about all this as you probably have done too. I can only try to understand how tragic and traumatic your wife's mental illness must have been. That said, I will never be able to understand why you could not tell me the truth. I can't accept that you had to sacrifice honesty and openness with me, whom you say you love, for your need to keep control of our relationship. As someone you loved, surely I should have been told the truth. The fact is I have lost trust in you and I won't be able to recover it. I don't think there is any future in us continuing to meet. I am sorry."

Ron sat back into the sofa and took a few moments before responding.

"I was hoping you would be open to a discussion about this. I had hoped that we could talk this through and repair things. I admit I should never have concealed this and lied to you. Meeting and getting to know you has been the best thing that has happened to me in years. I did not want to do anything that could result in losing you. Can't we find a way through this?" Ron pleaded.

"After what happened with Eddie, you more than anybody else should know that deception and loss of trust is what I cannot recover from. It's how I am. You must understand that this makes it impossible for our relationship to continue. There is no way back for me."

"But we have had such happy times together. We are good for each other – you have said that yourself often enough. Surely, that means something?"

"It means a lot to me. Always will. But that was then and this is now. It can't be like that again."

"But it can! Just accept that I made a terrible mistake and that I never will again – I promise!"

"No, it's not as simple as that."

"Don't you have any forgiveness? I have been in a dreadful state for the last five years with my wife's illness. I have struggled to cope with it all. Then I meet you and fall in love.

I didn't want anything to happen that would bring that to an end. Yes, I shouldn't have kept all this from you, but people make mistakes. I made a mistake. I haven't wronged you! I haven't committed a crime."

"But you lied to me! And lied to me for a very long time."

"But for good reasons, or rather, understandable reasons."

"So it doesn't matter what you did, as long as you did it for good reasons, which you decide on."

"That's being unfair," he replied with anger in his voice for the first time.

"I don't think it is. You are saying that actions should be forgiven if the person had good intentions, as defined by them alone. What about my feelings and thoughts in all this web of secrecy?"

"I have said I am sorry. I have said I made a mistake. What more can I say?"

"I don't think we are going to agree on this."

There was a silence before Ron spoke.

"Maybe I haven't made it clear just how much I love you. I would do anything for you. I want to marry you, Cassie. Can't we just put a single, albeit a big mistake, behind us? Please say yes!"

"No, no, Ron. It would not work. I would always have doubts in my mind; you can't love someone if you know you are always going to have doubts. If you are to marry again you deserve to be happy and secure in that marriage, especially given the tragedy that has happened to you. That could never be the case with us," she finished, looking away to keep herself from breaking down.

"You are not going to change your mind, are you? There's a hardness about you that I did not appreciate until now. For you, it can't be undone, because you are so rigid in your views. I still think it can. I am going before you make me say something worse," Ron said, leaning forward to stand up.

"Yes, I think it's best that you go."

"Goodbye, Cassie. If you ever—"

"Oh please don't! This is hard enough for both of us," interrupted Cassie as she walked to the front door and opened it.

"Goodbye. I wish you well and I do hope you find the happiness you deserve," she said in a trembling voice. He walked through the doorway into the night without looking at her or responding. When he got into his car, he slammed his fist onto the steering wheel. He felt angry and humiliated. After sitting motionless behind the wheel for a few moments, his shoulders began to shudder as he let out a howl of deep despair at the outcome he had so dreaded. After a few more minutes, he gathered himself and drove off into the night at speed, with tears streaming down his face.

On closing the door behind him, Cassie had sat down on the staircase and began to weep. After several minutes, she stopped. There was a calm and relief that it was done. She went upstairs to check on Neil. He was sound asleep breathing in a soft, rhythmic manner. Toys and books were strewn across the floor and the only order was his clothes on the bedroom chair that his mother had left folded in a neat pile. How innocent and carefree a child's life was, even for one whose father had left him, she thought, as she sat on the edge of the bed looking at him for several minutes before bending down and kissing him. As always, he made her feel that life was so much worth the living.

A few moments later Cassie found herself slumped on the stool, looking at herself in the mirror of her dressing table. She recalled that night of finding the money in the drawer after Eddie had left when she sat there feeling as exhausted as she did now. A profound sadness had enveloped her, like then, but she was aware of having none of the desperation or fear for the future that she remembered with a shudder from all those years ago. Cassie knew she would have a sound and peaceful sleep tonight for the first time for weeks.

Part 2 – Chapter VIII

By coincidence, there had been a programme on the BBC Home Service about the International Brigades in the Spanish civil war, during the week before Jim was due to come round to tell her Laurie's story. It was part of a series on the rise of fascism before the war. Jim arrived in the early evening with a bundle of letters and notes.

"Cassie, you asked to be told the full story about Laurie. In the past I have often felt unable to talk about him. Sometimes it still hits me like that. But what is the most important thing for me now is to ensure that Laurie's story is told, and told as it happened in reality, without hyperbole. I have come prepared to do that – I have written out all my notes setting out the story – but I can only tell it after I have eaten. The dinner smells delicious."

There was little chat between them over dinner as they both recognised this was going to be a hard story to tell and to listen to. After eating they settled down on the sofa as Jim got his papers out from the folder that he had brought with him.

"I have been looking forward to hearing Laurie's story. After listening to that radio programme, I am fascinated by the Spanish civil war and those working people who were so committed to fighting against fascism," Cassie said as she gently touched Jim's arm. He cleared his throat and began.

"The story I am about to tell you is based mainly on the letters I received from Laurie, and my conversations with Jack Findlay, a friend and comrade of Laurie's in Spain who survived and returned home. It is also informed by newspaper articles and books I have read about the war. From all those sources, it's been possible for me to form a detailed account of Laurie's part in the Spanish civil war."

"Where does Jack Findlay live? Is he from Aylston?"

"No, he's from Westpool and returned there after his time fighting in Spain. He told me so many harrowing things. He struggled with the horror of his war. I don't know where he is now. Nor does his brother, with whom I still have some contact. Jack suffered from depression for years; aggravated by excessive drinking, in my view. Many years ago he just disappeared. His brother doesn't know if he is alive or dead. Poor Jack."

"Another man that's disappeared, then," Cassie retorted.

"I didn't mean to remind you of that. I'm sorry."

"I know you didn't, Jim. Yes, let's get started."

He began by setting out that Laurie was only twenty-five years old when he died but he had packed a lot into such a short life. From the age of seventeen, he had been active in the Young Communist League and then the Communist Party. He described how the General Strike in 1926 had been bad; but times had gotten even worse after the crash of 1929. It resulted in a big increase in unemployment and also under employment, with working men being cut to two or three days work per week – if they were lucky enough to be chosen. That had caused so much misery for working people and Jim concluded that this was a primary reason that Laurie had decided to become an activist. Laurie had worked in No. 3 colliery south of the town, as a face worker and was active in the union there. He had a fearless quality about him, but there was never any occasion that he was rash in his actions.

"I can recognise his father in him, already," Cassie interjected, which caused Jim to smile.

"Anyhow, he would take up workers' cases and grievances with the owners no matter what. He was always calm and determined to argue the case and never went into any meeting without preparing the facts and arguments. He was so effective and persistent that it resulted in him being sacked and blacklisted. For a good period of time, he was unable to get a job in any other mine in the region because of his reputation. Like father, like son, as you said, Cassie. The mine owners were ruthless in stamping out any opposition to their power to act, as they saw fit. The union helped out by giving him some paid hours as an organiser but it wasn't much. Laurie spent a lot of his time reading and educating himself."

"That must have been difficult living in Aylston back then."

The explanation given by Jim was that Laurie had been able to improve his learning only because of the Workers' Educational Association, the WEA. Without the WEA, he and so many other working class men and women would never have been able to access any education. Jim's son had also become active in political causes, helping to organise marches in the National Unemployed Workers' Movement, and in campaigning against Mosley and the Blackshirts in the cities, although the fascists had never been active around Aylston. Laurie had also worked hard for the Communist Party in elections so with the fascist uprising against the Spanish republican government in 1936 and the central role of the Communist Party in the recruitment for the International Brigades, it was inevitable that he would end up enlisting to fight.

"When was that? When did he leave?"

"He left Aylston in early November 1936, with the British government announcing its intention to pass the Foreign Enlistment Act, which would make volunteering to fight in Spain illegal. That was what swung it for him. The Non-Intervention Pact signed by all the main European countries was bad enough – but the British government now planning to actively prevent anyone fighting fascism was the last straw. So Laurie decided to go and fight. He told me he could not pass up the opportunity to fight on the side of the people's government against the fascist military coup. I don't think he ever really entertained a thought that he might not return."

"And how did he go about that? How did Laurie get from a place like Aylston to eventually end up fighting on the front line in Spain?"

Jim set out the very complicated process. The first stage was going to London where the Party had its recruitment office. With the imminent Foreign Enlistment Act, everything had to be kept as discreet as possible. After arriving in London, Laurie had written to say that he had been interviewed by a fierce military man, who interrogated him about his motives and capabilities. Initially he was rejected but after a lot of arguing and pleading over the following days, he was accepted. After being recruited, the first obstacle was to get from London to Paris, without being stopped by either the British or French police. Jim highlighted the degree of effort put in by the British and French governments to stop anyone joining the fight against fascism – barely two years before the start of the Second World War against fascism.

"It's incredible they would put so much effort into stopping volunteers," Cassie agreed.

"Once he was in Paris, I got another letter from him. He wrote that when they arrived there by train, they made their way to a so-called secret address that they had been given in London, which according to Laurie, every taxi driver in Paris appeared to know of. In Paris, the recruits were subjected to further testing of their health and their views. If they passed that, as my son did, they would spend about a week in Paris before boarding a train for Perpignan, down in the far south of France, near to the border with Spain and the Pyrenees. In his letters from Paris, Laurie wrote how grand the centre of the city was and that Montmartre, where he stayed, was his favourite district with its bars, cafe terraces, and street artists. He sounded so excited about life there that I suspect he may have fallen in love. At least I hope he did, given what was to come."

"Did he mention anyone's name, in particular? That's often a sign. A young man sometimes slips in a girl's name before getting round some time later to making it known to his parents he has fallen in love," Cassie said with a smile on her face.

"No, he gave no name, but I could tell he was enthralled with someone. But let's get back to what happened next. It was a long train journey from Paris to Perpignan. Laurie liked it there as it felt like a Spanish town and the locals were so supportive and welcoming to the International Brigades' recruits. However, once they were transported in lorries from there to the foot of the Pyrenees, they had to be wary of the police and border guards who worked hard to prevent recruits getting over the mountains into Spain."

"That's difficult to take in. That radio programme I was listening to said that the Italian government was bombing Malaga, and Nazi Germany heavily bombed Guernica, in early 1937. That means that while they were bombing Spanish civilians, the British and French governments were pouring all their efforts into preventing anyone from their countries going to fight against those fascists. How could they get away with calling their policy neutral?"

"Yes – indeed. Meanwhile, at the foothills of the Pyrenees, they disembarked from the lorries. From there, they had to trek on foot over the mountains under the cover of darkness – from dusk until dawn – off road, on remote, stony paths. The Pyrenees are big mountains and they had to get over high passes of snow and ice. Laurie wrote that it was the worst experience of his life, up until then. It was bitterly cold and the exhausting climb went on, and on, and on. Silence had to be maintained throughout the endless climb and for the early part of the trek they weren't even allowed to light a cigarette, in order to prevent them being spotted by the many border guards deployed on the foothills, who were determined to stop and arrest anybody trying to make it to Spain."

"What a hard climb that must have been"

"It was. He wrote that the high point, in more ways than one, was when they eventually got to the top. In the dawn twilight, they could see the Mediterranean and Spain shrouded in the thin mist of dawn. It was probably the only time he ever experienced peace and tranquillity in Spain. They then sang 'The Internationale' on the way down off the mountains."

"I would have loved to have been there on that descent, but certainly not on the climb up to the top of the pass."

"Coming off the foothills, they were transported by lorry to the first Spanish town any of them had ever entered, Figueres. It was mid December 1936. Laurie was struck by two things in his early days in Spain. Firstly, how the Spanish people were so welcoming and grateful for their presence. Secondly, he was amazed at how many Spanish women were involved in the militias fighting the fascists. He realised probably for the first time in his short life, just how important and just how capable, women were in the fight against oppression. He wasn't long in Figueres but when there they were again tested for their commitment and only if the officer in charge was satisfied, were they then transported, via Barcelona, on a long journey to Albacete, the headquarters of the International Brigades."

"Did he write about Barcelona?"

Jim explained that Barcelona had been memorable for Laurie. He spent the best part of a week in the city and wrote that he felt like a hero there; and that was before he had done any fighting at all, which in Jim's view was the only time a soldier ever feels like a hero. Across the city there were so many flags flying; the red flag of the Communists, the black flag of the anarchists, and the national flag of Catalonia. The walls were covered with posters exhorting people to fight against fascism. There, he met and socialised with a great many men and women from different countries.

"If Paris was the first place my son fell in love, then I am convinced, from the tone of his letter, rather than anything explicit that he wrote, that Barcelona was the second and probably last place where he fell in love."

"Jim, you are at heart such an old romantic. I think Laurie must have been so like you. You have always struck me as one of those few men who genuinely like women; not because of how they look, though I am sure that comes into it, but because you tend to prefer their company to that of men's – not exclusively but generally. That's what I think anyway," said Cassie with a glint in her eye.

"I don't honestly know. That's the thing; I only have these few letters. Not enough to really know the man he had become. But if he was like me, then yes – you would be right. I do prefer women's company. For as long as I can remember I have thought that women, not every woman obviously, tend to have an honesty and courage that many men don't. So a physically attractive woman with those qualities – yes, I would have been entranced. Anyhow, back to the story," he said taking hold of the his papers again.

Jim continued the story with Laurie's arrival in Albacete where his war started for real. Albacete was clearly no Paris or Barcelona. It was in effect a training camp. He learned to become a soldier there though Jim was not convinced the training was as good as that for those fighting on the other side. The recruits were grouped by nationality so he was living, and would eventually fight with, people who spoke English, although there was contact with a mix with people of all nationalities. He learned to dismantle, clean, and shoot a gun – though ammunition was limited – as it would be on the front itself. They had some items of uniform but because of shortages not everything. After several weeks, they were then dispatched to the front in Madrid, ill-equipped with old rifles, a few old machine guns, limited ammunition, and inadequate clothing for the climate they were to fight in.

"That lack of equipment was mentioned on the radio programme I listened to about the International Brigades," Cassie confirmed.

"Laurie and his inadequately trained comrades arrived in Madrid in January in the middle of winter. I think Madrid is the highest capital city in Europe; it is certainly bitterly cold in winter and then unbearably hot in summer. The warm welcome of the people contrasted with the bitter cold they had to fight in, day and night. There is not a lot of detail about conditions in his last two letters from Madrid and Jarama, where he would go to next. Those last letters were brief compared to earlier ones. I think he was hiding the misery of it from me. The conditions were so tough and relentless, as I found out from a first-hand witness subsequently. It was only in conversations with Jack Findlay, a good few years after, that I got a full understanding of just how bad it actually was."

"That would be why Jack found it so difficult to cope when he returned from the war, I suppose," suggested Cassie.

"Things were only to get worse for them. The fighting took place in trenches just west of Madrid. It was freezing cold and the noise of mortars and machine guns was deafening and incessant. Most of all, it was bloody. They witnessed terrible injuries and the brutal deaths of so many comrades. Artillery hits would leave body parts strewn over the ground, with men and women wailing and whimpering in indescribable pain. According to Jack, it became clear that the brigades were outmatched, in terms of training and equipment. But in terms of courage, they were never lacking. After many weeks of constant fighting, they succeeded in repelling the fascist forces from the outskirts of Madrid. That brought a respite, an attempt to delouse themselves, and a welcome break off duty in the city for a few days."

"What an amazing achievement. They must have been euphoric at forcing the retreat of better equipped forces."

"I am not sure they felt euphoric, but if they did, it was not for long. Soon after that battle they were dispatched to Jarama. Jarama is on the road connecting Madrid to Valencia, which the fascists were trying to take control of. If the fighting on the outskirts of Madrid had been bloody, Jarama was even worse for bloodshed and horror. They were up against crack troops from Morocco as well as German troops firing on them endlessly with far superior machine guns. They managed to hold out for hours without any relief. It was more a massacre than a battle, according to Jack. Laurie was mown down by machine-gun fire. Well over half the battalion were killed in the battle. He and his dead comrades were left there – dead, in the mud and mayhem – as the few remaining members of the brigade managed to retreat to safety."

"When did you find out, Jim?"

"On the 11th March, 1937, I received a brief note by post from the commander of Brigades simply stating that Laurie Reilly had fought bravely and died on the battlefield on 12th February, 1937. The day I received that stark telegram, is the one I will never forget – the worst day of my life. He would have been dumped in some mass, unmarked grave. His war was short, though there must have been times when it felt like a never-ending nightmare for him. Ironically, the fascists were actually repelled at Jarama. The Republican side won – at least for a while. But I lost my only son that day; my irreplaceable son."

There was silence in the room. Cassie's throat was aching as she tried to stop herself from crying. Meanwhile, Jim was bending down from his chair in order to seek comfort in the stroking of his dog that was lying at his feet.

"Oh Jim, what can I say? How heartrending. No wonder you are so proud – and so sad."

"Do you want to read Laurie's letters and my notes?"

"No, I couldn't. Maybe someday I will. I know as much as I need to know for now."

As Jim got up from his chair to leave, he turned to her and said, "A while back, I was thinking that I'd like to do that journey – to retrace his footsteps – travelling from this town to his journey's end on a hillside near Jarama. It would be a sort of homage to my son's life. But no, I am too old to do anything like that now. Although somehow it feels like it should be done – for Laurie."

"I will do it someday. I promise," Cassie responded without hesitation.

Jim looked at her and took her hand.

"You know, I believe you will," he said as he walked in slow and unconfident steps, down the garden path leading to the gate onto the footpath. The light was beginning to fade with the outline of the Leidan hills now barely visible. She stood on the doorstep watching an old man, with his dog in tow, struggle home in the drizzling rain with the aid of a walking stick. Taking a slow, deep breath of the air scented with pine, she closed the front door. That was the last time that Cassie saw Jim Reilly.

Part 2 – Chapter IX

A short time after his death, Jim's daughter called on Cassie and asked her to make the main speech at the social event after the funeral. She said that her father had requested this in a letter he had left for her to open only after his death. Feeling honoured to be asked, Cassie accepted without hesitation, although her response was then followed by anxiety. She had never spoken in public. Determined to deliver the speech that Jim Reilly deserved, she sat up late for several nights in a row before the funeral, spending many hours preparing the speech and making an endless number of changes to it. Afraid of being unable to get through the speech without breaking down, she resolved that whilst reading it her sole concentration would have to be on paying homage to Jim's life and avoiding any focus on his death. When she was satisfied with what she had written, she practised reading it aloud, over and over again.

The funeral took place on a day when it never stopped raining from dawn to dusk. It was a unique burial with no religious figure officiating; but a speech was given at the graveside by an old friend, who had been a fellow trade union activist. He gave a short account of Jim's life and ended by stating that his friend had never believed in a god but what he had believed in was fighting for social justice – to a degree that made him stand out among his peers. There were a lot more people in attendance than Cassie had expected, most of whom she did not know. She had taken Neil with her as in her opinion this was an important life event not only for her, but also for her son. Although they had not known Jim well, Ellen and Jenny had decided to come because they appreciated just what a loss Jim was to Cassie, which had been exacerbated by the recent ending of her relationship with Ron Bates.

The brief event at the cemetery was followed by a gathering in a room in the Miners' Institute. It was a place Jim had loved, and where he had spent a lot of time – and not only at political meetings and events. He had set up a reading room there with a small library, which he had built up with contributions from individuals, local organisations, and the local council. His daughter gave a brief speech thanking everyone for attending and then invited Cassie to speak, adding that that was what her father had requested. Cassie stood up, walked to the front, and started her speech in a calm and assured voice. She paid tribute to Jim as a father, a life time social justice activist, a self-educated and erudite man, but above all as the most kind and sensitive man she had ever come across. It was delivered as well as she had hoped and when she finished, the room erupted into loud applause.

Afterwards, she was approached by several people, mainly unknown to her, who congratulated Cassie on a great speech and on how she had delivered it. The Labour leader of the county council, Peter Johnston, was one of those being complimentary and he was keen to persuade her that she should get involved in the party. He praised her public speaking ability and suggested that if she were to join the party he would strongly support her becoming a councillor. Still feeling relieved that she had gotten through the speech without breaking down, she thanked him, but took little notice of what he was saying. It was only when Neil, Ellen and Jenny approached her and told her how proud they were of her that Cassie succumbed to her loss. Tears began to roll down her cheeks. She felt a release, which she had not allowed herself in the period leading up to the funeral. After spending some time chatting to Jim's daughter and several of his closest friends, it was time to leave. As she was moving towards the doorway, Peter Johnston again approached her and reminded her that if she was interested in joining the party, she should come to see him in his office. He also remarked that he could now understand why Jim had thought so highly of her.

The evening, after Neil had gone to bed, was spent thinking about the day. There was an acknowledgement that for some considerable time there would be a sense of loss to a degree that she had been distracted from in the last week by all the thought and effort put into preparing the speech. Those positive feelings about how well the speech had gone down now ebbed away, as the depth of her loss began to sink in. Sitting in the armchair by the fireplace sipping a whisky while staring into the flickering embers of the dying coal fire in the grate, she was realising that there would be no more times spent with Jim discussing politics or literature that she had so looked forward to and enjoyed. Most of all, there would be no more of the man who had cared so much about her, who had built up her confidence in herself and in her potential, and who had never ceased to encourage her to read, learn, and give expression to her passion for life.

There was no point in spending any time hoping for someone who could take his place in her life. How could she ever find anyone to replace someone so unique? She wondered whether her life would ever again be so vibrant as it had been in the last few years – in the main because of the loss of Jim, but in part also due to the ending of the relationship with Ron Bates. Half-hearted thoughts drifted through her mind of how she had to face up to the fact that an important and much loved era had gone forever. It was time to move on, but the trouble was she didn't much feel like moving on. And to what? She began to think about what Jim would be saying to her now; of him chiding her about her pessimism and then extolling how she was a woman with the heart and soul to overcome anything and with the capabilities to achieve so much. What Peter Johnston had said to her came back to mind. Jim Reilly must have been effusive in his praise of her to a lot of people, which she had never been aware of. Maybe Jim was right about her, she mused, as she broke into a smile for the first time that day.

The decision was made to have one more whisky before departing to bed, as it was beginning to stir an energy to work up some thoughts on how to adapt her life and move on from this huge loss. She was forming the view that perhaps it was time to embark on the things that her mentor was convinced she could and should do. Maybe this was the time to find out her potential and also to discover through new experiences what was not for her. Fetching a notepad and pencil out of the cabinet drawer, she began to jot down some ideas on how to start this new era in her life. First to come to mind was Peter Johnston's suggestion to meet up with him. But then she thought that before doing that, she should get involved and established in her trade union. After all, Jim had always stressed that trade unionism gave one a sound grounding in struggle, which was essential before moving into party political involvement. Besides, there was an uncomfortable feeling about using a short cut to political power through the patronage of a male politician. No, she would never be beholden to any man in that way, she vowed.

Her energies in the first instance would be put into getting established within her union. The first priority would be to talk with Bob Andrews, the union organiser where she worked, and to aim for a position within the local union branch. The second priority would be to join a political party. Although not convinced that the Labour Party was radical enough for her, nevertheless the decision was made to join Labour rather than any other party. After all, the Labour government had achieved a huge amount after the war and what she wanted to be part of was a movement that would actually make improvements for people, her people; not just sit on the side lines criticising others for not being as 'pure' as they were. She would just have to make the Labour Party radical enough, she decided, smiling to herself.

Having come up with plans for her political development, Cassie turned her thoughts to what else she wanted from this new era. Widening her knowledge was the first thing that came to mind and she committed herself to continuing the two Saturday mornings per month she spent attending WEA courses that interested her. With regard to reading, there were difficulties that appeared impossible to resolve. Jim had not only been the source for recommending books, but had been invaluable as someone with whom she could discuss books and also programmes of interest on the radio. That was one of the most treasured benefits of Jim's friendship and she could see no way of filling this gap in her life. After some more reflection, she resolved to continue to read, as it was now woven into her evening regime after Neil had gone to bed. The focus now would be on reading other books by the authors Jim had recommended to her, but she would now start to look out for book reviews both on the radio and in a relevant journal.

Companionship was the next thing to come to mind. A big loss in her life was not being in an intimate relationship with a man. She would always continue to have close women friends whom she knew were second to no one in her life, but she also recognised how much she missed the company of men who liked her for the person she was and to whom she felt a physical attraction. Not long after she ended her relationship with Ron, she had started to miss the intimacy; she wanted the sex, which she considered to be important to her sense of well-being. On some late evenings in the recent past, she had found herself lying in bed longing for an interesting and attractive man to come into her life. Cassie had talked to Ellen and Jenny about these episodes and Jenny had joked that if Cassie got really desperate, she could send her Alex round, as she seldom allowed him any sex these days. Laughing about it with her friends had helped.

Tonight, she felt an intense loneliness and was in need of comfort. She was attractive to men; that was clear to her as there had never been a lack of interest, but how to meet men whom she liked was another matter. It would be ideal, she mused, if she were to come across a man who embodied Jim's kindness and intelligence, with the energy and physical attractiveness of a younger man. But what chance of that, especially a woman with a child! That was a depressing thought. After a number of fruitless attempts to think of new ways to expand her chances of meeting such a man, she decided there was nothing specific to be done to improve her chances of doing so. While accepting that there was nothing more to be done, she vowed to herself that were a suitable man ever to appear then she would be decisive. That meant she would make the first move if the man didn't. On that affirmation, Dr Mike Bennett at Furlong hospital came into Cassie's mind. The conversation with him at the hospital had left her intrigued and attracted. He was intelligent, of independent mind, and young. Of course, little or nothing was known about him – she couldn't even remember if he wore a ring on his finger or not. She vowed that the next time they met through work, she would check the wedding ring finger of his left hand and if there was no ring, she would generate an opportunity to meet up outside work. After this alcohol fuelled burst of planning, Cassie was overcome with tiredness. Having arrived at such a positive outlook – one that was some distance from the gloom in which she had started the evening – she toasted Jim's memory with the remaining whisky in her glass and departed to bed.

Part 2 – Chapter X

Despite having ended up positive and optimistic about her future on the night of Jim's funeral, over the following months Cassie fell into a prolonged depression. Only Neil, Ellen, and Jenny, kept her from fully succumbing to it. There were many periods of anxiety, at the weekends in particular, when she was unable to pull herself out of a despairing loneliness. Nevertheless, Cassie had not abandoned the plans she had made, despite encountering this long depression which she had not foreseen. She had become a union steward and had started attending monthly union executive meetings, but she had met with a lack of respect and sometimes open hostility from most of the other delegates, who were all men. They would often make belittling remarks and some of the men had a tendency to speak over her when she made an intervention in a discussion. She had talked to the union convenor, Bob Andrews, about it. Although he was very encouraging about her getting involved, his response was that it would soon stop and that she just needed to put up with it until that happened. Although dissatisfied with that response she lacked the energy to confront him or the men who gave her such a hard time at the meetings. It got to the point where she was even considering bringing her union career to an early conclusion.

What stopped her was the arrival of a woman steward onto the union executive committee. After yet another man had talked over her, Cassie had got up and gone to the toilets. There she broke down with the frustration of it all and was considering going home, when a woman came through the door. She was the only other woman on the union executive and this was her first meeting.

"Hello, I am Nora. Some of those men around that table are just pigs, in my view."

"They are and I am not sure I want any more of it. I have complained to Bob about it but he says I just need to ignore them. He wouldn't ignore it if he was subject to that."

"I can see why you may want to pack it all in, but maybe we can do something about it. I am certainly not going to put up with behaviour like that. Why don't we sit together and see what we can do together?"

"Oh I don't know if I can be bothered, Nora. Do you really think we can do something that would put an end to it?"

"I am not sure, but there's no loss in trying for a bit. If we don't then I may join you in packing it in."

They agreed to give it a go and went back into the meeting. Nora was true to her word. She turned in anger on a man who interrupted her when she was speaking in support of a motion to join a campaign within the region, fighting against the threatened closure of so called uneconomic mines in Aylston and neighbouring villages. The impact of Nora's challenge was immediate and sparked an energy surge in Cassie. With colour flooding into her cheeks, she backed up Nora's comments, complaining of the way women were treated at these meetings. She went on to decry the condescending attitude of the men around the table, whom she accused of being nothing more than bullies and of trying to maintain a 'closed shop' of only male representation within the union. Defiant in declaring that Nora, herself, and other women members were here to stay and that they had better get used to that, the men sitting around the table said nothing in response, as if struck dumb by the onslaught. She and Nora exchanged a fleeting smile and then moved that a vote be taken. The meeting decided to support Nora's motion and it was agreed that the two women would be responsible for organising support and working with other organisations opposing the closures. Apart from bringing a respite to the condescending behaviour of most of the male delegates, it also resulted in Cassie having something practical to do, with the added bonus that she would be working closely with another woman. From then on, Nora and Cassie always sat together at executive meetings, and while their frequent challenge to offending behaviour made the meetings bearable for them, they knew that it was always going to be a constant battle that they would just have to get used to.

In contrast, the reception at Labour Party meetings was welcoming from her first attendance. The members, many of who had been at Jim Reilly's funeral, were respectful when she contributed to any discussion. There were many more women involved in the Labour Party, which was not the case with the trade union. In her view this was due to the huge reduction of jobs for women that followed the end of the war. After her first six months in the Labour Party, she stood for the role of branch secretary and was voted in. This coincided with the most important issue for the town in decades coming to the fore. The National Coal Board had put out a report for consultation, on the future of the local coal mines. The report concluded that most of the mines in Aylston were uneconomic and that no mine had a long-term future. Although there was an acknowledgement that a few mines were economic, it went on to argue that the closure of those deemed to be uneconomic would lead to the unavoidable flooding and subsequent loss of all the mines in the district, including those that had seams of coal that otherwise would be economic to work. The report then stated that the closures could be achieved without any compulsory redundancies, with miners being relocated to mines situated beyond the district, but still within the region and thereby accessible by bus.

Although the report was termed a 'Consultative' report, the local party and trade unions saw it as something that the NCB would adopt and act on, if they did not resist. Given that the town was dependent on the local mining industry for employment, the fear was that the closure of the mines would lead to the permanent blighting of what was in effect a single industry town, with no local jobs available for future generations. Cassie put herself forward to be the local party representative on the regional steering group for resistance to pit closures and won the vote at the meeting of the local party. The group comprised representatives from all the local trade unions and political parties in the region, so she was aware that it would be a far bigger undertaking than anything she had ever been involved in.

It would mean much more time spent at evening meetings but this was no longer the problem it would have been when Neil was younger. He was now almost twelve years old and in the last year of primary school. Although still going to Ellen's for tea after school, he had been given a back door key and more often than not, Neil would be out playing football with his many friends in the local park or on the street near his home, by the time his mother got back from work. The main roads through the town had little traffic and it was seldom that one saw a car on the roads in the housing estates. Consequently, Cassie never worried about her son being exposed to traffic dangers; in fact she was confident and trusting in him on most matters now. Neil was doing well at school without having to work very hard. He was one of the few in the class of almost thirty children who were expected to pass the eleven-plus examination, which determined which school a child went to and in effect whether they would leave school at aged fifteen and enter the world of work or stay on to do entrance examinations for higher education. Being a star at football meant that Neil was never short of friends and in the restricted horizons of the mining town of Aylston, being good at football was not only a source of popularity but also a saving grace, given he was also doing so well at school. For the majority of children in the town, academic achievement was expected by neither their teachers nor their parents, so there was little encouragement for those children to do well at school. The following year after the eleven-plus examination results, Neil was likely to end up being one of the very few to achieve a place at the high school in Westpool, where the ethos of academic achievement would mean that doing well at school would have a different connotation among his peers.

Soon after attending her first steering group meeting, Cassie decided to have a phone installed at home, as she found herself having to do a great deal more liaison and planning with officials and organisations. Few households in the town had a home phone so there was little motivation to have one installed for social purposes. Not only did the campaign against pit closures require her to plan and attend a great deal of meetings and protest events locally, it also involved the occasional trip to meetings further afield and sometimes even outside the region. After a short time in her role, by common consent she was accepted as the best public speaker in the group. The most exciting trip that arose was one to London in order to lobby Parliament and to attend and speak at meetings with the national leadership of the Labour Party and the NCB. Cassie was chosen as one of the three delegates to go to London. The thought of going there filled her with excitement and only a little trepidation. Her confidence had grown in abundance since her period of depression in the months following Jim's death. The London trip would require her to be away for three days and would be the first occasion when she had been away from home on her own without Neil. For Neil it scarcely seemed to matter as he would be staying at Jenny's, whose son was a few years older, and with whom Neil loved to spend time.

The impending trip to London triggered thoughts of Eddie for the first time in a long time. On several evenings prior to the trip, after Neil had gone off to bed, Cassie sat by the fireside wondering if he would be living in London now. The letter, which she had received all those years ago, informing her of the monthly payments to be made by him, bore a London postmark. Those payments had increased every year and now enabled her to live with no money worries in contrast to most families in the town. Long since, she had given up trying to work out what sort of a man Eddie was. There was no forgetting the way he had left, and for never trying to contact her or their son since that traumatic event. Yet now she found herself thinking how dutiful he had been in providing large maintenance payments every month. These two extremes of Eddie's character were difficult to reconcile. It was clear that he was earning well and could be living in London which made her wonder what she would do if they were ever to meet again. In her mind, there was a clarity that, were he to apologise, she would still not get back with him. On further reflection, she concluded that everything has its time but then time changes everything.

There were a number of planned events in London to get excited about. The delegation would be meeting with the national Labour Party leadership, the National Coal Board, and the local Labour MP in the Palace of Westminster. In addition, there was a rally in Westminster Hall organised by the National Committee for opposing Pit Closures, which Cassie was to speak at. She spent less than an hour writing her speech in preparation. Her competence in public speaking had increased several fold since her acclaimed speech at Jim Reilly's funeral; something that she considered Jim would not have been surprised about, given how much he had believed in her.

On the day before leaving for London, she had a work meeting at Furlong hospital concerning a woman who was soon to be discharged back home and lived within Cassie's work patch. From the case notes, she had seen that Dr Mike Bennett was the woman's consultant psychiatrist. There was an expectancy as she walked down the main corridor, knocked on the door of his office, and entered on being invited.

"Hello, Nurse Gallagher, it's a pleasure to see you again. Take a seat," the doctor said as he shook her hand.

"It's good to see you, Dr Bennett. Are you well?" replied Cassie, as she checked if he was wearing a wedding ring. He was not.

"I am, thank you. And you – are you still battling away for the best interests of your clients?"

"I like to think I am. Though not only for clients these days."

"Who else are you fighting for?"

"Oh, I am involved in the Labour and trade union movement now. Can't seem to stop battling. You probably think that strange."

"Good heavens, no. I spend a great deal of my own time battling, though unlike you, not with colleagues but against them in the main. Maybe you could give me some advice about how to get my colleagues to come alongside me, as I find myself more often than not on the wrong side of them," he said with a chuckle.

"More than happy to; after we have dealt with the matter we are meeting about today – the return home of Mrs Lees."

Dr Bennett nodded in agreement and proceeded to set out the situation with Mrs Lees. He said that she had responded well to medication and to individual and group therapy sessions. He then explained about a new outreach service that Mrs Lees would benefit from. After a long period of pressure from him, the Hospital Management Committee had agreed to provide funding for a team of psychiatric social workers, who would also undertake outreach work when patients had been returned to the community. Dr Bennett advised that from now on, district nurses would be able to call on their specialist services and should contact his secretary when they needed to do so. Cassie was impressed by his enthusiasm for what he called a more personal and community approach to psychiatric services, rather than the traditional hospital based model. He made it clear that the setting up of this new approach had been done in spite of the lack of support of many of his consultant colleagues. For that reason, he was keen to do all he could to make it a success and would be depending to some extent on the support of the District Nursing Service to that end. She assured him that she would speak to her manager in support of establishing close cooperation and liaison.

"Putting in place a new community focused approach for people with mental health problems is something I think is well overdue. Anything I can do to support that, I am more than happy to do."

"Thank you, that's very much appreciated. I felt sure that would be your attitude. On another matter – a more personal matter – would it be okay to talk on first name terms? That's how I like to work. I don't like hierarchies and the normal top down authority approach," Dr Bennett added.

"Of course. My name is Cassie."

"And mine is Mike," he replied as she got up to leave. "I know you are probably very busy but I am going to ask anyway. Would it be possible to meet up sometime – outside of work I mean? I'd like to – but obviously only if you would," said Mike.

For a moment Cassie thought she was imagining what she had just heard, as that was what she was about to ask him.

"Well I am busy, but not only with political commitments. I have a son who is eleven years old. I am a single parent, you see, but if that doesn't scare you off then I would be happy to meet up with you," she replied in hope that this would not disappoint him.

"That does not put me off at all. If you have a child to look after, you will be much busier than I am in the evenings, so I think it's best if you suggest the time and place."

"I am happy to do that, but tomorrow I am off to London for a few days as part of a delegation fighting against the proposed closure of mines in Aylston and the surrounding district. I need to talk with my son and my friends who can look after him in the evening when I am out. After all that, I will come back to you with a suggested date and time – if that's okay with you?"

"Certainly. Here's my telephone number at work and my home number. London – what a trip that will be! I look forward to hearing all about it."

In return, Cassie gave him her home phone number, and strolled out of the hospital amazed that she had never foreseen her new phone line to be a means of developing a romance. She sat in her car for a few minutes, feeling a sense of achievement and excitement. The immediate future could not be better. A fascinating trip to London starting tomorrow, followed by meeting up with a man whom she found attractive in so many ways.

After driving home from work, she took Neil and a bag of his clothes and shoes to Jenny's house, where he would be staying while she was in London. Jenny commented on how happy she looked. Cassie confided that it was not only the London trip that was exciting her, but the fact that she had just met a man who was as close to anything she could wish for; adding that all would be revealed to her and Ellen shortly after her first date with him, which she expected to take place within the next two weeks. Having returned home to clean the house, the final task was to pack the new suitcase, bought for the trip, before then being able to relax by the fireside with a glass of whisky. Although feeling tired, the excitement about all that was imminent had not dissipated. Her thoughts wandered back to Jim Reilly. How she wished that he was here tonight, to share her feelings and aspirations. There was no denying just how important he had been in building her confidence and capabilities, whereby a new reality had formed for her, opening up these unexpected opportunities that now lay ahead. She vowed to herself that she would do everything possible to win the fight on pit closures, as it was clear that the future of her town depended on the winning of that battle. At the same time, there was a stirring conviction within her that on returning from London, a relationship with Mike Bennett would begin.

Part 2 – Chapter XI

The regional delegation for the visit to London included two men from the local branch of the miners' union; only one of whom Cassie felt comfortable with. The other was prone either to find fault with what she said or tried to flirt with her. Having refused to engage with his provocations for most of the journey, she could put up with it no longer and told him in front of the other delegate to stop trying to chat her up because she wasn't interested and never would be. That seemed to have the desired effect, as he was careful in what he said to her from then on.

At the end of a long train journey, they had arrived in London in the afternoon of a sunny day in early autumn. From their first steps after disembarking from the train, they were entranced by how different the city was to anywhere else they had ever been. Everything appeared to be on a colossal scale with so many people in a hurry to get to somewhere they needed to be. There were so many first time experiences. Travelling on the Underground was one of them where they were struck by the accelerating draught of air which preceded the train before it burst out of the tunnel in a deafening roar. The escalators aroused both a sense of marvel and a source of nervousness. The London streets were as wide and as busy as had ever been seen, with unbroken traffic flows, including more buses passing every few minutes than would be seen in a week in Aylston, or even in Westpool. The city's unique noises and smells generated excitement and intrigue. The air was an exotic mix of traffic fumes, coffee aroma, and of so many foods smells that were unfamiliar to Cassie and her colleagues.

Having booked into the hotel at London Bridge, overlooking the Thames, Cassie took a leisurely bath. She then did her make-up taking twice as long as usual, followed by a long period spent sitting at the window looking out onto the river below. The river appeared as busy as the London streets, with tugs and ships going in and out of the riverside wharves, to deliver or load up with goods. The deep bass sound of the ships' horns brought thoughts of far off places around the world where all these ships travelled to and from. There was no doubt – London was the hub of the world.

On the first evening, the delegation had a meeting with the National Union of Mineworkers' leadership at the head-quarters of the Trade Unions Congress. They walked over Westminster Bridge, then passed by the Houses of Parliament, stopping to take in the views before arriving at Transport House in Smith Square. The meeting was informal and they were taken through the detailed arrangements for the next couple of days. There was a briefing on the order of speakers and for how long one should speak at the Westminster Hall rally, due to be held on the last day of the trip. They were told that almost two thousand people were expected to attend, which at first unnerved her but then the challenge of speaking at such a huge event generated excitement. Following the meeting at Smith Square, they were then taken to a nearby restaurant, which was yet another revelation for the delegates. Wine was served with the food, which they had never had before. It was also the first time any of the delegation had eaten Italian food. By the time that Cassie got back to her room at the hotel and prepared for bed, the trip was beginning to feel dream-like. Sitting at the dressing table, she looked at herself in the mirror and could not help but smile. Here she was in London, meeting important and interesting people, playing a key role in the future of her community, and yet with the expectancy of a new relationship, awaiting her on the return home.

The two days spent in London seemed to last so much longer with all that they were involved in. They met and spoke with leaders of the Labour Party as well as those of the national union, who were gracious and encouraging to an extent not expected. In contrast, the meeting with the National Coal Board generated a feeling of impending defeat. There was no movement on withdrawing or reducing the scale of the threatened pit closures. The NCB management provided endless data of their technical assessments, which they were adamant showed there was no economic future for the mines around Aylston. At every opportunity they stressed there would be no compulsory redundancies; with a choice of early retirement packages or redeployment opportunities for every miner.

For the first time, Cassie began to have doubts about the ultimate success of the campaign. She even began to wonder whether it might be best to switch the focus onto investment in new industry and jobs for the town, rather than dwelling on the preservation of coal mines. When this idea was broached with the NUM officials and the two other delegates it was met with stern disapproval and earnest warnings that such thoughts would undermine the resistance built up back home. She did not pursue it further but was left wondering why the battle for jobs and for the future of the town had to be one solely for mining jobs. After all, working in the mines was a hard and dangerous life. It had taken her father and caused untold misery to her mother and so many others who had to pick up the pieces of their lives following each and every tragedy in the mines.

The rally in Westminster Hall took place on the last day of the trip. Cassie was the speaker following the president of the NUM and before the Labour shadow minister of employment. Her speech was delivered with a passionate appeal to support local communities in their struggles to secure a future for their children. She had changed her draft speech on the evening before to focus not only on mining jobs, but on secure and better paid employment for working people – men and women.

Thunderous applause followed the end of the speech. The view of many delegates was that her speech got the most applause of all the speeches and one important official remarked that she was the refreshing new voice of working-class communities. That generated a strong sense of pride and privilege that she was fighting for 'her people' – both men and women. Following the rally, a sightseeing trip was organised for all the delegates from outside of London. It included all the major sights, but Cassie found herself most interested in people watching. She was intoxicated with the buzz that the city generated from the heavy traffic and from so many people filling the streets and rushing to places they had to be. There were people of different nationalities and she realised this was the first time she had ever seen black people and Asian people. London was a thrill to all the senses, but the idea of living in this forever busy and noisy city, was not all enticing. Might she take the opportunity to move here, were it ever to arise, was a question that was left unresolved in her mind.

On the last evening, the delegation and the leadership of the NUM, dined with a Labour Shadow Cabinet spokesman and his wife. They had both come from mining communities and had almost as many stories as Jim Reilly had on the struggles during the 1920s and 1930s. The chat with the Shadow Cabinet's minister's wife, Jessie, was engaging. In particular, the Minister's wife was encouraging of her as a lone parent and complimentary of what she called her passionate way of communicating. Jessie told Cassie that she was a reminded of herself when younger. There was agreement between them that a woman's looks often remained the key factor in the limited opportunities that there were accessible for women; it was still a man's world – including within the Labour and trade union movement. They ended their discussion expressing the hope that this would not last forever, although Cassie was left with the impression that opportunity for women was more important to her than to anybody she had been in discussion with over the last few days.

The train journey back home to Aylston was spent reading a novel, *The Grass Is Singing*, by Doris Lessing. She had been alerted to the book while listening to a late night radio programme in her hotel and had gone to a book shop on her last day in London to buy it and also to buy a present for Neil – a book on London football teams. Reading the novel on the train journey back home was a trip into a world very different to any she had ever experienced. It was not a book that was enjoyed as it had no characters that she warmed to. However, each one of the characters generated a fascination, because they were so troubled and damaged. The novel introduced her to racial prejudice, of which she had no awareness until then. It took her mind far away from the last few days in London and filled her with unease, which remained even on departing the train in her home town, just as the sun was setting. She was feeling tired for the first time since leaving Aylston, which felt like an age ago.

It took several days to return to the normality of life. Neil was much more interested in the book she had brought back for him than in hearing about what she had been doing in London. Jenny and Ellen were interested in hearing the account of her time in London. They listened to all the stories about whom she had met, the places she had seen, and the things she had done. Cassie had spent several minutes talking uninterrupted about her trip when Jenny intervened.

"How your life is changing. I can hardly keep up. I suppose the way things are going, you may not be living in this town for much longer."

"What do you mean by that? I have no plans to go anywhere."

"Well, with all this politics and trade unionism, and being so good at it, I just wonder where it might take you," replied Jenny.

"I don't intend to be taken anywhere," Cassie said with a little irritation in her voice.

"Jenny's not criticising you. It's something I also think about. You are so good at speaking and all this politics you do. We don't think you should stop doing it. But whether you intend it or not, you are bound to start spending a lot of time in far more attractive places than Westpool, never mind Aylston. I suppose we are concerned about you drifting away," Ellen said.

"Sorry, I didn't mean to be snappy. Maybe deep down I am worried myself where it will end up. All I can say is that I have no intention of moving anywhere else and more importantly, I can honestly say that I will never abandon my friends."

"We can't stop change; none of us can no matter how hard we try. But there are some things we will always fight not to lose. The future will bring what it brings – for each one of us. What about this new man you were so excited about before you went to London?" Ellen asked.

"I am meeting him next Thursday evening, if you can do some child minding, Jenny?"

"Yes, no problem."

"I am excited, though it will only be after our meeting that I will know if it is going anywhere or not. He is a psychiatrist at Furlong hospital whom I have gotten to know a bit through work. He asked me out, so I suppose that is promising. I have told him that I am a lone parent so given he is not put off by that, I am optimistic. I do like what I know of him."

"It sounds like you are well and truly hooked. Of course, you are required to let us know everything no later than the day after you meet up with him." Ellen joked

"Or no later than the morning you get up with him!" Jenny added.

They all laughed, although her friends then proceeded to advise Cassie to take her time before deciding to get involved in a serious relationship again.

Part 2 – Chapter XII

Mike Bennett lived alone in a four-bedroom detached house on the northern fringe of Westpool. He had lived there since he first moved to Furlong hospital over three years ago. London was where he was brought up although he had been born in Hamburg, Germany. He was a child not yet two years old when his parents, who were German Jews, had fled to London in 1933. In that first year, the family name had been changed by his parents from Bennigsohn to Bennett, having decided that change to be essential to the family's well-being, at a time in 1930s Britain when Jewish immigrants were often made to feel unwelcome. Pursuing what had been their line of business in Hamburg, his parents had managed and then had taken ownership of a big hotel in north London. It had been an affluent upbringing, although throughout his childhood Mike had lived under the shadow of his parents' anxiety and then in his youth with the permanent sadness for relatives who had been left behind and perished in Nazi Germany. All contact had been lost with their relatives in Germany before the war started in 1939. Within two years of the end of the war, his parents had come to accept that none of them had survived.

In 1949, he had gone to university to take a degree in medicine. Within a year of qualifying, he had moved from general medicine into psychiatry. He would joke this move was because he was more interested in the person than in body parts. After completing his training in psychiatry, he had taken up a post in a hospital in north Kent. Less than a year later, he applied for the job as consultant psychiatrist at Furlong hospital, just outside Westpool. He knew nothing of the area, but the attraction was that it was a considerable distance from London. Of particular importance, it was a long way from the darkness of the Holocaust that his parents were forever locked into now. Despite having been immersed in Judaism, there had been a drifting away from both religious belief and Jewish cultural life ever since he went to university. This move away from living within a Jewish community had distanced him from his parents, his mother in particular. She was forever pushing him to meet and marry a 'nice Jewish girl' and have children in order to preserve their Jewish heritage. The more she repeated this, the more resistant her son became to acquiescing in her wishes. Within a short time of escaping that pressure and arriving in Westpool, he had come to love the area and the local people. Being able to live life as he wished and having made good friends with neighbours and a few colleagues, he felt a growing attachment to where and how he lived and worked.

For him, the garden was the main attraction of the property he had bought. During the spring, summer, and autumn, he tended it with care on most days often for an hour or so after work. In winter he would read horticultural books and plan what changes in the garden were to be embarked upon the following spring. In the main, he lived a solitary life after work during the working week. Following his short stint of gardening in the evening, he would cook himself a simple meal, while listening to the radio. The evening meal would be followed by settling down to read. He always had a book on the go, mainly non-fiction, often a book on European history or on the history of art, both of which he knew a great deal about. Those interests he accredited to his upbringing. His parents had often taken him to art galleries and museums in London when a child, but after the war when they travelled in Europe, they took him on art and history tours to cities such as Paris, Florence, and Venice. How they had somehow managed to get a boy interested in art from a young age was something that never ceased to astonish him.

The improvement of psychiatric services had become a mission. Although he would complain about a lack of cooperation from senior colleagues, the truth was that most of the changes he wanted in the hospital were achieved without a lot of difficulty. There was an understanding of the importance of energy, preparation, and staying power, which he would always have more of than his superiors, who valued a quiet, unchanging professional life more than anything else. Weekends and holidays were an important counterbalance to his dedication to work. There was seldom a weekend that he didn't spend a great deal of time in the garden and holidays were researched with care and determined well in advance. He preferred to travel abroad every summer; exploring the history of places that had caught his interest and enjoying the local culture.

Since moving to Westpool, there had been a few affairs, none of which that had lasted more than several months. That had caused him no concerns until the last six months when a worry emerged about his capability of maintaining a long-term relationship. His not remaining with any woman for long was only partly explained by the fact that most of his energies were poured into his work. Preparing for bed, tomorrow's first date with Cassie Gallagher was on his mind. He had a hope for this to be different yet he feared that it would last no longer than his previous affairs. However, there was no doubting that there was a strong attraction to Cassie Gallagher; much more than there had been for any woman in a very long time. So much so that it was causing him trouble in getting off to sleep that night.

The venue for their first date was a restaurant in a hotel in the centre of Westpool. Mike was already seated at the table when she arrived, five minutes after the agreed time. As Cassie approached, he got up and pulled out the seat opposite for her to be seated, which struck her as an indication that he was very keen that all would go well.

"Sorry, I am a bit late. Unusually, my friend, who child minds my son, was delayed. How are you?"

"I am well, thanks. Five minutes is not what I call late. Especially given all your responsibilities. How was London, then? Tell me all about it!"

"I don't know where to begin. It was wonderful – like nothing I have experienced before. Let's order drinks and some food first."

They ordered their meal and Mike suggested a bottle of red wine from the wine list, which Cassie agreed to, admitting that she knew nothing about wines.

"That's good. I have something of real value to get you interested in. I do like a good wine. Anyhow, London. How did it go?"

Cassie set out the main events from their arrival to their departure three days later, describing the effect it had on her, in particular the traffic on the streets and on the river, the noises, the unique smells, and the relentless pace of life. The trip had been so exhilarating, although she was unsure of ever wanting to live there. She detailed all the meetings they had and whom they had met; culminating in her successful speech to almost two thousand people at Westminster Hall.

"At the end of the day, though, I am not sure that any good will come of it, in terms of stopping the programme of pit closures. I think they will announce the start of them soon."

Cassie sat back and looked at Mike for a response.

"Sounds amazing! I know just what you are talking about with regard to London. I was brought up in north London. My elderly parents still live there so I go down several times a year and speak to them on the phone every week. I also spent four months working on placement at Guy's hospital, by London Bridge, when doing my training in general medicine."

"Really?! I must have bored you with my account of a place that you probably know like the back of your hand."

"Not at all. You described it so well. I don't think it is possible to know London like the back of your hand. When living there you can become immune to how amazing it is."

"Do you think you will ever return to live in London?"

"I don't know. It's not something that's on my horizon. I have grown to love it round here. You must be an accomplished public speaker, Cassie. I don't think I could stand up before two thousand people and give a speech as well as you clearly did. I love the way you can be so exhilarated by your personal experience yet still be grounded in the political purpose you were there for in the first place. Do you really think they will close all those mines?"

"I think they will. They'll make sure that no one faces compulsory redundancy. That is a good thing of course but it also makes it more difficult to resist pit closures. We are talking about a lot of people who lived through a period before the war when redundancy and short time working was the norm. The closure of the mines will be a blow. However, if everyone has a guaranteed job or is offered enhanced terms for early retirement, then I cannot see them turning down a deal like that."

"I can see what you are saying. An outcome of nobody losing their job is an achievement in itself, though. It's a sign of how things have changed and how much pressure the unions can bring to bear. An employer, or indeed the government, now knows that it cannot simply close things down and throw people out of work."

"I appreciate your interest and your support, but let's talk about other things. This is supposed to be our first date to get know each other, so that we can each decide if we like each other enough to continue."

"Well, I have heard enough to know that I like you. But yes, you hardly know anything about me, apart from my tendency to be a bit bolshie and outspoken at work."

"And I like that – I like that a lot. But yes, I don't know much about you so carry on where I left off," joked Cassie with a broad smile.

Mike proceeded to give a potted history of his past. He told of his upbringing and of his parents' flight from Nazi Germany, and the loss of all their relatives. He made it clear that while his parents were practising Jews, he was not. He did not believe in a god.

"How terrible the murder of all those millions of innocent families! I am not sure I could ever get over something like that if I had lost family and friends."

"In truth, I am not sure my parents ever will. Time does not so much heal, as lessen the suffering caused by such horror. For some, the despair is eternal. But let's not be negative on our first date. Is there anything else you would like to know about me?"

"What about relationships? You haven't told me anything about those."

"I have had a few relationships but nothing that has lasted that long. Probably down to me being so obsessed with work! I hasten to add that I am beginning to realise the limitations of short-term relationships and that is not what I am looking for from you. You have intelligence and a drive that I have never come across before – and you are attractive. What is not to like about that combination!"

"Thank you for the compliments. My past relationships have been different to yours. Ironically, I am not sure if I am up to a long-term relationship at this point in time. That's not to say that I would say no if it felt right."

Cassie then told him about her marriage and Eddie's sudden behaviour change and unexplained disappearance many years ago. She explained that Eddie was still alive and right from the start had provided money to support Neil and her. Whether Eddie's behaviour change and disappearance was related to some mental illness had been something that she had wondered about in the past. She ended by telling Mike about her more recent relationship and the reasons she had ended it.

"That's fascinating – about your husband that is. But I can tell you that it's highly unlikely to have been caused by mental illness. If he had a mental illness, including clinical depression, then he wouldn't have been able to plan his disappearance in the way that he did, especially the arrangements for leaving you money. That sort of planning is just not possible if suffering from mental illness."

"So what explanation is there?"

"Well I obviously don't know the precise reason, but it strongly indicates he was a victim of trauma. His sudden change of behaviour suggests that something awful happened to him."

"But there was nothing awful that happened there and then. Surely any traumatic event that happened in such a small community would have become apparent. It couldn't be hidden. His parents were dead, and his twin brother is alive. So, there was no the death of somebody close," said Cassie with a touch of exasperation.

"That may well be so but remember trauma does not have to be caused by something that happens there and then or indeed solely by the death of someone close. It can be caused by suddenly finding out something that has a massive impact on you; something that was unbeknown to you but which you have just come to discover."

"Oh, I had never thought of that, but I don't have a clue as to what he came to discover. Will I ever?"

"That's as may be; I didn't mean to get into a discussion about your past, nor to cause you any renewed distress about things that have brought you so much pain. From what you said about your last relationship, I get the message loud and clear that nothing less than honesty is an essential requirement for you."

"I'm glad you can appreciate how important honesty and openness are to me. That's never going to change."

"I also prefer an approach of no secrets. I won't be keeping anything from you. Let's get back to the present. I'd like to meet regularly. Of course, I do understand that it's a bit more complicated for you, with a son to look after. I accept that his welfare should come first, but I cannot see why it need stop us meeting. I like children – for what that's worth," Mike said as he awaited a response.

"I really like you and I find you attractive in lots of ways. Neil won't be an obstacle, but I need to have confidence that our relationship is strong and likely to last before I introduce him to you. Can you see that?"

"Of course."

"Good. Let's take things as they come and not rush things. To the future!"

They clinked glasses and smiled at each other. They agreed to meet every Thursday evening.

Part 2 – Chapter XIII

The phone rang at seven thirty in the evening. It was a union official telling her that confirmation had been received late that afternoon that the Aylston pit closure programme would start in two months' time. All pits in the central district, including all of the mines around Aylston, would be closed within a nine-month period. A scheme including voluntary redundancy, early retirement, and a guaranteed job on no less pay would be offered to all who wanted that. Anybody choosing a job in other mines beyond the district would have to travel but free transport would be provided.

Almost six months had passed since the trip to London and this was the outcome always suspected. Nonetheless, the confirmation filled her with foreboding for the future. The branch secretary of the local executive of the NUM had convened a meeting the following evening of all local union representatives – to which delegates from the Steering Group against Pit Closures were invited. Cassie confirmed that she would attend. Immediately after putting the phone down she phoned Mike to tell him the news. The discussion was of what she saw as disastrous consequences for the town – not in the immediate future but in the longer term. Aylston would be a town without industry and devoid of local jobs in less than a year's time. There would be no long term future for the town; those young people who were able to, would leave, and those who couldn't, would be left in a town with no prospects.

"That's a bleak future you are foretelling. You must be feeling angry after all the effort you and others have put into resisting this outcome."

"I feel flat... powerless, to be honest. So much effort put in by so many. I don't think they had any intention of consulting – they had made up their minds before they had even published the so called consultative report," replied Cassie.

"You, and the others, did your best, darling. Don't lose sight of that. What do you think will be the reaction of the men – of the miners themselves?"

"Well, I can't be sure but I would be surprised if the package on offer is not accepted by the overwhelming majority. I don't blame them. They have to look out for their futures. It's not their responsibility to prioritise the future of the town over the needs of their own families."

"What do you mean by that, Cassie?"

"My view is that this is fundamentally about the town's future – about the future of this local community – and not primarily about mining jobs. And it's not about simply keeping coal mines running no matter what. There should be a properly funded economic plan with training and employment programmes for towns like ours. That's the only way to sustain a future for this town and towns like it. It's the government's responsibility. But they are not interested and I am not sure the Labour Party is either. Too radical by half!"

"You are probably right. There's your next battle; getting the Labour Party to adopt more radical policies on a range of matters. In the meantime, how about getting together the evening after your meeting? I know how to cheer you up."

"You do know how to do that, and I need cheering up. Let me check with Jenny and I will confirm later this evening."

The atmosphere at the union meeting was one of resignation, apart from a few representatives exhorting everyone to fight on and claiming victory was in sight, if they did. On the vote, the vast majority of the union representatives opted to recommend acceptance of the package on offer. There would be a meeting at each mine in the coming week where each miner would have a vote to finally determine the union's stance.

Cassie then spoke with a passionate anger to a motion that called on the Labour party to campaign for properly funded economic plans and programmes to be developed at regional level to focus on those communities that were blighted by the loss of their local industry. The motion was adopted with only three votes against. A few weeks later, she was successful in getting the Constituency Labour Party to adopt her motion and press for it to be submitted to the party's annual conference with the purpose of making regional employment plans and programmes a national policy.

Over the coming months, many of the older miners opted for early retirement, but most of the workforce chose redeployment to other mines. For the vast majority not within 5 years of retirement age, the voluntary redundancy packages on offer were not attractive enough. Only a few of the younger miners, who considered they had a reasonable chance of getting a job elsewhere, chose the option of voluntary redundancy in return for a lump sum the equivalent of six months' wages.

It was only two weeks after the miners voted to accept the package that something far more immediate occurred. There was a loud knocking on Cassie's front door at seven thirty in the morning. She opened the door to find Jenny in a frantic state. There had been an explosion at the River Colliery and five men were missing, including Bill, Ellen's husband.

"Alex has gone down to the colliery with Ellen. I have the girls around at mine but Ellen wants them to go to school so they'll be doing so in about an hour. I will join Ellen after that. God! It doesn't sound good. Obviously I needed to let you know," Jenny said, her voice trembling with emotion.

"I'll come with you. I need to phone work to tell them why I won't be in. I'll come round to yours after Neil goes off to school. Is that okay?"

"Of course! I'll wait for you."

Cassie felt a deep dread on closing the front door and needed to take a few deep breaths before going back into the kitchen where Neil was having his breakfast.

"Neil, something's happened. There's been an explosion at the pit where the twins' dad works. We don't know yet what's happening but Bill is missing. I'm going down there with Jenny, to be with Ellen. Can you get off to school a bit early today?"

"Of course, Mum. Is he going to be okay?"

"I don't know, darling. I hope so. I won't be going to work today and I should be here by the time you get back from school," replied Cassie, as she kissed Neil on the forehead.

After Neil departed for school she phoned her work to let them know what had happened and that she would not be coming into work. That was followed by a phone call to Mike, catching him just before he departed for Furlong hospital.

"Listen, Cassie, I have something I need to do at work this morning but after that I can come over and join you at the pithead."

"Oh you don't need to, Mike."

"I know I don't need to, but I want to. This must be awful for Ellen especially, but also for you and Jenny. I'll come over if that doesn't cause you any problem?"

"No. No problem. Yes come over. I would like you here," replied Cassie surprised with her response.

Jenny and Cassie arrived at the pithead where there were lots of people around including several ambulance crews. They headed towards a small group of people that was gathered in front of the bleak looking building that housed the winding gear descending down into the pit shaft. The group was made up of family and close friends of those missing. In the background, the dirty blue slag heaps stood steep and high, erasing any glimpse of verdant countryside beyond. Trickling up from the gap where the thick steel ropes emerged from the pit shaft, there was a trail of smoke that had made the air acrid around the pithead. Only an occasional murmur of broken conversation could be heard. The huge black winding wheel was still. Steam engines and coal wagons that would be in constant motion with the loading and transporting of coal, looked like they had been frozen in time. The eerie silence seemed to highlight the stress on the faces of all those awaiting news of what was happening.

They spotted Ellen standing forlorn on the far edge of the group. The three women hugged each other in turn.

"Any news, Ellen?" asked Cassie.

"Five men are missing. There was an explosion at about six o'clock this morning and there is a fire burning in the main tunnel connecting to the coalface. They can't get down the pit shaft because of the fire so they're trying to get down an auxiliary, or maybe it's a ventilation shaft, about half a mile from here," replied Ellen as she looked away, trying to keep herself together.

"Do you know where Alex is, Ellen?" asked Jenny.

"He's gone to help with the group of about thirty miners who are going down the auxiliary shaft. He's relaying messages to the pit management here on what is happening down there. How kind of him to come down here after finishing his morning deliveries."

Every thirty minutes, a manager came out to the group to give an update on what was happening. The regular briefings continued unchanged; he reported that nothing more was known but that they were hopeful of soon getting a rescue team to where they thought the missing men were. The relatives and friends in the group were beginning to feel the penetrating cold of a damp grey November morning, when a car pulled up with a screech of brakes just by the group. Out of the car jumped Mike Bennett and signalled to Cassie to come over. He opened the boot of the car to reveal a gas urn, tea, milk, sugar, cups, and a large box of sandwiches and biscuits.

"I stopped off at a cafe and got these made up. The tea urn I managed to get from the hospital store," Mike said.

"You're something else, Mike Bennett," said Cassie as she threw her arms round his neck and kissed him.

Mike proceeded to set up the gas bottle and urn on a small table he had also brought. After the water was boiling, he went from person to person offering tea, sandwiches and biscuits. When he approached Cassie and her friends, she introduced him to Jenny and Ellen for the first time.

"I am so pleased to finally meet you both, but it should have been in better circumstances. I have heard many good things about you. Hope the tea and sandwiches can fend off this damp cold," Mike said as he shook their hands. After he had wandered off to others in the group, Jenny turned to Cassie.

"What a kind, thoughtful man. Are all psychiatrists like him?"

A smile flitted across Ellen's face as she looked at Cassie, awaiting her response.

"Who knows? I've only met the one and now I can't be bothered finding out what the others are like."

Just after midday, the manager emerged from the building looking agitated and approached the group. He stopped in front of them, cleared his throat and read in a faltering voice from a sheet of paper:

"I am so sorry to tell you this. The rescue team that entered the mine by shaft D3 have discovered five bodies. We believe them to be the missing men who are: Ralph Dobson, Tom Elliott, John Hodge, Keith Lyle, and Bill MacDonald. They will be brought up and taken to the mortuary. We hope to have that completed by this evening. Words can't describe how sorry I am."

A low wailing started, grew louder, and then exploded into a howling anguish. Ellen slumped forward and was caught by Jenny and Cassie before falling to the ground. She was crying out, "NO! NO! NO!" as her friends held her up, with tears streaming down all their faces. There was no comfort to be had. Nobody could come to terms with the outcome they had been dreading. Mike stood on the fringe, feeling powerless to do anything but witness the relatives and friends broken with grief. Cassie turned and signalled him to come over.

"Can we take Ellen home in your car, Mike, please?" Cassie managed to say through her tears.

"Of course. I'm so sorry, darling. I am ready to go when you are; let me get this stuff back in the boot of the car."

On the drive to Ellen's house, Ellen continued to wail as her friends tried to comfort her as best they could through their own unstoppable crying. Mike was thinking about the overwhelming despair of those who have just lost loved ones. He thought of his parents. The car pulled up at Ellen's house and as Ellen was being helped out, Mike turned to Cassie and said, "I won't come in. It's best Ellen has those she knows closest around her. If you can, please phone me before the day is out."

It was 11.30 at night when Mike Bennett's phone rang. Cassie had returned from Ellen's, having spent all day there with a stream of friends and neighbours coming and going to give support to Ellen. All the children, including Neil, had spent the rest of the day there, having been taken out of school in the early afternoon by Jenny. She told Mike that she had had a lot of trouble getting Neil to go to bed and had only managed to do so fifteen minutes ago. Neil was very upset, as were the other children, and he hadn't wanted to leave his mother's side all day.

"What a dreadful day, Mike. A day that we will never forget," said Cassie in a weary voice.

"It's hard to imagine a worse one. How is Ellen now?"

"In a better state than when you left us; being the wonderful mother she is to her twin girls. That wailing was unbearable. Ellen is such a kind, well-meaning person. How cruel this world can be."

"It is cruel. Endlessly cruel!"

"I don't know how Ellen and her children will ever get over this."

"Grieving is so exhausting. It is like a long episode of vomiting that keeps coming in crescendos; it drains the energy from you. There will be an end to it eventually but it's not healthy to try to contain it before it has run its course."

After a short pause, Mike added, "Cassie, I love you so much."

"Don't set me off again. I love you too. After what you did today… Well, what can I say," she managed to get out before breaking down.

They agreed to meet at a lunchtime the following week as Cassie was of the view that she could not be away from home in the evenings, while Neil was so upset.

Following the results of the post mortem, the funerals of the five dead miners took place ten days after the explosion. All five men had died of multiple injuries. There had been two explosions, almost simultaneous; one caused by fire damp and the other by coal dust ignition. It was reported that Bill MacDonald had come across the high methane levels and had been organising the evacuation of men from that area when the explosions occurred. The funeral of Ellen's husband was attended by hundreds of people. On a bleak day, when the town was as sombre as anyone could ever remember, it was small comfort to Ellen that Bill MacDonald was highly thought of among the townsfolk.

Two weeks after the funeral, Neil's behaviour had returned to how it was before the disaster. After school, he was playing football on the streets with his friends and was no longer showing the need for physical closeness to his mother. Cassie decided that she could spend her first evening for some time with Mike. As was now the established practice, they went for a meal at an Italian restaurant. At the start of the evening, she was very talkative, recounting how Ellen was coping and how the pit closure programme was being started sooner than planned on account of the disaster at the River Colliery. Confirmation had come through that this would be the first to close, in a programme that would see no mines around Aylston in less than a year. She fell silent on making that point.

"What are you contemplating? I know this is such a hard time for you," Mike said as he took Cassie's hand.

"I have been doing a lot of thinking about several things in the past couple of weeks. I haven't told you this as all I have been concentrating on has been Ellen and her girls. A strange thing about the disaster is that two of those killed were men whom Eddie knew. The police initially suspected them both of doing Eddie some harm, even of possibly killing him, given their criminal records. They soon dropped that idea as Eddie clearly was alive and had left of his own accord."

"Really? Did you ever have any contact with them after Eddie left?"

"Only with Ralph Dobson. Shortly after the start of the monthly payments to me from Eddie, I bumped into him, or rather he stopped me in the street. Smelling of drink, he told me that Eddie had recently paid him what was owed, but he had no more idea of where Eddie had gone than I did. He slurred something about never understanding why Eddie left as he did and in particular, why he would leave someone as beautiful as me."

"I would agree with him on that. What did you say?"

"I just said thank you and walked away. I didn't like his leering. So I didn't ask him what Eddie owed him money for. Their deaths have left me thinking again about Eddie. What did he owe them for? I suspect that like Ralph Dobson and Tom Elliott, I will die without knowing the full story."

"Whoever dies knowing the full story of everything that has happened to them in their life?"

"You are philosophical tonight. Other things have been on my mind. These two disasters happening; the deaths of those miners and the pit closure programme – it's left me feeling that I don't want to live in Aylston anymore."

"I can understand that. Emotions are very raw after something so terrible. Give it a bit of time and you may start to feel differently."

"I don't think I will. It's as if something has come to an end; that it's time to move on. Understandably, it's the deaths of those miners that everyone is thinking about, but what I can't get out of my mind is that Aylston has begun a slow death that is unnoticeable at this stage. The closure of the mines will kill the life in this town – not now and not next year – but slowly and surely it will. Young people will drift away to greater opportunities. That will leave a shell of a community where only those for whom there is a bleak future, remain."

"I can see what you are saying about the town. If you are thinking of moving, where would you want to go?"

"I don't ever want to lose regular contact with Ellen and Jenny," Cassie said looking distraught.

"It may be that after a period of time things will look different, but it's always worth letting time pass after such a trauma before making any firm decisions about the future. If you do end up deciding that you want to move away, it is possible to move on and yet stay in contact with friends."

"Yes, that makes sense. I am certain of two things at this point in time. Firstly, I won't move anywhere that prevents me seeing my friends on a regular basis, and secondly, and at least as important, I wouldn't want to move anywhere without you, Mike."

"I am relieved to hear you say that. I was worried you might be thinking of moving to London or somewhere far away from here. I can't imagine a life without you now."

"There are other factors for moving. Neil's teacher is saying that he will be one of the few in his class to pass the eleven-plus and that would mean he will go to Westpool high school, while his Aylston friends will go to schools in other towns. It won't be long before all his friends will be from outside the town – probably mainly from Westpool."

"Then that sounds like you should move here, to Westpool. I would love it if we were to live together."

"Really? That had crossed my mind. I do love you – certainly enough to live with you. Maybe we should start sleeping together first," said Cassie as she leaned over the table to kiss him.

"I thought you'd never ask," Mike said, as they smiled at each other.

"There are other reasons why it would make sense to move to Westpool. My work is here. Besides, I have been approached to stand as a councillor on the county council and all the meetings would take place here in Westpool."

"If you lived here, you'd still be able to see Ellen and Jenny probably as regularly as you would were you to stay in Aylston."

"Indeed. The timing of such a move is important, though. I wouldn't want to move until Neil was established with new friends at Westpool High. Also, he needs to get to know you more and feel comfortable with you. He also needs to get used to us sleeping together."

"I agree with that. We have a plan then. Realistically we are probably talking no sooner than this time next year before it's best to move Neil. Would you agree?"

"I think that's about right. We may have got tired of each other by then, of course. If we haven't, then yes I would want us to move in together. I don't want to get married though, so it will mean living in sin. That's a lot less problematic when not living in a small town," Cassie concluded before starting to laugh.

"Living in sin sounds hugely appealing to me. Let's go soon and do some sinning. You have no idea how desperate I am to get you into bed."

"The feeling is entirely mutual."

It would be almost two years before the plan to move to Westpool came to fruition. In that time, Mike worked hard at building his relationship with Neil. He took him to football or rugby matches most weekends. In the summer holidays, Cassie, Mike and Neil went on holiday together and Neil was allowed to choose a friend to come along on holiday with them. Mike would stay over in Aylston occasionally during the week and always on Friday nights. As expected, Neil started at Westpool High in early September 1959. Before the end of his first year in high school, Neil was keen to sleep over at Mike's house on a Saturday as he could then meet up with his new friends who all lived in Westpool.

The move to Westpool had been held back further than the original date planned. Ellen took over a year to return to anything like the person she had been prior to the tragedy. Her husband's death had taken a long time for her to come to terms with. This in turn had an impact on her twin daughters. As a consequence, it was decided the move had to wait as they did not want to do anything that could make Ellen and her girls more upset than they were. In the spring of 1959, Cassie was elected onto the county council. Although she was still very keen to move in with Mike in Westpool, at least now that they could overnight together, with Neil being accustomed to having Mike around the house, so the delay was of no serious consequence. Mike had also taken on responsibility for Cassie's garden, which had fallen into a state of neglect after Jim Reilly's death. There was a confidence building that when the move did take place in the early 1960s, they would all be embarking on a happy and fulfilling period of their lives.

PART 3 - RESOLUTION

Part 3 – Chapter I

Neil was sitting on the sofa absorbed in the song playing on the radio in the front room of their new home, which he and his mother had moved into only one month ago. He was tapping his foot to the hop and skip beat of the Everly Brothers' song 'Walk Right Back', the lyrics of which brought his father to mind for the first time this year. As the song ended and another began, his mother entered the room.

"Do you want anything to drink, darling?" she asked.

"Mum, can I ask you something?"

"Of course you can."

"Did Dad leave because you loved someone else?"

His mother was taken aback and after a moment's hesitation, she sat down on the sofa by Neil's side.

"No. What makes you think that?"

"Oh nothing really. I was listening to a song that set me thinking about why Dad left all those years ago."

"As I have told you when you asked before, I don't know why your dad left. He didn't give me any explanation. If he had I would not have hidden it from you, Neil. Maybe us moving in with Mike has triggered this. Is there anything you are unhappy with?"

"No, I like it here. Is Mike the first man since Dad that you have liked?"

"No he isn't, but he is the first man I have really loved since your dad left."

"Didn't you love that policeman that used to call round at night time years ago?"

"I didn't know you knew about that. That's so long ago!"

"I didn't until a boy in my class in primary school started saying that my mum hung about with policemen. I stayed awake then and heard him downstairs once or maybe twice. I got into a fight with that boy about it."

"I am amazed. You never mentioned that back then. Yes, I did see a policeman for a bit but it didn't work out. It wasn't anything important. Not like now, with Mike."

"I was wondering if I could write to Dad. He sends money every month, doesn't he?"

"He does provide money every month, but he pays it into a savings account, he doesn't send it. He has never given me his address, so I don't know where he lives. I would give you his address if I had it."

Neil did not say anything.

"Listen, Neil. I know it is hard to understand – I have spent so much time in the past thinking about it myself. Your dad must have left for some reason but whatever it was, he never told me. He clearly cares about you as he pays the money every month. I know he pays it because of you. When he first started making the payments, he sent me a note to say that. I have it upstairs. It's the only note that he has ever sent."

"Can I see that, Mum?"

"Of course, if you want to, darling."

She went upstairs and few minutes later brought down the typed note and gave it to Neil. Neil read and reread it several times.

"And he's never sent anything else?" asked Neil.

"No, that is it. Nothing else. If he were to send anything in the future, then I would definitely let you see it."

"I don't understand, Mum."

"Neither do I, Neil. Maybe someday we will. He does care about you to be not only sending the money every month without fail but to be increasing it as his wages go up. Not many dads would do that."

"You think so, Mum?"

"I know so."

Cassie raised the discussion with Mike when he returned from work. He expressed the view that this was all part of a child's maturation process, rather than any indication that Neil was unhappy. Given that Neil was now fourteen years old, he would ask different questions as he developed and it was unsurprising that he would have such thoughts and questions at his present age. The important thing was that he was asking the questions rather than feeling not able to, Mike advised.

In that first year living in Westpool, there were other changes to their lives. They could now watch television; albeit they were each interested in very different types of programme. Being used to a wide cinema screen with films in technicolour, the porthole screen in grainy black and white was disappointing in comparison with the visual experience at the cinema. The positive side was being able to watch a range of programmes and the occasional film at the flick of a switch, in the comfort of their own home. Cassie remained much more of a radio listener and spent little time watching television, claiming that radio allowed the engagement of the imagination more than television did. On a cold winter's day in Westpool, Mike switched on the television as the new American President, John Kennedy, was making his inaugural address in Washington:

"The world is very different now. For man holds in his mortal hands the power to abolish all forms of human poverty and all forms of human life."

At the end of the speech, Mike turned to Cassie and asked, "What did you think of that then? Did it inspire you?"

"Made me think more than inspire me! He is a good speaker but he champions liberty over equality and fraternity. That's not my way of thinking. I can only understand liberty as freedom from oppression; not some laissez-faire freedom to exploit others."

"What do you mean?"

"He made a good point that in our age, at the start of the 1960s, we have the means to abolish poverty at the same time as we have the power to wipe out all forms of life on this planet, not just human, as he probably meant to say. However, rather than setting out how to free the planet from nuclear weapons and how we are to eradicate poverty he invoked liberty as the guiding principle, which means allowing the rich and powerful to protect their interests as they see fit."

"You and other CND supporters managed to commit the Labour Party to unilateral nuclear disarmament at the last Labour Party conference. At least on this side of the Atlantic we may be free of nuclear weapons when a Labour government is elected."

"Yes, but for how long is that going to be the party's policy? Not long, I predict. Yet nuclear war feels imminent. As for abolishing poverty, that's so distant it's not even on the horizon."

"You seem unduly pessimistic today."

"I am just being realistic. Don't worry, I am not about to throw in the towel for what I believe in. Those in the party who talk about the need to spend millions on arming ourselves with nuclear weapons and at the same time stress the need to water down radical action on poverty and exploitation – they do get me down at times."

"How is it going at county level?"

"It's interesting. Although I haven't been a councillor for that long, it's clear that too many councillors have been – for far too long. There's little dynamism to do things in a different way but I am hoping that I get the opportunity soon to get some of the things done that I and a few others are keen on. I am due to meet Peter Johnston tomorrow about this."

Having been a county councillor for over a year, Cassie had thrown herself into it, sitting on several committees, although her main interest was in services for children. The leader of the

Labour group, Peter Johnston, never failed to show he liked her and at every opportunity in Labour group meetings he was fulsome in his support when she spoke in a discussion. The process to decide the chairmen of committees for the new municipal year was about to start and she had received an invitation to meet him in the leader's room at County Hall to discuss his ideas. He was sitting at his desk when Cassie was shown into the room by his secretary, who invited her to sit at the small coffee table in the corner. After concluding a telephone call, Peter Johnston got up from his desk and joined her.

"Cassie, you must know that I am a great admirer of yours. You have added a great deal to the group since you were elected. As you know I am meeting all members to discuss positions in the new municipal year. What would you say to becoming Chairman of the Children's Committee? I know you have a particular interest in those services."

"Really? I didn't expect such an offer. Thank you! I'd love to take that on."

"So, you'll accept my nomination at the group meeting when we vote on this?"

"Are you sure about this, Peter? I am not going to be someone who just does what has always been done, in the way it has always be done. You may regret this."

"I am sure you won't let me regret anything, I think we will get on really well. It will mean us spending a lot more time together. You're a free spirited woman; I like that about you," he said as he placed his arm round her waist.

Feeling uncomfortable, she leant forward to pour herself a glass of water which meant that he had to drop his arm from her waist.

"Can I think about this and get back to you?" she asked, intending to bring the meeting to an end and leave.

"I was hoping you would give me an answer today. I really need to finalise my nominations. Would you like to go out to lunch so we can talk further? I do like being in your company and you have always indicated that you like being in mine," he said as he placed his hand on her knee.

Cassie pushed his hand away and turned to face him.

"What do you mean – I have always indicated I like to be in your company?"

"You must know what I mean, Cassie. You always smile at me when—"

"That's a lie! Why is it that so many of you men presume that I have some sexual interest in you, just because I smile when we meet? I smile at every person I meet – men, women, and children! The truth is it has nothing to do with how I behave, but it has everything to do with your sense of entitlement."

"I am sorry. I assume that means that you are turning down my offer," Peter Johnston said as the smile fell from his face.

"You can assume what you want. I'm going to put my name forward for Chairman of the Children's Committee. If you want to put someone up against me then don't expect me to stay quiet about what you have done today. I am finished with putting up with this type of behaviour," stated Cassie as she got up and walked out of the room.

When she got home, she told Mike everything. Her anger had not dissipated.

"Why is it that this always seems to happen to me? Well not always; but it's not the first time it has happened to me, as you know."

"And probably not the last! I am sure you have got him worried about ever trying that again, with you or any other woman, hopefully. Are you going to put your name forward as you promised?"

"I am. I am determined to make sure he doesn't get away with behaving like that. I have a bit of support within the group – and he knows it!"

"Good. I think you should."

There was a pause before Mike continued.

"You probably don't realise but I come across so much sexual abuse of women in my work."

"Really? I'd never connected women being abused, with mental health."

"In our work at the hospital, the team has found out that more than half of the women who suffer from mental health problems, have been victims of some sort of sexual abuse."

"I'm shocked. Do you mean that the abuse has caused their mental health problems?"

"No, I'm not saying that. There are some women where sexual abuse has certainly been a major contributory factor to worsening their mental health problems, but it is not the primary cause in most cases. A lot of women have experienced sexual abuse and assault before and after they have become mentally ill. What is clear is that abuse amongst mentally ill women is a lot more widespread than people think."

"It's not surprising, thinking about it. After all, the more vulnerable a woman is, the more likely she is to be abused."

"Exactly. Sometime in the future, when we have more evidence from casework and group sessions, the team and I plan to write about this for the psychiatric journals."

"You telling me all this – it makes me even more determined to follow through on what I told Peter Johnston I was going to do. You're so good for me, Mike Bennett."

"On another matter; you know we've talked about the house being in my name and how we could do with an arrangement that gives us all security into the future. Well today I went to discuss options with a solicitor and he is going to put them in writing with the aim of giving you part ownership in this house. He will send them this week so we can discuss them and come to some agreement. Is that okay with you, Cassie?"

"I still feel that it's not quite right for me to have half ownership, as you were suggesting."

"Well let's look at what he sets out. I want a solution that leaves you feeling secure. If things do go wrong between us then you should have something to fall back on in your own right. You are the one with the child, or rather adolescent. I love you and I wouldn't want it any other way."

"Are you thinking that we may be about to split up then? I was just thinking we could take advantage of Neil being round at his friends and go upstairs to bed and discuss this further, amongst other things."

"You always come up with the best suggestions. Who am I to turn that down?"

"Good. But before we go up; it's Neil's birthday next month. Let's have a big party. I think that will help him feel at home here."

"Sounds a good idea to me. How about I get him a record player for his room. He is getting into pop music in a big way, some of which does not suit my tastes."

"Good idea. I'm sure he will like that. The party will also be a good way of getting all our friends together – yours, Neil's and mine. Do you think yours and my friends will get on?"

"I can't see any reason why not. Your friends are good people and mine have been good to me. If one or two of them don't get on by any chance, then it's not the end of the world. It isn't for me anyway, as I know I'll be in bed with you at the end of the party."

"You can be a bit presumptuous, Mike Bennett," said Cassie as she took his hand and pulled him towards the stairs.

A few months afterwards, she was elected unopposed Chairman of the Children's Committee. In her acceptance speech Cassie made clear her intent on introducing new policies and practices into the Children's Department; all of them aimed at reducing the instances where children were taken into care. Her friend and now long-standing colleague Nora Bateson, stood for and was elected the Vice-Chairman of the Children's Committee. Together, they set about devising a plan to change the management of the department including visits to several other councils where the policies and practices for community service provision were already in place to support struggling families. By the middle of the year, they had a detailed plan for how they were going to effect the change they were set on, although they were aware that there would be difficulties ahead.

Part 3 – Chapter II

In his bedroom upstairs, Neil and a few of his friends were playing at high volume the recent album he had bought – *The Times They Are a-Changin'*. They knew all the lyrics and were singing along in their best Dylan drawl. Downstairs in the kitchen his mother and Mike were listening to the radio news which was reporting that the previous day had been the first of the year when there was no frost in any town in the country.

"At long last, it's come to an end. What a hard winter that has been! I intend to start on the garden this weekend. There's so much to be done," Mike said.

"I don't suppose I'll be seeing much of you for the next few months then; as you immerse yourself in your garden," Cassie remarked.

"Our garden now! Yes, it is going to take much more time and effort than in previous years. There has been a lot of damage done by a long winter of temperatures below-freezing. You're going to see a lot of change in the garden this year."

"Now that we can see unbroken green countryside for the first time in months, how about going for a walk through Beuly wood, up to the top of the hill?"

They set off well wrapped up against the cold air of early spring and were soon breathing in the pine scented air of the wood. Cassie talked of matters that were at last generating change in the council. She, together with Nora Bateson, had spent the last two years chairing the Children's Committee. The two women councillors had set out to reshape what they saw as an inflexible and at times damaging approach to children and families at risk. The Head of the Children's

Department had been managing the service for the last ten years and had applied a policy, almost without exception, of taking children into institutional care where families were struggling to cope. For her and Nora, this blanket policy was what they had wanted to change, seeing it as too often causing unnecessary damage to the welfare of the child as well as to that of the family. It was also an expensive policy for the council, leaving little resources for the development of the support services that they wanted to see in place. Cassie's experience as a district nurse had left her convinced that by providing more practical support and assistance for some troubled families, they could be kept together without resorting to taking the children into care. The two women had investigated alternative approaches and practices, with the result that they were both convinced that big change was only going to be possible through the introduction of new, senior management from outside the department.

For a large part of the first year of their tenure chairing the Children's Committee, they had worked to persuade the Head of the Children's Department to retire. She had resisted and it was only after some months that they discovered that her resistance was being encouraged by Peter Johnston, the Leader of the Council. From the start of their tenure, he had taken every opportunity to express doubts about their proposed changes. However, they had not expected what they referred to as his skulduggery. Cassie was convinced that Peter Johnston's motivation was as a result of her refusing his advances. She had spent hours discussing with Mike how to respond in the face of his political intervention to undermine what she and Nora were trying to achieve. The outcome of her discussions with Mike and those she had with Nora, was to apply a bit of their own illicit scheming and avoid an open clash with Peter Johnston, which they would lose in all probability. After all, the Leader continued to enjoy the support of many long established councillors, who had been councillors for much longer than Cassie and Nora had. Instead they embarked on a strategy of applying constant pressure on the Head of the Children's department. Their demands increased, requiring that she present all reports to them in person and that she alone had to respond to their questions, instead of delegating to junior officers who had written the reports and knew the case in much more detail. They also adopted a practice of demanding an assessment of alternative approaches used by other councils, rather than agreeing to take a child into care in every instance. Ongoing reports were also required on the progress achieved to help the parents improve their care and thereby have the child returned home. After almost six months of this pressure, the Head of Department agreed to take early retirement. Peter Johnston was furious but was unable to stop that outcome.

Having achieved their goal with considerable difficulty and no little stress for all concerned, they had recruited a new Head of Department, whose approach was in line with their own. By the start of their second year's tenure, the council had contracted with a national organisation, called the Family Service Unit, which would set up a local service in the county. Its innovative methods of working with problem families, whose plight was often caused or exacerbated by poverty as much as anything else in their eyes, was the direction that Cassie and Nora wanted the council to take. By the start of the new municipal year in May, the results had justified their decisions to adopt radical change. Within a year of the new service arrangements being in place, the cost of the contract with the local Family Service Unit had paid for itself, through savings to the budget for placing children into care. As a consequence, the council had provided services to forty per cent more families than it had done in the last ten years of operation. Cassie was feeling both vindication and unease. She was feeling uneasy about the deceit and ruthlessness that being a politician appeared to demand and which she was not immune to using herself.

On reaching the top of the hill, Mike and Cassie took in the view down across the south of the county to the sea in the far distance, with occasional patches of thin mist obscuring the land in between.

"That's something we have in common. When we come up against obstacles, it just makes us more determined to find a way round them. Don't you think so?" asked Mike.

"I suppose we do. I don't understand why some people are so afraid of challenging the status quo. Nobody is going to take you outside and shoot you if you ask questions and disagree."

"I would have thought that being taken out and shot is marginally less frightening than to find oneself on the wrong side of an argument with you, darling."

"How can one not act if one has the power to make a difference, given the staggering level of injustice and harm done to vulnerable people in this world?"

"Just joking! I know how strongly you feel about people who are more interested in occupying positions of power, than on focusing their energies to get things changed for the better."

"It's true though that my vehemence masks some self-doubt. I often feel uneasy about what being a politician may be doing to me, without me noticing. I'd hate to turn into one of those who has stayed in it too long and extols the virtue of experience to hide their own inertia. At the same time I fear becoming someone who criticises the values and actions of others with unashamed self-righteousness, while their vanity prevents them noticing the flaws or inconsistencies in their own stance."

"I know you found it hard to do what you did to get rid of that Head of Department, but that is a positive thing. None of us can be allowed to continue to occupy a position of power and influence, just because it would cause personal hurt to be removed."

"I can see that, but the danger in being guided by your conscience is that it is you who is the sole guardian of it. Self-justification is much easier to slip into than self-criticism."

"I promise to let you know promptly if you ever get corrupted. You should do the same for me. Anyhow, what do you think will be the next stage for you in local politics?"

"Peter Johnston is a shrewd operator and has more support in the Labour group than I do. So, I am not planning to challenge him for the leadership as I was thinking to do last year. My support base is more within the party membership. George Turley, our Labour MP, has indicated that he is likely to stand down when he is seventy in a couple of years' time. Perhaps I'll go for that, but I need to have specific aims with a clear timeframe for achieving them. I don't want to climb on the political career ladder just for the sake of it."

"That would be a big decision. Not only politically, but for us personally. London is a long way away, even if you were to come home to the constituency at weekends."

"Now there's an example of me slipping into self-centred mode. I just didn't think to make it clear to you that any decision will have to be one that we are both happy with. I wouldn't have it any other way," said Cassie as she kissed him and took his arm.

On the way home, Mike talked of the new regime that he had managed to get established in his work. The changes introduced at Furlong hospital several years ago were now a catalyst for the adoption of a similar service model in hospitals in other parts of the country. Just over a year ago, this approach had been given a major boost by the Minister of Health attacking the tradition of incarcerating those with mental health problems in isolated hospitals. In its place the Minister had advocated a move towards community-based services and the eradication of the psychiatric asylum. Encouraged by this change in national government policy, if not practice, Mike Bennett and his team had invested time in recording the results of their new methods of therapeutic services delivered as much as possible in the community rather than being purely hospital based. They had produced a substantial amount of information on the outcomes for patients and their families, from this new approach. As a consequence, the hospital had become a magnet for training placements in both psychiatry and social work. Mike and his colleagues shared the increasing demand for attendance at conferences and seminars, to explain and promote what they were doing. The only activity that he retained sole control of was the editing and publication of reports and articles for journals. He was able to turn out written material much quicker than any of his colleagues. This last year had brought a welcome development. His professional life had become easier to manage following his appointment as the lead consultant in the hospital. It meant that he was no longer required to spend an inordinate amount of time convincing the hospital management to adopt his latest idea for changing traditional practice.

Life at home was also changing. Neil was now sixteen years old. He was performing well in sport and school work. This was in no small measure due to constant encouragement from both his mother and Mike. At home disagreements and preferences were aired and resolved, as and when they arose. Neil accepted that Mike's view was of equal value and interest as that of his mother's in any issue under discussion. Nevertheless, Mike tended to not take part in any argument that arose between Neil and his mother, unless asked for his view by both. Neil was on track to pass all his O levels, which he was due to take in the next couple of months. His intention was to do languages at university. The only doubt in his mind was whether he would do a degree in both French and Spanish or in only one of those languages. Despite all the positives, for his mother, it felt like there had been a war of attrition going on to get Neil to do his agreed chores within the household. Because Neil did sport on Saturday mornings, he could not do a Saturday job as many of his peers did. That meant he had no money so his mother had agreed to pay him pocket money for his undertaking of several household tasks, including cleaning, washing up and hoovering. All of a sudden, his performance of domestic chores had shown a remarkable improvement, when his mother stopped his pocket money and agreed to pay it from then on, only on the basis that Neil completed his chores in full; no later than one day after she had issued her first reminder.

By the end of May, all the areas of the garden that had been damaged by the ferocious winter had been redesigned and replanted, with the intention of creating a cottage garden. On the north facing wall, Mike had cut back the climbing roses that had been damaged and he had planted a variety of new roses and clematis, both there and along the side wall. Many of the border shrubs and flowers had to be renewed and replanted, and an extended vegetable garden was already progressing well with lettuces, potatoes, leeks, and onions. A fish pool and fountain had been installed and a small orchard of apple and plum trees added at the bottom of the garden. Mike had also engaged a gardening contractor to construct a terra cotta brick patio with a stone barbecue in the far corner. In effect, the damage caused by the long hard winter had given him the opportunity to re-plan the garden in ways he had always wanted to but would never have embarked on, had it not become necessary to do so.

"I am excited by how the garden is going to look in full summer and early autumn. If it is okay with you, Cassie, can we keep our holidays this summer to only a few long weekends away? I need to be around more to make sure everything turns out the way I want it," asked Mike.

Cassie thought for a few moments before giving a response.

"I'll go along with that – on two conditions. Next summer, I want to honour the promise I made to Jim Reilly to make a trip from here to the battlefield in Spain where his son died. I feel we should do that at long last. Second, can we have a party in late August to celebrate Neil passing his O levels and also to celebrate Ellen's girls getting their grades to go to university? I think there is little if any risk of any one of them not doing as well as expected."

"The party sounds a great idea. If the weather is good we could have a barbecue in the garden. Did you tell me that Ellen may have a new man in her life now?"

"Yes, she does. It's Phil Simpson – a policeman who was involved in the investigation of Eddie's disappearance. I remember him as a really nice man. Ellen got to know him at the time of Bill's death and the inquest that followed. He was ever so supportive. Such dreadful times. It is amazing how time melts away even the bleakest moments."

"That's good. And that trip to Spain in memory of Jim's son, I'd love to do that next summer. I know how much Jim means to you, even now. It will be the trip of a lifetime, I promise."

The party was held in the redesigned garden on a beautiful day at the end of August. Mike had worked almost every day in it since early March, following the end of the long winter that had caused so much damage. The impact was impressive with the garden displaying a variety of colours, mixed and matched in informal yet coherent arrangements. He had managed to revive the 'Madame Alfred Carriere', one of his favourite climbing roses now covered with heads of white, tinged in pink. The pink and white flowers of the clematis were also in bloom. The flower beds were a mix of blue Campanula, red roses, the burnt orange of Helenium, Phlox in shades of pink, white, and purple – all interspersed with white Cosmos. There were also rows of sweet peas supported on bamboo canes in a riot of purple and pink, and the range of scents as one moved through the garden was as captivating as the mix of colours. Mike completed the last of the dead-heading of shrubs and flowers and returned indoors where the final preparations for the party were almost complete.

"The civil rights march is taking place in Washington today. I know we have the party to attend to as the hosts, but

I don't want to miss that. It's on television and it is being shown live," Cassie stated.

"I didn't know that you were interested in that, Mum," remarked Neil.

"I have been for some time now. I knew nothing of racism until I read a Doris Lessing book on the way back from my first trip to London years ago. It left a deep impression on me. Since then, I have taken a keen interest in the civil rights struggle of black people in the United States. It never fails to shock me just how ingrained racism is there. Mind you, it now happens in this country, with immigrants being discriminated against at every turn."

"I will watch the march on television with you, Mum. I've learned about the civil rights struggle in the States – from the papers and television, but also from listening to the songs of people like Bob Dylan, and Joan Baez. In fact, they are due to sing at the rally following the march in Washington today."

Several of the party guests gathered around the television to watch Martin Luther King. As his speech proceeded, a silence fell over the group. Everyone, young and older, was captivated by what was unfolding on a small television screen in the corner of the living room. At the end of his speech there was spontaneous clapping from all who had sat entranced by what they knew was a dramatic event.

"Has anyone ever heard a more inspiring speech than that? Not only was that brilliantly put together, but his delivery – building to that emotional crescendo – it was so uplifting!" Cassie exclaimed, as she and the adults returned to the party in the garden. Only Neil and a few of his friends continued to watch the event, in order to see the singers perform.

Towards the end of the evening, Cassie gave a speech congratulating the children on their examination results and made a special point of acknowledging Ellen and her daughters, who had come through such terrible loss after the mining disaster. On finishing, she made her way to the patio on the far side of the garden where Ellen and Jenny were talking with Jenny's husband, Alex, and Phil Simpson. Ellen introduced Cassie to Phil Simpson.

"Cassie, you remember Phil from all those years ago, don't you?"

"I do. Phil, you were very kind to me back then and you have been so considerate to Ellen and the girls. It's good to see you. Still in the police?"

"Yes, still there – for my sins. As you would expect there have been a few changes since back then. I am now a sergeant and mainly work at the Westpool police station."

"Is Sergeant Bates still there?"

There was a silence for a few seconds.

"No, he isn't. You can't have heard. He retired last year and I am sorry to say he was found dead two weeks ago."

"Dead? How?" Cassie heard herself ask.

"He died of a heart attack."

"I can hardly believe it. Was he not in good health?"

"No, he hadn't been for years. The reason for his retirement was his alcohol problem, which was affecting his performance at work. The heart attack would appear to have been caused by excessive alcohol intake, according to the post mortem. He was a heavy drinker for as long as I worked for him. What I didn't know about him was that he had been married to a woman who had severe mental health problems. She was in hospital for years before she died. Believe it or not, that only became known to his colleagues after his death."

"Sorry, I need to go inside for a moment," Cassie said as she turned and walked off in haste.

Ellen and Jenny followed her inside, to the kitchen where there were no guests.

"I know what you must be feeling, Cassie. But as Phil said, Ron Bates was a heavy drinker well before you were involved with him. His death is nothing to do with you," Ellen stated.

"Ellen is right. You have no reason to feel responsible for any of this. Sad and shocked yes; but it was nothing to do with your ending of the relationship," added Jenny.

"I do feel guilt. Maybe this would never have happened if I had stayed with him. I can be hard-hearted at times."

"You left him for good reason. As for his drinking, that was his responsibility. It's only the alcoholic who can take responsibility and stop. That's what Alex realised a few years back, thank God," Jenny added.

"That's the truth of it, Cassie. It's all very sad, but you are not responsible in any way for Ron Bates drinking himself to death," said Ellen.

"Where would I be without you two? And thanks for your discretion. I told you about his wife years ago, although I notice it has only now become known to Phil and others. What tragic lives Ron Bates and his wife lived."

Later, she recounted what had happened to Mike and Neil. Mike was understanding as always and reassuring that such an outcome could not in any way be linked to what she had done all those years ago. What made her feel better was her son's response. He hugged his mother, told her he loved her, and without further delay went out on the town with his friends.

Part 3 – Chapter III

They were sitting round the table after Sunday lunch when Cassie raised her promise to Jim Reilly to retrace his son's journey from Aylston to Jamara, in Spain, where he had died fighting for the Spanish Republic. She was convinced that this year was the time to fulfil that promise and wanted to do the journey with Neil and Mike. Her view was that it was not essential to take the exact route that Laurie Reilly had taken almost thirty years ago; not least because she worried that they wouldn't get back home until the autumn, if they were to. Turning to Mike she asked,

"What do you suggest? You have travelled abroad a good few times so you are best placed to advise on how best to do the trip."

"Well, I've given it some thought since you raised it last year. The route I suggest is to overnight in London, possibly at my parents' house, before going on to Paris. We ought to stay maybe a week there as there is so much to see. From there we take the long journey to Barcelona and spend about a week there before going on to Madrid. From Madrid, we can visit the battlefield at Jarama where Jim's son was killed, before travelling down to Malaga to relax by the sea for a week or so. I suggest we travel by train all the way to Malaga but that we fly back home from there, to save travelling time."

"That sounds great! I really want to come but I am worried that on such a long holiday you two will get sick of me – or I may get tired of being with you for so long. What about someone my age coming with us? One of my friends, perhaps?" Neil asked.

"Is there anybody you are thinking of? Would they be able to pay something towards it?" his mother asked.

"I haven't got anyone specific in mind. I thought I should ask you both before talking to anybody."

Mike then intervened.

"I think it's a good idea. Perhaps we can kill two birds with one stone. We need to have someone with us to help with the language in Spain. My French is passable but not my Spanish. No disrespect, Neil, but although we want you to practise your French and Spanish when out there, we will struggle in Spain without a really good Spanish speaker. I have an idea."

He then told them about one of his colleagues at the hospital who for the last year had a Spanish au pair stay to look after his children. At the end of June, she was due to return home to Tarragona. Mike suggested that they offer to pay for her expenses to accompany them on the trip, in return for her providing translation services while in Spain.

"A girl – wow! How old is she?" Neil asked.

"I think she is nineteen; a couple of years older than you but that would be okay, wouldn't it?" Mike replied.

"Perfecto!" Neil exclaimed.

"You are not going to turn this trip into chasing a girl, are you? You have to come with us to the places we want to see; and not complain about it. You have to agree to that, Neil," Cassie said.

"Yes, Mum. I've already agreed to that. Remember, I do French and Spanish at school so there are lots of things I want to see on the trip. I won't be spending all my time watching or chasing girls."

"Glad to hear it!" replied his mother.

Cassie thought that Mike's suggestion had the added advantage of there being female company for her on the trip. The following week, Mike organised a meeting with the au pair. She spoke good English. Cassie's concern that she may not be sympathetic to the purpose of the trip soon evaporated on hearing that, although going back to Tarragona to visit her family, she would not be staying in Spain because of her wish to not live under the regime there. She had an uncle who had fled the country at the end of the civil war in 1939 and who now lived in London. With his help, she would be attending university there from late September. Neil sat mesmerised as she spoke. Rocio smiled a lot and from time to time would turn her brown eyes towards him while running her fingers though the lustrous dark hair that tumbled down over her shoulders.

By the end of May, all the arrangements for the trip were in place. It was going to be expensive but Mike was insistent that they could afford it and it would be money well spent on fulfilling the promise made to Jim. Consistent with his well-ordered approach to life at home and at work, he set up the arrangements for someone to tend to watering, weeding, dead-heading, and grass cutting in the garden while they were on holiday. As the date of departure approached, so increased the anticipation and excitement. For Cassie and Neil this would be their first trip abroad, which would culminate in their initial flight on an aeroplane.

On a Saturday in mid-July, they boarded a train for London. A decision had been made that they would not stay with Mike's parents but instead would have dinner at their home in north London and then stay overnight in a hotel near to London Bridge station, from where they would depart for Dover early the next day. Although Mike had been nervous about the meeting, his parents were as charming and welcoming as he could have hoped. Cassie saw none of the oppressive behaviour that Mike said he had been so keen to free himself from, but she did not doubt just how difficult it had been for him, when living so close to them in London. His parents were attentive to her when she responded to their questions about her work and political activism. They were also interested to hear about Neil. Mike's mother became tearful as Cassie told her how popular he was with his peers and how she had good reason to believe that he would fulfil himself in life as he knew how important it was to work hard at everything he did. Cassie was intrigued and discomforted by her display of emotion. How fragile his mother must be, she thought.

Rocio had stayed overnight with her uncle, before meeting them the next morning at London Bridge station for the train to Dover where they would board a ferry to Calais. From there they caught a train to Paris. On arrival, the immediate impression on Cassie and Neil was the different language that could be seen and heard at every turn. They had never been anywhere where English was not the spoken language. Mike's French was better than he had said and they located their hotel and checked in with no difficulty. The grandeur of Paris felt overwhelming on their first visit into the centre. The streets were wider than any they had ever seen. Majestic terraces of limestone blocks five storeys high with uniform, wrought iron balconies on the upper levels, stretched out in an impressive symmetry on both sides of the boulevards. At ground level, there were frequent cafes and bars, full of people chatting in an animated fashion and others sitting on their own watching the world unfold on the ever active streets. To add to the wide expanse, there was no shortage of large, open squares, often devoid of trees, but dominated by grand monuments or fountains. It was a city full of noise, with the streets generating a constant rumbling growl from vehicle tyres passing over the cobbles. Cassie was relieved that they were residing in a small hotel in Montmartre, as it had less traffic noise and was much more relaxing than the centre of the city. By the time they left almost a week later, Montmartre had become like a home.

Mike was keen to take them to many of the historic sites in the centre of Paris, becoming most animated when viewing art galleries. They visited the Louvre together with the Picasso exhibition and the impressionism collection at the Jeu de Paume gallery. His knowledge of art was wide ranging, both in respect of the paintings and the artists. Neil loved Mike's passion, which would brim over into veneration when holding forth and he liked to do impressions of him to make Rocio laugh. Neil and Rocio much preferred the paintings of Picasso and the impressionist art to the more classical art in the Louvre. For Cassie, the visit to the galleries in Paris left her in a mesmerised state. It was the first time, she had experienced that catharsis induced by great art, both sculpture and paintings, which she had only read about up until then. Having done a short course in art appreciation several years before at the WEA in Westpool, to view such collections of art in the grand galleries of Paris was something she had never foreseen. A high point was visiting the Pantheon, with the specific purpose of paying homage to Emile Zola. In the crypt, which also had the remains of Victor Hugo, Cassie explained to the others why Zola's great novel, *Germinal*, would forever be associated with her hometown, Aylston.

Rocio was beginning to enjoy the company of Neil, who had fallen in love from the day he first met her. He would engage her in conversation in his limited Spanish as a means of attracting more of her attention. She in turn was patient and encouraging when he attempted to converse in Spanish. On the last night in Paris, Rocio and Neil had gone out to the bars and cafes on the Place du Tertre, where artists displayed their work late into the evening. Cassie and Mike had taken the opportunity to spend the time on their own, in a little restaurant in Rue des Trois Frères.

"Have you enjoyed your time in Paris?" asked Mike.

"It's been everything I could have hoped for. I'm so glad you chose Montmartre for us to stay. I can see how one can fall in love here without effort; like Laurie Reilly did all those years ago."

"That would be almost thirty years ago. Just think of all that has happened since he was here, in love for a brief period in his short life. In effect, Jim's son was one of the very first to fight against fascism on the battlefield. The end of the Spanish Civil War only preceded World War Two by a few months."

"Yes, he was one of the first of countless millions to die in that war and in the other much bigger ones to follow on shortly after."

"Last year, I read that in that period 1936-45, the estimated number of dead killed by violence, famine, and disease caused by the Spanish Civil War, the Sino-Japanese war, and World War Two, is well over seventy million – the vast majority in China and Russia. And six million Jews were wiped out in Europe just because they were Jews."

"And every single one of those seventy million was an individual. All that brutal ending of lives – lives hardly begun for many. And the unending loss for relatives and friends – it doesn't bear thinking about. I will get more than enough sadness and loss when we are in Madrid and Jamara. Tonight, I want to immerse myself in the romance of this city. After all, I am here with the love of my life," Cassie said as she reached over to kiss Mike.

"Yes, let's do that. After the meal, we can stroll round these streets thronging with people then go back to the hotel and make love on our last night in this enthralling city."

"And we can do it with abandon, now that I am on the pill," added Cassie as she gave Mike a lingering, passionate kiss.

They left Paris the next day and embarked on the long train journey through much of France to Barcelona. There was a foreboding as they travelled; trepidation about entering a country with a fascist government. Rocio had told them that the killing and persecution still continued despite the civil war coming to an end twenty-five years ago. Trade unionism and left wing political parties remained illegal. There had been famine in a lot of the country during the 1950s, which had been kept hidden from most of the population and foreign countries, by the government controlled press. She recounted that Barcelona and the Catalan region were subject to the added repression of the Catalan language and culture.

According to Rocio, for years the Franco government had been facilitating a big influx of people from poorer regions of Spain into Catalonia. She claimed this was a deliberate attempt by Franco to undermine Catalan nationalism, which was still very much alive and on occasion defying the regime.

A short while after their arrival, they realised with relief that Barcelona was far from the austere city cowed under the heel of fascism that they had expected. It was every bit as lively as Montmartre and had architecture and art that was different but at least as striking as they had experienced in Paris. It was apparent that many young people from a mix of north European countries were visitors to this city, like they were. The only visible signs of being in an authoritarian society were the Guardia civil police in their tri-corner hats who patrolled the streets with their sub-machine guns at hand.

The old town was a particular attraction for Rocio and Neil with its clubs and bars selling beer and wine so much cheaper than in Paris. Cassie and Mike were more attracted by the city's landmarks and sights. On the first day they strolled from the city end of La Rambla to the port end by the Mediterranean. The highlight was La Boqueria food market. The cacophony of competing human voices within the market left one exhilarated and at times disorientated. They had never witnessed such a sumptuous scene. There were open slabs covered with a plethora of fish and seafood most of which they could not identify. The meat section was stacked not only with cuts of beef, lamb, pork and chicken but with countless types of cold meats and sausages, although only a few cheeses. As for the fruit and vegetable section of the market, it brought the Garden of Eden to mind for Cassie.

The following day they visited some of the city's famous monuments including the Sagrada Familia Cathedral, which they were surprised to see was still very much in a state of construction. This was followed by a tour of several other Gaudi buildings including Casa Vicens and Casa Mila, before ending up with a stroll through Parc Guell.

"I have never seen anything like this style of architecture, Mike. It evokes something out of a dream where straight lines and sharp angles have melted into a distortion of curves and bulges. I am not sure I like it that much. Unorthodox though it is!"

"It does strike one as at odds with Spanish fascism, with its emphasis on control and tradition. I wonder what Laurie would have made of this city. Nothing like anything that he grew up with in Aylston, for sure."

"Barcelona is the last place Laurie was before he entered the war proper. Jim suspected that, as in Paris, he fell in love here – and for the last time. Laurie didn't know that of course. I have always thought that not knowing is the worst state to be in, but I suppose there are things that are best left unknown in this life," Cassie mused.

"What would you most like to know that you don't know presently?"

"It would be good to know when fascism is going to come to an end in this country. It has gone on for twenty-five years now – that's a very long time."

"Had the Allies declared war on Spain, as they did on the other fascist regimes, then the dictatorship here would have been ended in 1945. It's hard to understand why Stalin didn't make a declaration of war on Spain, given that Franco sent Spanish troops to fight with the Germans on the Russian front. How ironic that fascist Spain is now treated as a treasured ally of the West in the fight against communism."

"Politics is a dirty business! Don't hesitate to tell me if I ever claim that there are circumstances where there is a benefit to setting one's principles aside. I'll be sorry to leave Barcelona for Madrid tomorrow, but it will be satisfying to at last fulfil my promise to Jim, when we take the day trip from there to Jamara where Laurie died."

The trip by train to Madrid was relaxing. Rocio's willingness to take the lead in translating, removed the anxiety that Mike and Cassie would otherwise have had, in what they expected to be a more austere city than Barcelona. As in Barcelona they headed for a hotel in the old town – on the Plaza de Santa Ana. Unlike Barcelona, there was little architecture that was arresting, but the streets of the old town were lively, at night in particular, much to the approval of Rocio and Neil. They were struck by the frequency of seeing nuns and priests on the streets in Madrid, which they took to reflect the eminent role that the Catholic Church had in Spanish society. However, it was the cauldron of heat on the streets that had the biggest impact on them. They had never experienced such high temperatures before. Rocio advised them not to go out in the afternoon sun and at other times to wear a hat and to dress in clothes that protected their skin from exposure to the sun.

On their first full day in the city, Mike was keen to visit the Prado art gallery so they set off down the hill and through the narrow streets of old Madrid, passing the church and convent of Las Triniterias Descalzas, which was constructed of narrow, slab bricks, the likes of which they had never seen before. Neil pointed out that the convent was where Cervantes, the great novelist, had been buried, which he had learned in Spanish class. He suggested to his mother that perhaps she should read *Don Quixote*, as his Spanish teacher had said it is known as the first novel written in Europe and one of the greatest. At the bottom of the hill, they crossed the busy Paseo and arrived at the gallery, which would not have been out of place amidst the grandeur of central Paris. The attraction for Mike was viewing the work of the great Spanish artists for the first time; El Greco, Velazquez, and Goya. The visit did not disappoint any of them – Mike in particular. After spending almost two hours viewing many but by no means all of the rooms, they left to take a stroll in the Retiro Park behind the Prado where they sat down on a bench in the shade under a tree by the lake, to protect themselves from the fierce sun.

"That is the fulfilment of one of my ambitions. Several times I have seen the work of Picasso, undoubtedly a genius, but never that of the old Spanish masters. It's hard to imagine I will ever see another art collection as good as that. Surely Velazquez must be one of the greatest painters. And as for Goya, I don't think I have ever seen a more arresting depiction of the terror of war than that painting: El Tres de Mayo," enthused Mike.

"I agree!" exclaimed Cassie. "I loved the expressions on the faces of those drunkards in the Valazquez painting, The Triumph of Bacchus. It captures brilliantly how merry alcohol can make you feel. But yes, that Goya painting; with such terror on the face of the man about to be executed – that was chilling! It seems apt that we have seen that painting before going to Jamara tomorrow!"

That evening they ate in a restaurant on Calle de Las Huertas, around the corner from their hotel. When they entered, they were hit by the pungent aromas of garlic, smoked paprika, and grilled meat. The walls of the restaurant were tiled from the high wooden ceiling to the stone floor. Each Azulejo tile had the same complex geometric pattern, painted in blue with an off-white background, which generated an impression of the restaurant walls extending into infinity. Hanging from the rafters of the ceiling were at least twenty legs of serrano ham, turning black as they dried out. Only Rocio and Neil wanted to try the dark red ham from the leg mounted on the bar counter, which a waiter was skilfully cutting sideways with a long thin knife. At the end of the meal Neil asked his mother to recount the story of Laurie's death in Spain. Cassie had brought the letters Laurie had sent to his father and proceeded to tell the story as she remembered old Jim had told to her, all those years ago. When she had finished there was a silence around the table until it was broken by Neil.

"To Laurie Reilly! Made in Aylston!"

They all raised their glasses to toast his memory. Cassie noticed what Mike could not from where he was sitting; Rocio and Neil were holding hands. She smiled to herself at the thought that her son had fallen in love, for the first time in his life, with a young Spanish woman, as in all probability, Laurie Reilly had done all those years ago. Later that evening, Rocio and Neil befriended a young Madrid woman and her boyfriend in a bar on the Plaza de Santa Ana. The woman was advising them on how to get to Jamara and in particular the battlefield, where they were planning to go the next day. She then explained that they were seated in the bar where Ernest Hemingway used to drink during the civil war; even pointing out the table that he used to sit at, which the bar staff confirmed. Neil knew that he needed to fetch his mother from the hotel on the other side of the square as he realised how significant this would be for her. After Neil arrived back in the bar with Cassie and Mike, he asked his mother to explain the significance to the group.

"One of the last books that Jim Reilly read was Hemingway's *The Old Man and the Sea*. He loved that book and I never heard him being so effusive about a book again; probably because it was written about an old man nearing the end of his life. Isn't life so amazing? Here we are in a bar in old Madrid that generates a connection with the much missed Jim, who lived and died thousands of miles from here. To the memory of the extremely well read Jim Reilly!"

They all raised their glasses as tears filled Cassie's eyes while she smiled.

On their last day in Madrid, they made their way to the Casa de Campo parkland situated to the west of the city centre, where there were still open trenches of what had been the front line in Madrid during the civil war. That was where Laurie had first fought and had been shocked to the core by the horrors of war. Afterwards they took a bus to Jarama, a few kilometres east of the city. There, they climbed a hill and stood overlooking the river valley, with Madrid just visible in the distance and the Sierra de Guadarrama, soaring up to the sky on the horizon beyond. There was no evidence that a battle had ever been fought there. Cassie knew that somewhere in this valley, Laurie lay buried in an unmarked grave, with so many others. She bent down and placed a bunch of red roses on the ground, with a card that read:

In memory of Jim Reilly, to whom I owe so much, and to the memory of his son, Laurie, who had the courage to fight and die for what he believed in. A promise fulfilled.

Early the next day Rocio departed. She planned to spend two months with her family in Tarragona, before then leaving for London to start university. Neil saw her off from the Atocha railway station. On the platform, they exchanged addresses and promised to meet up in London, before embracing and kissing goodbye as the train was about to leave. Neil walked back up the hill to Plaza de Santa Ana, vowing to study Spanish at university in London and to become fluent in the language. He was daydreaming of long days and nights spent with Rocio there.

Later that same morning, the remaining three departed on a train for Malaga, to spend their last week of the trip by the sea. On arrival, Neil showed his confidence and competence in the Spanish language that he had built up through spending so much time with Rocio. They travelled by taxi from the station to their hotel overlooking the city beach – with all the transactions done by Neil. Cassie felt a huge pride that compounded the feeling of satisfaction that had stayed with her on completing the trip to Jamara. She was realising that Neil was no longer a boy but was growing into a confident and independent young man. When he was very young, there had been nagging worries that he would be damaged by his father leaving him at such a young age, but now she could tell herself that this was not the case. Next year, in all probability he would be leaving home to go to university. She had honoured her promise to Jim and now she was close to completing her long standing vow made when Eddie Gallagher left all those years ago; that of bringing up a child whom she would not only always love and protect, but one who would be well equipped to go out into the world and achieve his potential.

On their opening stroll along the city's Paseo, Neil suggested that they had arrived in a tropical and exotic land. For the first time they were viewing palm trees, swaying in the gentle sea-breeze that offered some respite from the heat. Atop several church towers and electricity pylons, they spotted graceful storks taking off from and landing into huge nests. By late afternoon, there was little relief from the relentless sun that burned in the cloudless sky. The only thing to do in such conditions was to take refuge in one of the many cafes or bars that every street appeared to have. The air in the centre of the city was heavy with aromas of garlic and grilled fish, but on occasion one was overcome with wafts of foul air from sewer vents. At night it was still hot and humid, making it difficult to sleep in the never-cooling air of their bedroom. As a consequence, Mike and Cassie would get up and sit on their hotel room balcony looking up at the stars, with a chorus of cicadas chirping in the undergrowth below; and the reassuring sound of waves lapping on the shore in the near distance. Beneath a yellow crescent moon hanging in the star strewn sky and casting a shimmering light on the silver Mediterranean sea, the enthralling scent of jasmine sparked in Mike an association with his ancestry.

"I haven't told you this before but my ancestors lived and thrived here in Andalucia for centuries. They were Sephardi Jews, that is Jews who lived in Sepharad, the Jewish name for the great Arabic civilisation in Spain, Al Andaluz."

"Such an exotic past you have! Why did they choose to leave this paradise?"

"They had to leave in 1492, when all Jews were expelled from Spain by decree of the Catholic kings. They had just taken control of the last Arab kingdom in Spain, Granada, and then paradoxically they expelled the Jews from Catholic Spain and not the Moslems, whom they had just defeated.

That came later! My Sephardi ancestors were living in Cordoba when they had to flee with little more than the clothes they had; eventually making it to the Netherlands."

"Why there?"

"That was one of the few safe places for Jews fleeing Spain, though many fled to North African countries or the Ottoman Empire, which also offered some degree of security. My ancestors lived in several towns in the Netherlands for almost a hundred and fifty years before moving from Amsterdam to Hamburg. My parents can still speak some Ladino, which is the language that dates back to those Jewish communities living in Arabic Spain."

"That's incredible! A language still in use by the descendants of Sephardi Jews expelled from Spain almost 500 years ago."

"I'll tell you something else that will seem even more unbelievable. My parents knew of some Sephardi families who had possession of keys to the homes that their ancestors had to leave behind when fleeing Spain, in the late 15th century. The keys had been passed down over generations. The retention of the keys was more a symbol of a great wrong that had been done to them by being expelled from a place they loved and had thrived in, rather than an intention to ever repossess what had been theirs."

"What a fascinating story. On this trip, I have been thinking about what defines identity and how important identity is. Obviously, key elements are one's parents and ancestors. But in my view, what is at least as important is what one has become in this life. Identity is dynamic rather than merely something passed on unchanged down through the ages."

"I would not disagree with that. Nevertheless, I still struggle to settle on my identity. I am clearly Jewish by a long line of ancestors; yet I am not now, in terms of belief and custom. It is strange to think that I am German by birth but that doesn't feel part of my identity. I like the idea of being Sephardi but how does that impact on my identity? It may be important to know one's past but what do you do with it once you know it?

Don't get me wrong, I don't spend time worrying about it, but it does distract me from time to time."

"What has triggered my thinking about identity is the memory of Jim and Laurie, and why they became the people they were; in many ways different from others who for generations shared their time and place. Besides that, I have had Neil on my mind, now that he is on his way to becoming an adult. Specifically, I have been thinking about his father's birth parents and ancestry, which he and I know nothing about. At least you have records of your past and where you came from."

"Yes I do. However, the records of identity largely remain hidden in one's genes and they have a seldom noticed impact on shaping the person we turn out to be. I think that one's genes, as well as factors such as class, upbringing, and life's experiences, they all have a significant impact. I would never suggest that genes are the only determinant of who you turn out to be; just one of several contributory factors."

"Maybe when we have more time in our lives, we should do a bit of research into our pasts. Your ancestry is exotic and fascinating. Have your parents got keys to a former home in Spain? Now that would be interesting – trying out ancient keys in order to unlock one's distant past," Cassie enthused.

"That would probably result in expulsion from Spain all over again. I like the research bit but not the trying to break into what are the homes of others now. Anyway, no, my parents never had any keys to an abode in Cordoba. We ought to visit that ancient city some time. It has the great mosque and a synagogue dating back to those centuries when the Arabs ruled this land. The street layout and the exteriors of many of the buildings apparently remain largely unaltered. It was the capital of a unique civilisation in this world; one of great learning and development; with Moslems, Jews and Christians living together in a surprising degree of cooperation."

"Yes let's do that some time. It certainly appeals much more than going all the way to Western Australia to track down Eddie's ancestors."

Towards the end of July, they returned home from Malaga. Cassie and Neil had boarded their first ever flight and three hours later they disembarked in London. It struck them as miraculous that they could cover such a long distance in so short a time and that the plane could find its way from a tiny spot in Spain to its destination in an equally small spot just outside London. They decided that air flight would be their preferred mode of transport for holidays abroad in the future, which was something they saw themselves doing on a regular basis.

Part 3 – Chapter IV

George Turley, the Labour MP for Westpool and District, announced in early January 1965 that he would be retiring at the next election, which was expected to be held sometime in the following year.

"This is it, Cassie. This is your opportunity and you must take it," Nora Bateson stated.

"Now that the chance of becoming the MP has arrived, it doesn't feel as straightforward as I assumed it would be. If I do decide to go for it, will you be my election agent, Nora?"

"It would be an honour, dear. I cannot see how you won't be selected, as you are so well liked amongst the membership. With the majority Labour has in this constituency, the selection process is in effect the election itself."

"Before I make a final decision, I need to talk this through with Mike. He has a strong commitment to his job here and it would be difficult for both of us to be apart for much of the week. Besides, I should be absolutely clear in my own mind about what I want to achieve by being an MP, rather than just having a general aim of supporting the Government's programme. The Party's policies never go far enough for me – or you for that matter!"

"Okay, but we need to move without too much delay. I reckon that Peter Johnston is considering standing but I don't think he will make a serious bid if you put your hat in the ring quickly, as he knows he would not win in a vote of the membership."

The discussion between Mike and Cassie spanned several days of talking through the difficulties that her standing as an

MP may cause to their relationship. He was not inclined to raise an objection to Cassie putting her name forward, but he had concerns about how this would change their lives, which he wanted to raise and then see if there were ways that these could be alleviated. His main worry was that he would be cast adrift from the family. In the last few years, Mike had grown used to living in a family and it was now something he did not want to lose. With Neil likely to go to university in London in the autumn, and were Cassie to become the MP the following year, then they would be in London together for most of the week whilst he would be in Westpool on his own. His other concern was that of losing Cassie to another world and possibly to another man. Despite Cassie providing reassurances, the impression was forming in both of them that maybe there were more difficulties than benefits to her becoming an MP. They had agreed that each of them would give further thought to the matter before talking again soon, with a view to making a decision one way or the other.

On a cold and damp Saturday afternoon, they set off on a walk up Beuly Hill, clad in several layers of winter clothing. The air was fresh but devoid of any fragrance which added to Mike's unusual feeling of melancholy. They negotiated the muddy path up the hill, to find the ground becoming firmer and the frost turning more intense the higher they walked. The thick mist began to restrict visibility to no more than ten yards, with the condensation from their breath growing more dense as they ascended. The countryside was frozen in a wintry hibernation with an eerie stillness all around, which accentuated the sound of their voices as they began to talk about what had been hanging over them for the last few days.

"Mike, I wouldn't feel any resentment if you don't want me to stand as an MP because you feel it may damage our relationship. I have always been clear in my own mind that this is something that needs to fit comfortably with both of us or not all. That has not changed."

"I appreciate that; but I think that you, indeed anyone in your position, would begin to feel some resentment about their legitimate ambitions being curtailed. I will not stand in your way. I just needed to raise the worries I have and to work them through with you. I've settled on what I think is a solution. Were I to feel so alone during the week when you are in London, then I always have the option of applying for a job and moving back to London so that we can live together the whole week. We could keep the house here and return together at the weekend for you to do your constituency work."

"That's generous of you. Things would have to be bad for you to leave your work here given how committed you are to what you have built up. As for me, I am still uneasy about not seeing you from one weekend to the next for a good part of the year. I am not sure I could do that for any length of time."

"It would be a big thing for me to move back to London but I would do it if need be. Let's see how things go for both of us, if and when you become an MP."

"I have been thinking about our future beyond all this. I want to get married. I love you. With Neil about to turn eighteen, it feels like the right time. In truth, I've wanted to marry you ever since that morning of the pit disaster. That's when I knew you were the one for me," Cassie said with her voice faltering.

"How could anyone ever turn down a marriage proposal from you? I have never wanted anyone like I want you, but I have held back asking as I knew that seeing Neil through to eighteen without formally ending your marriage to Eddie, had a significance for you."

They stopped on the hill with the view both downwards and upwards restricted by the mist and no sound from either the town far below or from the bleak landscape around and above them. Standing, looking at each other in what felt like the middle of the clouds, tears formed in their eyes from both the cold air and the surge of emotion they felt.

"There's a first and last then – proposing to a man. It could only have been to you. On Monday, I will start divorce proceedings on the grounds of desertion. After so many years, no consent will be required so it should be agreed within a couple of months. We could be married by the end of April."

"The end of April is not far off."

"What sort of wedding would you want? I am happy for it to be either a registry office wedding or a Jewish wedding – if that's allowed without me having to convert to Judaism. Wouldn't that make it easier for your parents?"

"I certainly don't want to cause offence to them at their age. Notwithstanding that, I believe in no God, so I don't want a religious wedding. Perhaps we can incorporate some Jewish wedding customs into the celebration after, but I am happy with a wedding at the registry office. How about the second Saturday in June – a late spring wedding!"

"That's it then. That'll be a good time as Neil will have finished his exams by then. Can we go back home now? It's so cold and damp up here. What I really want is to be in a nice warm bed with you. I need to make sure the decision to get married isn't going to harm our sex life," replied Cassie as she took his arm and turned back down the hill.

"What a day this has turned out to be! We venture out into this bleak landscape where one can hardly see more than a few yards ahead, both a bit troubled, and we manage to work out a way ahead for ourselves. I end up marrying the Right Honourable Member for Westpool. I feel like Moses coming down from the mountain."

Neil was the first to be told the news. As expected, he was unconcerned and it touched them both when he said that he could not think of a better stepfather to have. He then pointed out that it would be good if his mother and his MP could push for the voting age to be reduced to eighteen from twenty-one and then she may get his vote. Nora Bateson's response to the news was one of relief. After congratulating them, Nora admitted that she had been worried that Peter Johnston may have tried to engineer opposition to her selection amongst party members, citing the moral disapproval of voters for a woman living with a man she wasn't married to. As the election agent, she now no longer had that to worry about, and she reiterated the view that Cassie's selection as the Labour candidate was unstoppable now. While aware of the potential controversy that her domestic arrangements could cause, Cassie had always been confident that it would make no difference to party members as it had never been concealed from them. As to the electorate, if it influenced any, then in her view it would only be a few, and certainly nowhere near a level that could undermine the huge Labour majority in the constituency.

Cassie wanted to tell Jenny and Ellen in person rather than by phone. A few days later, they arrived for dinner.

"Two bits of news! The least important first. I am going to put my name forward to stand as your next MP. The more important news is that Mike and I are to marry."

"At long last! I couldn't be happier for you, dear," Ellen said, as she and Jenny hugged Cassie in turn.

"What took you so long? How could any woman pass up a marriage proposal from such a man? But I am not sure about voting for you so that you can spend a lot of time away from us," added Jenny.

"I proposed to him actually. You know I wanted to see things through to Neil's eighteenth birthday and then get a divorce. So, that's what has come to be. Neil is happy with it. On the other news, if I am selected and get elected as the MP, I will be back here every weekend. It's always been the case that I need both of you to keep me grounded – that will never change. This calls for a drink."

"To yet another life, Cassie! You deserve nothing but happiness," Jenny toasted as they clinked their glasses, while they shared the memory of all those years ago when they had toasted her getting back on her feet after the devastation of Eddie's unexplained departure.

"Cassie, you'll remember you mentioned to us a few weeks ago that with Neil's eighteenth birthday coming up, you were wondering whether you should try to contact Eddie's twin brother in Australia. You were concerned about Neil having no knowledge of his father's family, as you think it is important for him to know his roots," Ellen recounted.

"Yes, of course I remember. What about it?"

"Well, I mentioned what you said to Phil the other day and he told me something you ought to know. Four years after Eddie's unexplained departure, the Australian police contacted them about Eddie's brother, Harry. Remember the police here contacting the Australian police when Eddie disappeared to check whether his brother had heard from him? Anyhow, the Australian police wanted to know if Phil and his colleagues had contact details for Eddie, as his brother, Harry, had been found dead. They said they knew of no other relatives. Of course, nobody knew where Eddie went when he left here."

"I didn't know that. I mean, I knew about the police contacting the Australians about Eddie, but nothing of his brother's death. Did they say what the cause was?"

"No, they didn't. I asked Phil about that."

"Well, that certainly puts an end to any attempt at tracing and contacting Eddie's brother. The gaps in Neil's identity will remain. I suppose it has not damaged him up to now so it's not anything to get concerned about."

Three weeks before Neil's eighteenth birthday, a letter arrived for Cassie from a London solicitors' office. The letter explained that the solicitor was acting on behalf of Eddie Gallagher, who had engaged the firm to trace his wife and son, so as to inform her that as stated many years ago, the monthly payments would stop on Neil's eighteenth birthday on 21st March 1965. There was a request in the letter that she and Neil inform the solicitors of any change of address in the future for the purposes of updating Eddie's will. The final sentence said that the solicitors could not divulge any contact details for Eddie.

After discussing the matter with Mike, Cassie then informed Neil of this and also the recent discovery that Eddie's brother had died many years ago.

"I still find it difficult to understand why Dad left with no explanation yet he has never failed to provide money for us all these years. Don't get me wrong, I don't think about it that often but it does come to mind from time to time. It's like he is a dutiful father – yet he isn't. As for Dad's brother dying, as you say there is nothing to trace in Australia; not that I was thinking of ever doing that. Mum, do you think we should send a letter to Dad and ask the solicitors to forward it to him?"

"I hadn't thought about doing that, Neil. I am not sure I would know what to say to him now, after all these years. But I can see why it makes sense for you to write a letter. From the start, the money he sent was primarily to see you through to adulthood. He is your birth father so your relationship with him is different from what mine was then and what it is now. If that is what you want to do, I think you should, darling."

Part 3 – Chapter V

In the weeks leading up to Neil's eighteenth birthday, everything appeared to be falling into place. The final monthly payment from Eddie had been made into the Post Office savings account. Cassie had withdrawn the money and closed the account that had been in her and Eddie's name since shortly after Neil was born. The selection of the Labour candidate for parliament was scheduled to take place in mid-May. The divorce was due to come through by the middle of April and the date for her wedding to Mike had been set for Saturday 14th June. A fortnight before his eighteenth birthday party, Neil sat down in his room and drafted a letter to his father, with the radio music turned up loud, as usual. In the letter he told his father what he was good at and what he wasn't and gave an outline of his life and friends, Rocio in particular, and how he had come to meet her. He ended the letter by telling him of the likelihood that he would be going to London University in the autumn to study French and Spanish, thanking him for providing money for him and his Mum all those years, and stating that he would like to meet up with him in London sometime. Neil showed it to his mother and asked for her opinion. His mother was moved by her son's level of maturity, however, she warned him that he should not have high expectations of a response right away, if ever. She advised that if he had not heard back by the time he was about to depart for London in the autumn, then perhaps Neil should send a further letter via the solicitors providing his London address, in another attempt to get contact with his father.

Cassie had decided that although reaching the age of twenty-one was by custom the occasion to celebrate becoming an adult, given that Neil was likely to be leaving home this year and that his father had in effect deemed turning eighteen years old as reaching adulthood, it struck her as more appropriate to have a special celebration of his eighteenth birthday. For the party, Mike had hired a sound system for the loud playing of music as Neil had requested, and comforted himself with the thought that the party would be over by midnight, at the latest. All of Neil's many friends were there but what pleased Neil most was Rocio's presence. Since the trip to Spain, they had kept in regular contact by phone and letter. In addition, he had visited her in London on several occasions. His application to London University to study French and Spanish had been accepted, subject to him achieving the required grades in his exams that he would sit in May. That provisional acceptance had acted as a huge incentive for Neil to put in many more hours work at his studies than he had ever done before. A few days before the party, Neil had raised with his mother the matter of whether he and Rocio could sleep together in the house. After some discussion between them, it was agreed they could, as long as Neil was using contraception. Close friends of the adults also came to the party, which added to the pride and emotion Cassie was feeling on the occasion of her son reaching the age of eighteen. Just as the party began, Neil opened all his birthday cards, one of which turned out to be from his father. After reading it Neil passed it to his mother. It had the following written message:

Dear Neil,
Thank you for your letter. I cannot express how relieved and happy I am for what you have become. I am forever grateful to your mother for bringing you up to be the impressive person you are. I will communicate in due course. I wish you nothing but happiness and fulfilment.
Your father.

"That's his writing. I am amazed that he responded, after all these years. Something must have changed, though he does not say what. It was ever thus. I am happy for you, Neil," his mother said as she continued to stare at the message in the card.

"There was a hundred pounds included, Mum. I am also surprised that he replied. I am pleased that he has, though it is going to be difficult for him to come up with an explanation for what he did. Anyway, that is for another time. By the way, Mum, he is not the only one grateful for all you have done for me," Neil added, as he hugged her.

Cassie called Mike aside to tell him of the card.

"Well, that's a turn up for the books. I think you are right; something major has changed. How does it leave you feeling?" Mike asked.

"My first reaction was intrigue and being happy for Neil but that has quickly turned to irritation. All this secrecy for all those years and it still continues! The chances are that if he ever does come up with an explanation, it may put me into a permanent state of irritation."

"That's another thing I love about you; no matter what happens, there is no lasting damage to your indomitable spirit."

"I feel a need to share this with Jenny and Ellen. Are you enjoying the party? We still haven't had a dance," said Cassie, taking another sip of wine from her glass.

"Yes, I am just about coping with the volume of the music. Perhaps, I am showing my age."

The sound system was blasting out the Rolling Stones' 'The Last Time' and Cassie began to sing the chorus as she moved off, dancing to the music, and smiling back at him as she went in search of her friends. She found them hiding from the music in the kitchen and told them of the letter that Neil had received that day.

"It sounds as if you may be about to find out why he left all those years ago," Ellen suggested.

"Maybe. You know, thinking about it now, isn't it strange that something that happened in a small town so many years ago still remains a mystery? Eddie departed without a word of explanation and not a single person knew anything as to why."

"The only person, whom I suspected of knowing something of the reason why, was that priest, Father Doherty. He denied it but I never believed him," Phil said.

"I never liked that man!" Jenny blurted out.

"It's so long since that priest left Aylston that I think I can tell you something that isn't widely known. We had two complaints about him behaving inappropriately with teenage girls. Sergeant Bates and I interviewed him about the allegations, but Bates was of the view that there was insufficient evidence to do anything. Nevertheless, the sergeant was convinced that the allegations were true so he contacted the bishop and told him to move the priest elsewhere or he would take action. He was moved within a couple of weeks," Phil recounted.

"To do the same elsewhere, probably," said Cassie as she looked from Jenny to Ellen.

"Let's not dwell on the past. Let's drink to Neil and his wonderful mother, who has seen him through despite all the difficulties. To Cassie and Neil!" Ellen toasted.

Later on, as a few of the adults were doing some clearing up after the young people had departed to a club in town, Mike noticed Cassie sitting on the sofa with the card that Neil had received from his father in one hand and a glass of wine in the other.

"I think it's probably time for bed, darling. You look a bit sad," Mike suggested.

"No, I'm not sad. It was a great party – I enjoyed it. I am a bit drunk, the truth be told."

"Yes, I know. I don't want you to end such a great evening feeling melancholic. Are you thinking of Eddie?"

"Kind of. I was thinking of the character of Mr Darcy in the book *Pride and Prejudice* and how Elizabeth Bennet misconstrued his intentions due to a lack of understanding about why he acted as he did. Perhaps Eddie Gallagher had some good reasons for leaving but for the life of me I can't think what they could possibly be," she said, slurring some of her words.

"That's a complicated take on the past to be thinking about; especially when a bit drunk."

"Yes, possibly. Before that I was thinking about that priest; you know the one I told you about, with whom I had problems. Tonight, Phil told us that he always suspected that the priest knew something of the reason why Eddie left and also that the police had received a couple of complaints about him abusing young girls. He was moved after Sergeant Bates had demanded as much from the bishop."

"Let's go to bed before you get on to something else that can't be resolved. I will finish the clearing up in the morning," said Mike as he led her upstairs.

Part 3 – Chapter VI

Shortly after arriving at work, Mike received the phone call from a friend of the family in London. Without delay, he phoned Cassie and they agreed to leave work and meet at home.

"Oh Mike, I am so sorry. What did your mother die of?"

"A heart attack early this morning, and she was dead by the time the ambulance arrived. I have just phoned my father and told him I will be with him by this evening. You may not know this but burial for Jews follows very quickly after death. The funeral will be tomorrow late afternoon. I am going to have to leave in an hour, I have checked the trains and planes and I'll get there sooner if I fly."

"I am happy to come with you but I need to speak to Neil first so I will travel very early tomorrow."

"I am grateful that you will be at the funeral and if you could stay for a bit of the mourning period, I'd appreciate that too. It's called Shiva and lasts for seven days, but if you could stay for a couple of days that would be sufficient. I intend to stay for most of the seven days, as I am the only child and it may be hurtful to my father if I do otherwise. We can stay at a local hotel – there will be close friends staying at the house for the first couple of nights so I don't need to be there overnight, until after you have left. Is that okay?"

"Of course. How is your father bearing up?"

"He was composed and resigned on the phone. His view is that she had been frail and in pain from crippling arthritis for such a long time, so in some ways it was a blessing that she was no longer suffering. He has good friends from the synagogue and the local community around him so he will be fine, with time."

Before leaving, Mike gave an outline of a Jewish funeral, the meal after at home, and Shiva. He explained a number of customs, including the washing of hands at the front door of the home, mirrors being covered, the prayer, Kaddish, being recited, a candle burning throughout Shiva, and not wearing leather shoes in the house. He also mentioned that she would notice at the funeral and during Shiva that the left-hand pocket of his suit jacket had been ripped, which would be done by his own hand. This custom, known as Keriah, was a symbol of the heart-felt impact of his mother's death. Cassie commented that she was fascinated by the customs and that she was relieved that all she had to say in the prayers was 'Amen'.

Mike was surprised at how easy it was to slip into a way of life he had long separated himself from. There was no re-emergence of religious belief in him but he found a comfort in the customs, and in the sense of belonging generated by the presence of so many family friends taking part in the mourning for his mother. The many stories told of his mother during Shiva not only compounded his feelings of being part of a community but also gave him a broader understanding of her. While she had been dutiful and kind, he had always felt that she was often distracted to the point of being distant during his childhood and adolescence. She had clearly been disappointed about his shedding of religious belief and about him distancing his life from the Jewish community. However, she had avoided having any argument or disagreement on the subject. The only sign of her disappointment was in her constant reminding of her desire that he marry a good Jewish girl. The stories told during the seven days of Shiva depicted a woman of extensive kindness and generosity, in particular to anyone, Jewish or not, who found themselves in difficulty. For the first few days, he found himself wondering why his mother appeared to be so sensitive to others yet could be distant with her own child; all of which he had no time to discuss with Cassie before she left for home on the third day of Shiva. Cassie had left a positive impression on his father and all his friends, with her willing contribution to the preparation and serving of food, as well as the clearing up. Mike admired how she had maintained a low key presence throughout, yet displayed an engaged and supportive demeanour to all who were in attendance.

It was only after she had left for home that his father told him the full and devastating story of the family's flight from Hamburg in 1933. When they were alone in the house late in the evening on the fourth day of Shiva, his father started the conversation by presenting the startling truth that Mike had a brother who was eleven years older and who had been left behind with close relatives in Hamburg, all those years ago. His brother was called Joseph and he had begged his parents not to be separated from his two cousins to whom he had been so closely attached since his first memory. They had spent their childhoods playing together with hardly a day missed outside of each other's company and the plan to leave Hamburg and be separated from his cousins had traumatised Joseph. What had come to pass in the days leading up to their departure was that Mike's parents, with deep reluctance due to the scale of Joseph's distress, had agreed with his aunt and uncle that Joseph move in with them, in the expectation that at some point in the not too distant future he would change his mind and would want to join his parents and baby brother in London. Despite his mother writing to him every week, Joseph had never changed his mind. Five years later, every Jewish family that had remained in Germany in the belief that the worst had passed, came to realise that they needed to flee to protect themselves, only to find that all escape routes had been blocked by the Nazis. From that time on, Mike's parents had lost contact with not only their son and relatives, but all the other friends who had stayed in Hamburg in the mistaken belief that the frightening times of 1933 would get no worse, if not improve in time. Two years after the war had ended, his parents could not escape the dreadful realisation that they had all perished in the nightmare of the Holocaust.

His father went on to explain that his mother had been overwhelmed with shame and grief at losing their eldest son ever since 1933 when they had left him in Hamburg, for what they assumed would be a temporary period. She had demanded that his father vow to keep this shame a secret from their young son and all the friends they went on to make as they built their life in London. He had done so out of his sense of duty and care to his wife but admitted that, despite the pain this would cause to Mike, he realised it was now his duty to inform him of the truth. Mike spent his last two days at his father's house in a state of shock, which was then followed by overwhelming grief. He felt that he was drowning in a sea of mourning for his brother, his mother, and every one of the six million Jews who had been wiped out by the brutality and cruelty of the Nazis and their many collaborators. On the penultimate day before he left to go home to Westpool, Mike could not stop crying, which caused alarm to both his father and friends of the family.

On the morning of the day when he was due to return home to Westpool, he had regained his composure and was able to give assurance to his father that he could work his way through this and that he would be in touch before the week was out. The journey home was one of total immersion in thoughts of his brother, his parents, and what it was to be Jewish. When he arrived home and was greeted by Cassie, he broke down. Through his tears, he recounted what he now knew would alter his life forever. Cassie took a tight hold of his hand and said nothing until he had finished telling the full secret that his parents had been too ashamed to make public for over thirty years.

"We will get through this together, Mike, I promise," Cassie said as she struggled to keep herself from breaking down.

"I know I will eventually but there is no short cut with grief. Anyhow, there is my father to look out for and I need to get through this to make sure he feels free of any guilt. In truth, I think my father has probably worked through the worst of it just by telling me and then his friends. There is a sense of release in him at having been able to divulge it, at last. I don't want to undo that in terms of how I personally cope with my grief. Can I have a whisky? If ever there was a time for a drink..."

For the next hour they talked and drank which, bit by bit, eased his grief and enabled him to begin to think about a resolution to his identity issues. Mike spoke of his need to at last resolve this matter in a way that felt right for him. He was clear that he was Jewish and would want to identify himself as such for as long as he lived. At the same time, he could never believe in a god so wouldn't ever practice Judaism. During the last week, he had recognised that while there was a lot of well-being from feeling part of the community, the reality was that it would be impossible to live a life embedded in those customs given he was not a Jew by religion and didn't live in a Jewish community. He acknowledged that he would have to find some other way of giving expression to being Jewish.

"If you take away the religion, what defining aspects of the identity are left? There must be some and maybe that is what you need to focus on and give expression to in your life," asked Cassie.

"That's what I have been thinking too. What is in my mind is the ability to survive, adapt, and thrive. Jews, because of recurrent persecution since the Diaspora, have had to uproot themselves again and again from societies that they had become a part of while still managing to preserve their historic identity within those societies. The impact of that constant adapting probably sharpens one's capacity to live and learn – only for those that survive of course."

"So where does that leave you in resolving the identity problem?"

"Maybe I should research and help to publicise some of the great achievements – intellectual and cultural – of Sephardi Jews in that great civilisation that was Al Andaluz."

"Well, your ancestry connects you with that time and place so there is the personal dimension to going down that route. It sounds like a promising way to give expression to what it is for you to be Jewish."

"Apart from making me feel better, I'd like to think there could be benefits in unveiling what is largely unknown about that amazing civilisation. There was so much cooperation and learning from different traditions and cultures when at its peak."

"It's fascinating. Makes me wonder why we know so little about it."

"With all my focus on my own grieving, I forgot to ask you how you found my mother's funeral?"

"I thought the customs were so interesting and I loved the story telling. What it has left me with, is how your parents' deep rooted generosity to others has played such a big part in forming the person you are. I love that about you."

The following months before their wedding, Mike worked through the worst of his grief. This was aided by how well his father was overcoming his loss. It was clear that he had been released from an onerous burden of having to suppress for half of his life, his desire to talk to both his son and his friends about what had happened to his lost son Joseph. His father was spending a great deal of time with his many friends, to whom he had now told everything. He was effusive about Cassie and was looking forward to coming to his son's wedding, accompanied by a few friends who had known Mike from when he was a child. Through discussions with both Cassie and Neil, Mike began to firm up how he would give practical effect to preserving his Jewish identity. He had decided that his primary aim over the next few years would be to become proficient in Ladino, the language of Sephardi Jews, and also in Arabic, given many of the historical texts of the period were in Arabic, which had been a second language for Sephardi Jews living and thriving in medieval Spain. On occasions during this period after his mother's death, the fear re-emerged of being isolated from his family should Cassie become an MP, which left him thinking that a move back to London would become inevitable. Nevertheless, he knew this was not what he would choose were Cassie to decide not to stand for Parliament.

Part 3 – Chapter VII

The selection process for the Labour candidate at the next General Election was held one month after the MP had made his announcement of retirement at the end of the year. As suspected by Nora Bateson, Peter Johnston had put his name forward. However a few days before the selection process, which comprised the two candidates making speeches followed by a ballot taking place, he withdrew from the contest, leaving Cassie selected unopposed. Nora's view was that he knew he would not win and decided that being seen to lose the contest could undermine his authority as Leader of the Council. While her supporters were full of congratulations and satisfaction at the success of the campaign, Cassie was concealing her continuing doubts about how becoming an MP may change her life in ways that she did not want. Nevertheless, she gave a rousing acceptance speech where she spoke of her commitment to ensure that the Labour government tackled social and economic injustice and to support only policies that were in the interests of working communities such as Westpool and the district.

At home the next day, Mike raised the matter saying that he had detected that she seemed less enthusiastic with the result than he had expected her to be.

"Yes, there's some truth in what you say. I've spoken in the past about my concerns for how it could change us and how it could change me. I've also been giving some thought to what our life could be like if I didn't become an MP and we continued life here as it is. What would you like from our life together that we couldn't have if I become the MP?"

"I suppose we would avoid moving to London. But I have got my head together on that and I am fairly certain and comfortable with the thought that I will be moving to London. I don't think there is anything else that would be different."

"Really? We are about to get married yet the subject of children hasn't been raised. I am forty-two years old but there's still the opportunity to have a child. You must have some views on that."

"Do you want to have a child?"

"I asked you the question first. I want to know what your thoughts are."

"Well I don't think it's a feasible option. I am never going to stand in your way to becoming an MP. You will be great at it. And anyhow, there are dangers for a woman in having a baby when in one's forties."

"I know about the dangers. I also know you are a kind, loving person who wouldn't want to stand in my way. But the question remains. Would you want to have a baby if we continued our life here as it is? I'm not saying whether I would want that or not before I know what you would want in those circumstances," Cassie stated with a hint of impatience.

Mike smiled.

"There is no hiding from you, Cassie. Yes, I have thought about having a baby with you. And yes, the idea is highly appealing were we in a different time and place. But I stress again, it's not that I am being honourably unselfish in not raising it. More than anything, I want to live happily with you for what you are and what you can become. I am selfish enough to see the dangers that my expressing a wish to have a child with you could generate for our relationship."

"I don't mind being selfish on this matter. It's clear to me that you would like to have a child, or possibly even more than one. I won't deny that the idea of having a child with you appeals to me too. So, I suggest I come off the pill and we see what happens. I will tell Nora and let her know that should I get pregnant then I will stand aside and support her becoming the Labour candidate."

"I love you for the many different sides of who you are, Cassie."

"Why is it that I always want to go to bed with you after we have a big discussion? My suggestion is that we take all this upstairs with us."

"That's another thing about you that I hope never changes."

The divorce came through later than they had expected. The delay had caused concern that the wedding would have to be postponed at a very late stage, but now they were relieved that the wedding could go ahead as planned. Cassie had decided to let Jenny and Ellen choose who between them would be the witness at the registry office and who would make a speech at the reception. They had agreed that Ellen should make the speech. The food would be a mixture of Kosher and traditional wedding fare. Mike told Cassie that his father would recite a Sephardi poem.

The wedding took place on a bright warm day in mid-June with the reception at the hotel where they had first met to have lunch. After the meal, the speeches began. Most of them were interspersed with humorous references to how forceful the bride could be and therefore how fortunate it was that Mike was so accommodating. Neil mentioned how greatly relieved he was to have his mother taken off his hands at last by a stepfather who could now rely on Neil for support. Ellen spoke of Cassie's loyalty to her friends and the community. The bride made nothing more than a simple announcement about just how happy she was and that with friends, both present and past and her now extended family, her happiness was assured.

The bridegroom started the final speech by declaring how happy and privileged he felt to have Cassie as his wife and Neil as his stepson. He then explained that it was important for him to acknowledge his Jewish identity, although stressing that he did not believe in a god. Giving a brief outline of his ancestral roots, he made reference to the expulsion of his ancestors from medieval Spain and to his parents' more recent flight from Nazi Germany, culminating in the loss of his brother, other relatives, and friends in the Holocaust. He then paid tribute to his parents for showing him how generosity and kindness to others should always be the response to adversity no matter how hard that may be. Turning to his father, he invited him to recite a Sephardi poem in Hebrew dating back to the 11th century. After he had finished, Mike announced that although the poem was written to God, he thought it fitting homage to his wife, and proceeded to read it out in English.

When all within is dark,
And former friends misprise;
From them I turn to thee,
And find love in thine eyes.

When all within is dark,
And I my soul despise;
From me I turn to thee,
And find love in thine eyes.

When all thy face is dark,
And thy just angers rise;
From thee I turn to thee,
And find love in thine eyes.[1]

He concluded by asking all to stand for a toast.

"*L'chaim*! To life!"

His father and several of the guests were moved to tears, as the gathering broke into a prolonged applause. The music and

[1] From Thee to Thee – Solomon Ibn Gabirol (1021-1058) Translated by Israel Abrahams (1858-1925)

dancing continued into the late evening. Towards the end, the family was sat at the table talking of what they had enjoyed most about the occasion. The references to Sephardi Spain had made Rocio realise how little she knew about the history of her country in those many centuries that the Arabs ruled in Spain.

"We have this annual event in Spain where we celebrate the Christians freeing the country from the barbarian infidels, but of course, like so much in my country, that is yet more lies and deceit. Isn't it so difficult to get at the truth of things?"

"That's the thing, Rocio. You have to put in the effort to find the truth. It's seldom offered on a plate; you have to dig deep and always ask questions of what is presented as truth," replied Mike.

"Next year, we are planning to go to Cordoba, Granada, and Seville. Those are the cities with the best remains of those medieval times in Spain when the culture of the Arabs and Jews flourished side by side for a good part of the time. It would be great if you and Neil could join us. We will help with the cost, of course," added Mike.

"I have never been to Andalucia so that's an offer I could not refuse. Wouldn't that be fabulous, Neil?" Rocio asked.

"Certainly would! And my Spanish should be so much better by then, as long as I get the grades to go to university."

Part 3 – Chapter VIII

Neil found out in late August that he had gained the exam grades that he required. He would be starting at London University in late September, where for the first year he would be staying in halls of residence, which he was keen to do, as it would better enable him to meet other students and make new friends. He had received no response to the letter that he had sent to the solicitors, which he had requested they forward to his father. A few weeks after he had sent it, the solicitors had confirmed that they had forwarded it, so the lack of response was down to his father. Neil decided that he would try one more time. He dispatched a letter via the solicitors, giving his father the address in London where he would be living and stating again that he would like to have contact.

The following week, while Neil was away in London with Rocio, a bulky package addressed to Cassie and Neil arrived in the post from Eddie Gallagher's solicitors. Inside the large envelope there were two copies of a document of several pages headed "An explanation" that had been typed out on A4 paper, and two envelopes one addressed to Neil and the other to her. There was a short covering letter from the solicitors, which informed them that Eddie had died of lung cancer on the 18th August, 1965 and that he had been cremated at Norwood crematorium on 26th August. His ashes had been scattered in the garden of remembrance there. The letter went on to state that in compliance with their client's instructions, enclosed were a document drafted by Eddie and two copies of Eddie's will, one for Neil and one for his mother. The letter ended with a request that each one of them confirm receipt of the solicitor's letter and the enclosures.

On reading the letter, Cassie slumped into an easy chair feeling faint. After a few moments she went outside to call Mike in from the garden and handed him the letter. He noticed that her hands were trembling.

"I am so sorry. How sad that is. Have you read any of the enclosed documents?" asked Mike as he hugged her.

"No. I wanted you around as I do that."

"I don't want to be hanging over you as you read through Eddie's letter. I think it would be best that you have a bit of space on your own for this. I'll make you a cup of tea and I'll be in the garden when you want me. Is that ok, darling?"

"Yes, thanks. I suppose we now know what changed and why he responded to Neil's letter in the card that he sent; he must have known he was dying."

"Yes, that does fit, although you will only have a full understanding by reading the documents."

"That was the worst thing right from the start; not understanding why. I never believed that I would ever get an explanation, although I always wanted one. Yet now that I have one in my hand, I feel too afraid to look at it."

"I can appreciate that but I hope that it will provide the closure that you have never had. Not immediately perhaps but at some stage in the future."

Cassie began to nod her head in agreement, then sat down at the table and started to read what had remained a mystery to her for so many years of her life.

Dear Cassie and Neil

I am writing this not to justify myself. I accept that my response to what I came to know fourteen years ago and my subsequent actions have caused a great deal of hurt. What I have set out below is my account of what happened and why I reacted in the way that I did all those years ago. I hope that this will give you some understanding as to the reasons for my behaviour, even though you may continue to think me wrong for acting as I did. I accept that.

Before I set out my account, I should say that it was never my intention to provide an explanation at any stage in my life. I had decided long ago that silence was for the best. However, in recent times I have been fortunate to meet someone who has led me to see that you and Neil deserve an explanation. I now realise you have a right to know; and that Neil in particular should not have to live his life without knowing who his father was, regardless of whether that knowledge leaves him more or less appreciative of who I am and of what I did. I decided to write this shortly before I became aware that my illness was terminal and I am grateful that I have had the opportunity to put it down in writing before I depart this life.

It all began on the morning of the 2nd May, 1951. As I was going out to work, I noticed that a letter had arrived for me, which I could see was from my twin brother Harry, in Perth, Australia. I was running late so I put it in my jacket pocket to read later. I was very busy that day and was due to work late that evening so before I started the overtime I went to the works canteen to read the letter. At this point I think I should say something of my brother and our childhood as I understood it up to the stage when my brother wrote that letter to me. As you were probably aware from the little I spoke about it, my brother and I did not have the best of childhoods. I don't want to get into detail but it's important to this explanation that I give an outline. Our adoptive parents were in their mid-forties at the time we were adopted by them. They were particularly strong Catholics, who played an active role in the local church and in the diocese. One or both of them were unable to have children but they desperately wanted to bring up a Catholic family. My brother and I were duly adopted as we had been baptised Catholic by our birth parents, whom we were told had died in a car accident in Western Australia. We were told nothing more and we were too afraid to ask. Our upbringing was not a warm one where we felt loved by our adoptive parents, but the saving grace was that we had good friends, whose parents were like aunts and uncles to us. The kindest thing I can say even at this stage of my life is that our adoptive parents must have had a similar upbringing for them to treat us as they did. They never knew how to relate to children.

Both my brother and I escaped home as soon as we were able. We were sixteen years old when we left home. My way of dealing with my childhood was to attempt to block it from my memory but my brother's way was different. Perhaps that is something to do with the fact that we were not identical twins. For many years he had been keen to find out who our birth parents were and something of their lives. This became an obsession for Harry as the years went by and he got more and more unhappy with not knowing anything about our birth parents. He stayed in Australia and eventually managed to find out that when very young we had been placed in a Catholic children's home in Western Australia that was run by nuns. That was for a short period of time before being adopted. With some help from a friend he broke into the home near Perth, Australia and searched the records and found information on our parents and background. The records revealed something that rocked him to the core. What he found out was that we were not Australian but British and that we had been shipped out when we were barely three years old from a Catholic home in the UK to an orphanage in Western Australia, both run by the same order of nuns. According to the records this was arranged and paid for by the Catholic bishop of Perth, Australia. The orphanage we were transported from in the UK was St Bartholomew's, just outside Westpool. The other information was our birth names and dates and also those of our birth parents, including where they lived when we were given up for adoption in the UK. When adopted our birth Christian names were retained but our birth surnames had been altered from Lawson to Gallagher.

What the records in that orphanage in Western Australia showed was that our birth parents were called Irene and Hugh Lawson and that shortly after our mother was widowed in 1923, she gave my brother and me up for adoption. The family home at that time was in Mapleside and the birth dates of our parents match those for your parents; 24th February 1897 for your father and 14th August 1898 for your mother. It is true, Cassie, unbeknown to either of us, when you and I met, fell in love, and got married – we shared the same parents. I was plunged into a state of disbelief and then shock when I read this information in my brother's letter. I found it difficult to take in and went through a short period of trying to believe it was not true. I felt as if I was trapped in a nightmare. But I knew that it must be true. How could it not be! My brother did not know your surname nor anything about you when he wrote that letter.

I couldn't think what to do for the first few days after reading the letter. It was unbearable to be at home with you and Neil. You will recall how cold and withdrawn I became and how late I stayed out at night. I shudder even now at how cruel that was to you both. I was struggling to cope. I was convinced that were this information to come out we would be broken up as a family; the worst being that Neil would be taken into care. I could not face the thought of that. I spent hours thinking about what I could do. It never felt right to not share with you what I had found out from the letter, but I decided that the best course of action was to keep it all secret and to disappear from your life and from Aylston. I knew you would suffer badly by my sudden, unexplained leaving, but I convinced myself that yours and Neil's suffering from my doing this would be considerably less than the alternative of making this public, which would tarnish and split our family up anyway and could mean us, you in particular, losing the child we so loved, to institutional care. In retrospect, it's also probably true that the horrors of war left me, as it did so many others, incapable of communicating on painful, emotional matters, even with those closest to me.

I was faced with trying to work out a viable way to do this while leaving you with enough money to get by for at least a few months, by which stage I hoped that I would be in a position to send you money on a regular basis. I negotiated an advance from my employer but knew that would not be sufficient. By luck rather than judgment, I raised another £50 through gambling on horses. I managed in the space of a week to win more than I had ever won since I had first started betting. That together with what we already had in the savings account, I reckoned would last you for almost six months at a push. As you know it took me a considerable period of time before I was able to start the regular monthly payments. I remain deeply sorry for that. It took me much longer than I hoped to get a job and to earn enough money.

The week before I left Aylston, in my desperation I began to think that there was a remote possibility that all of this about our birth parents was not true; that my brother may have mistakenly stumbled on information about other migrant children, not us. The only way of definitively knowing was to check any records at this end in the UK. I found out that records would be held in the parish church where my brother and I would have been baptised Catholic, and that there should be records in the children's home run by nuns just outside Westpool; assuming that we had ever been placed there. I engaged the help of a couple of acquaintances that I knew from the pub. They had some experience in breaking into properties. I had to pay them, but as with you it took longer than I had imagined to do that. With their skills and through the kindness of a work colleague who let me borrow his car for a couple of evenings, we set off to break into St Bartholomew's Children's Home and the St Peter's Church in Mapleside, with the sole purpose of checking the records in these two places.

My acquaintances were indeed skilled, causing little discernible noise or damage, and I was able to find the records I was looking for. They confirmed the information that my brother had obtained through his break-in to the children's home in Western Australia. In addition, I came across a record of the payment that the bishop in Australia had made for the transportation of my brother and me to the other side of the world. It included all expenses including the cost of having two of the nuns accompany us on the journey from the UK to Western Australia. It also included a contribution to the Order of Nuns who ran the homes. It subsequently dawned on me that the nuns accompanying us on that journey explained a recurrent dream I used to have as a youngster of a nun holding my hand on a ship's deck as we looked out over the ocean. There was no mention in the records that our birth mother was ever consulted or told of our migration to Australia. She clearly wasn't. I took all our records from the orphanage, which shall be bequeathed to you, in my will. The baptism registry in Mapleside Church should still be available for you to check if you so wish; it confirms the date of birth of my twin brother and me, our baptism date, and who our parents were.

At that point just before I was about to leave Aylston, it suddenly struck me that five years previously your mother, our mother, must have realised that I was one of her twin sons, whom she had been forced to give up after Dad had been killed in the mines. As you had told me not long after we met, your/our mother had had to return to her mother's home in Aylston because she was left destitute after no compensation was paid for Dad's death. On that morning of the day she died suddenly, you may recall that you had asked me to take her some groceries while on my way to work, as she had not been feeling well. I remembered my last conversation with her that day when in response to her persistent questions I told her my birth date and that I had a twin brother called Harry. I remembered that she fell silent and looked ill when I told her this information, but of course I did not know then what

I would come to learn later. There I was in the middle of what was a nightmare, now realising that my real mother had recognised me that day when I called on her, as one her children whom she had to give up to a children's home. I remain convinced that her recognition of me and that I was about to marry her daughter was what brought on the heart attack that killed her.

It was then that I felt a huge anger well up inside of me, like I had never experienced before. I was furious with the Catholic Church. The day before I left Aylston, I went to the presbytery and confronted the priest. I exploded with rage about what the Church does to orphaned and abandoned children, telling him that my brother and I had been victims of child migration to a far off country, with our true identities and birth families concealed from us. I ranted about the Church's cruel treatment of innocent children and of their often destitute parents, but did not mention the accidental incest as keeping that a secret was a must for me. I am not sure what the priest made of what I was saying to him, or perhaps he just would not accept that the Church could do wrong; but he said not a word to me in response.

I left you, Neil, and Aylston the following morning in the most broken state that I have ever been. I didn't think I would ever stop crying. I made my way to London with the plan to enlist in the Merchant Navy. It was not as easy as I had expected and I had to spend some time sleeping rough on the streets, as I had no money. However, with my engineering qualifications I believed that it was only a matter of time before something would come up. It did and since leaving my family in Aylston I have spent all of my life at sea as a mechanical engineer, endlessly travelling the world, and barely spending any time away from the oceans of the world. For twelve of those years I told no one of what only I knew. I saved money with the intention of giving most of it to you and Neil. I have earned a great deal of money but it was only in 1963 that I purchased a home and spent some time on dry land. I have made a home in south London.

There is one other matter that I should tell you about before I recount the final period of my life. After I left Aylston, I did not attempt to communicate with my brother, Harry, in Western Australia until three years later when I felt my mind had stabilised to the extent that I could talk to him and tell him the full story. I wrote him a letter and informed him that I would like to come to Perth in Australia to meet up with him. I got no response. After several months of hearing nothing, I decided that I would take a month off work to go there and find him. What I found was another cruelty of this tragedy. After a lot of searching and follow up of acquaintances, I eventually tracked Harry to a hostel for homeless men. It was clear that his heavy drinking had turned into full scale alcoholism. I never could bring myself to add to the immense sorrow he carried with him by telling him the full story of our birth parents. I simply told him that I had found out that our birth parents were long dead.

He had been drinking for so long that it was difficult to hold any length of conversation with him. However, he would frequently break down in tears crying out how cruel life had been for us, not to have known our real parents and families. I tried to get him off the streets and off the booze, but all my efforts were in vain. I left him on a hot day, arguing in the park with some of his drinking mates. We hugged as we said our goodbyes and I knew at that moment that he was beyond help and that I would never see him again. A year later I got a letter from an acquaintance in Perth who told me he had died of alcohol poisoning. He had gotten so bad he had taken to drinking methylated spirits. Our brother never got over the knowledge that he had been separated as a toddler from his mother and father; and the denial of any information on our birth family haunted him for most of his relatively short life.

For the first few years following my leaving you and Neil, I was forever cursing how coincidence and accidents had determined my fate. With nothing but work in my life, I began to read voraciously – both fiction and non-fiction. With time, I have considerably expanded my knowledge and widened my understanding of this world, and I have come to see that coincidence and accidents play a much smaller role in one's fate than ignorance tends to make one believe. The understanding I have arrived at is that there are two elements that shape our fate; firstly there are those powerful interests, be they religious, political, or economic, that determine the conditions we have to live in, and the second element is the person one becomes and the choices one makes. To an extent, the person that each one of us becomes is also shaped by what is outside our control, for example genes, impacting events, or nationality, but the little influence we are able to exert on our lives is in respect to our personal morality; specifically the choices we make from the restricted set of options that are available to us. Of course, being a man who could earn decent money I had options, whereas our mother, widowed with three children and facing destitution, had virtually none. There are only a few in this world who have the power and wealth to exercise influence over their own and other people's fates, while most people have no power or wealth, so have little or no control even over their own fate. Nevertheless, how one exercises the little influence one has, determines the value of a life – in my opinion.

For most of the last fourteen years, I have been consumed with a sense of injustice. Injustice caused by the actions of a range of Christian institutions, and certainly not only the Catholic Church; but also the injustice caused by governments that did nothing to stop, and in some periods actively encouraged, the inhuman child migration that has lasted for over a century and has involved tens of thousands of children. I have found out a great deal about child migration, although I suspect I may have only touched on the true scale of it all. So many of those children given up to institutions, most for the sole reason of their parents' destitution, have been taken from the UK and deposited in children's homes, not only in Australia but also in Canada and in other 'white' ruled countries of the British Empire. Unlike Harry and me, most of those migrant children never left those children's homes until they approached adulthood, and many suffered appalling treatment and damage whilst there. All of this was done not only without the permission of their birth parents but without their knowledge. Information on their birth parents and siblings has been consistently denied to all those migrant children; many of whom were old enough to know that they had birth families somewhere on this planet. This appalling treatment of the innocent is still going on now.

However, the final years of my life have been marked by two things that are as contrasting as darkness and light. I was diagnosed with lung cancer, which has progressed to a terminal stage. I can endure that without bitterness because of the light that has arrived in my life. Two years ago, I met a woman who for some reason has come to love and care for me – as I do her. She has reintroduced me to life after so many years existing in an emotionless desert. Most importantly, she has taught me how to love again. I cannot deny that the premature ending of our relationship is a source of great sadness.

Amongst the many things she has given me, she has convinced me of the importance of not leaving you and especially Neil, in ignorance of matters that have had and may continue to have a detrimental impact on your lives. Her encouragement and Neil's letter to me earlier in the year have prompted me to write this, which I hope will give you some closure on what happened all those years ago. Our son's letter has felt like an absolution, not in a religious sense, I have long abandoned the Catholic Church, but in the sense that it relieved me of the dread and worry about his welfare; of how he would turn out. His letter showed clearly that he is a son as intelligent, talented, and generous spirited as any parent could wish for. For that, I am eternally grateful to you. Consequently, I am no longer consumed by despair and injustice. To my own amazement, I approach the end of my life full of pride; a pride that could not be bettered with any title or honour bestowed by the powers that be in this world.

- *Proud to have known you and loved you.*
- *Proud of Neil, our son, who is so well set up to fulfil his considerable talents, yet is attentive to the needs of others.*
- *Proud of our mother, who lived through so much suffering and injustice yet raised such a wonderful human being as you.*
- *Proud of our father, who worked so hard in such dangerous conditions and for so little pay, simply to keep his family from destitution.*
- *Proud of our brother, who despite never making it through, had the courage to pursue what should be known to every child, as of right.*

For myself, I am at peace knowing that, despite my failings and errors of judgment, I have tried to make the best of the hand I was dealt in this life, not only for myself but for those I have treasured.

Yours always

Eddie Lawson
Brother and Father

Author's notes

1. **Child Migration** refers to children generally between the ages of three and fourteen. Most child migration occurred in the 19th and 20th centuries. Child migration removed over 130,000 children from the United Kingdom to Canada, New Zealand, Zimbabwe (formerly Rhodesia) and Australia. These children were sent away with the expectation that they would never return, to start new lives in a foreign land without their families and often in harsh, understaffed institutions. British boys and girls were shipped overseas by specialist agencies such as the Fairbridge Society, which sent young children to populate the Empire with "good, white British stock." Respected national child care charities such as Barnardo's, along with the Church of England, the Methodist Church, the Salvation Army and the Catholic Church, played major roles. The final child migrants arrived in Australia in the 1970s. Only in the last fifteen years have both the UK and Australian governments made public apologies for their sometimes active participation, but mainly their passive acquiescence, in child migration. For more information: https://www.childmigrantstrust.com/
2. **The coal mining industry in the UK** had undergone a significant contraction long before the final depletion of the industry that followed the miners' strike in 1984-85. At its peak in 1920, there were 1.19 million men employed in the industry, which had almost halved to 695,000 in 1956, and diminished further to 247,000 in 1976.

Bibliography

- *Empty Cradles* – Margaret Humphries
- *Unlikely Warriors: The Extraordinary Story of The Britons Who Fought In The Spanish Civil War* – Richard Baxell
- *Families and Social Workers: The Work of Family Service Units 1940-1985* – Pat Starkey
- *The Jews in Cordoba (X-XII centuries)* – Jesus Pelaez del Rosal
- *Capital in the Twenty-First Century* – Thomas Piketty (Pg. 505-508 – Confiscatory Taxation of Excessive Income: An American Invention)
- https://bradfordtaxinstitute.com/Free_Resources/Federal-Income-Tax-Rates.aspx
- https://www.nationalarchives.gov.uk/education/resources/attlees-britain/

Acknowledgements

Thanks to all those who have encouraged me in the writing of this book and those who read early drafts and provided comments that have helped me to improve the writing. In particular: Tricia, Jack, Kate, Penny, Chris, Odette, Josie, Anna, Terry, and Cathie.

Thanks also to Roisin Martindale for her inspiration and design of the front cover.

Lightning Source UK Ltd.
Milton Keynes UK
UKHW012206280820
368995UK00003B/55